Juliet

with love from Grandma

Christmas

1990

LOOKING FOR ILYRIAND

Looking for
ILYRIAND

Jay Ashton

Oxford University Press
Oxford Toronto Melbourne

Oxford University Press, Walton Street, Oxford OX2 6DP

Oxford New York Toronto
Delhi Bombay Calcutta Madras Karachi
Petaling Jaya Singapore Hong Kong Tokyo
Nairobi Dar es Salaam Cape Town
Melbourne Auckland

and associated companies in
Berlin Ibadan

Oxford is a trade mark of Oxford University Press

British Library Cataloguing in Publication Data
Ashton, Jay
Looking for Ilyriand.
I. Title
823'.914 [F]

ISBN 0 19 271646 8

Typeset by Pentacor plc, High Wycombe, Bucks
Printed in Great Britain

CHAPTER 1

THERE WAS a large crowd that evening in the great hall. With the approach of winter, people had come in from the outlying pastures, greeting friends they had not seen since spring. Osric was to tell a story.

A wind had risen, and howled down the corridors. Inside the hall, curtained against the night, it was warm enough. The firelight glinted on smoke-blackened walls, casting into sharp relief the carvings of animals, strangely patterned, and of dreams. Around the doorpost wound the scaly coils of a wooden dragon, and nearby sprawled the real one, fast asleep. Leaning against his back was Ronan, Crown Prince of Fallond, his eyes lost in some unreachable imaginings. On a chair carved from a single piece of wood, ornamented with birds, and snakes, and snakes that were becoming birds, sat Ronan's grandfather, Emerick, the King. He had the warmest place by the fire. Wrapped in a snug cloak, his beard spreading over his chest, he listened with an air of benign approval. Behind him, erect, arms folded, stood Conrad, younger son of the King, and uncle to the heir.

'When I'm king,' sighed Ronan, 'things will be different.'

The dragon opened one yellow eye. 'How, different?'

'Adventure. Excitement. Things *happening*.'

The dragon repressed a shudder. 'Long live King Emerick,' he murmured. His eye closed.

A buzz of excitement ran around the hall. The wizard had come, was there in the room, sitting with his stick beside him and staring at the ceiling. He was rarely seen within walls, spending his time, some said, up trees, or walking on waves, or sharing the caves of wolves and bears. He had not been seen at all one long winter, and had been given up for dead: but he had reappeared next spring, thinner than ever, but still alive. There

1

was cause for excitement: someone had heard the wizard talking to Osric, instructing him what tale to tell tonight; it must be something special, then.

Osric held up his hand for silence, and in the hush began. 'Long, long ago, before the memories even of dragons, our people came to this land. For we are not of this land, but came as strangers to it, though so long a time ago that now all that is left to us of the country that we lost is the thread of a tale, and a name—Ilyriand.'

He paused, and a murmur of anticipation ran round the hall. This was a story that Osric told only rarely: the youngest in his audience had not heard it before.

Osric closed his eyes for a moment, then fixed them on the ceiling, where the smoke drifted about the rafters. 'It is said,' he went on, 'that Ilyriand was a country of such plenty that our forefathers could want for nothing. They had no need to hunt or fish: they had only to stretch out a hand to the trees which hung ever laden with ripe, delicious fruit. The sun shone every day, every evening was cooled with soft showers; winter came not. Summer's warmth and autumn's bounty were constant and dependable as the night that followed every day, the day that followed every night.

'Their music was charming and their pictures pretty; their carvings elegant and their poems serene. They told no tales, for they had none to tell. As the fruit fell when it was ripe, so they died when they were old: tranquil, untouched, like a maiden unawakened.

'How many generations slipped by thus unnoticed none can now tell, nor ever could. It was bound to end at last. It took only one man to end it.

'Eldon was his name, King of Ilyriand. But not content to be so. From a child his eyes had been turned upwards to the stars, and outwards to the world beyond. Questioning, he was always questioning, and his tutors often had no answers. "It is not known," they would say, or, "We cannot tell." And ever the child said, "Why?"

'As he grew to manhood he began to study magic. Some knowledge they had of amusing tricks, diverting fancies to while

2

away an hour. But Eldon found here a frightening skill, and a magic which was not only one of seeming.

'The old King, his father, forbade it; but then the old King died.

'On the evening of his coronation, Eldon left the feast and vanished. They found him at last, standing alone on top of the highest tower of the palace.

' "See!" he cried. "The stars travel, seek out new horizons. Why cannot I?"

' "But Sire," they said. "You are King . . . "

' "King? Of what? To what end? What tasks are there for me?"

' "Sire, look about you. All you can need is here. What more can you want?"

' "I want the moon," he said. "Here in my hands. If I had it I might not like it, but I want to know what it is made of. I want the stars. I want to know what lies outside the bounds of Ilyriand."

' "But, Majesty, it is impossible. No man can touch the moon, nor climb the mountains that surround our land."

' "How do you know?" he asked. "Have you tried?" '

Osric paused, running his eyes round the room, past the drowsing dragon, the wizard's dark shape.

'Who can say how these things happen? Night follows day, the plant springs from the seed, one man has an idea and soon all men must follow.

'The years passed, but no longer in tranquillity. Men scurried around the mountains in search of a pass to the outside world. Preparations were made for a long journey, lights burned late in the palace where Eldon wove his magic.

'An heir was born. Tancred he was called, for even as an infant he seemed to ponder deeply before he wailed for his food. He was an only child, for the King forgot to father others.

'Twenty years passed, and all that men thought of was ways to escape from a land where they had everything.

'And, of course, a pass was found. To keep the land safe while they were gone—for they always meant to return—the pass was sealed with a secret door, a door which could be opened only

3

with a magic key wrought of pure gold.

'Tancred alone spoke against their going. "We have all we need here," he argued. "Why go elsewhere?" But no one listened to him. They left Ilyriand.'

The story unwound in a comfortable hush. It was but a fireside tale, a shiver of horror to take cosily to a warm bed. Ronan's sympathies were with Eldon. Why sit at home being bored when there was a chance of adventure in the outside world?

Conrad listened in impassive silence, unaware of the stirrings of his neighbours. He knew of no other story so potent with loss and longing. He saw Ilyriand and smelt its fragrance. It was the freshness of a spring morning, leaves uncurling into life. It was an enchanted land, spangled with flowers, sun-kissed. Angrily he thrust the vision aside. He must be brain-sick, wallowing in illusions.

'They journeyed on, through many lands, and came one sunny day to a river idling in great loops through lush meadows bright with flowers. They stopped to drink and bathe in the dark slow water. Children played at hide-and-seek in the bushes, unawares. Very hot it was; a haze shimmered over the grasses where bees drowsed among poppies.

'Time dozed in the languid peace of midsummer. There was no breeze. The birds were silent. There was no sound but the humming of insects and the laughter of children. A mother watched proudly as her son, who had but newly learned to walk, toddled through the long grass on some infant voyage of discovery. She would, she thought, always remember the joy in his face as butterflies danced about him.

'At last, somnolent, sun-sodden, they wandered on. The path left the meadow and plunged between dim, mossy banks, into dark forest. They shivered in the sudden chill. Still blind from the sunlight, they did not see death coming.

'It fell on them from the trees. Men with axes, leaping, shrieking.

'Our people had never known fighting. Within minutes, most lay dead on the ground. Tancred escaped by diving under a bush. Hiding among the leaves, he watched helpless as the screeching axemen carried off his father, still alive and struggling.

'A terrible silence fell as the cries of the axemen faded into the distance. Tancred searched among the bodies for any left alive. There were none. He drew his knife, and followed after the killers. The trail was not difficult to find: death and desolation ran in the tracks.

'As the sun sank low he came to a fortress, walled all around, its back to the sea. And even as he gazed despairingly at the tall towers, hefting his knife in his hand and longing for some chance of revenge, he saw something thrown from a high window. It caught the sun as it fell, glinting with a yellow light. He knew what it was: the golden key of Ilyriand. He ran to find it, but could not, try as he might. And as the sun went down he heard from the fortress one last appalling scream.

'He wandered away then, to nurse his grief alone, but though he sat down to die he lived, despite himself. One day by chance he met with others who had escaped the massacre. Then they built ships, and left that land; they travelled far, seeking a new home, wishing always that they might find the golden key, and the way back to Ilyriand.'

Osric ended. The audience applauded and began to think of refilling their cups.

'So why don't we?' said Ronan, suddenly jerking upright.

'Ouch,' said the dragon. 'You kicked me. Why don't we what?'

'Find the key. Go back to Ilyriand.'

'For a prince,' said the dragon, 'you do talk an awful lot of nonsense.'

'And you, Prothero, are the most poor-spirited dragon I've ever met.'

'I'm the only dragon you've ever met. Anyway, I'm just biding my time. You wait and see.'

Then the wizard rose to his feet. He made no other sign, but gradually an uneasy, waiting silence fell. When at last he spoke his voice was quiet, conversational, and his words all the more disconcerting.

'There is a doom on this land. I have watched it in dreams.

5

Cold, so cold . . . Even the sea will freeze, and ice smother all. No green, no blue, only white. No life. Slow ice grinding at the rocks . . . ' His voice trailed away, his eyes were closed. He shivered. Around the hall, despite the warmth, people pulled their clothes closer.

The wizard shook himself and opened his eyes. 'If you stay here you will all die,' he said, briskly matter-of-fact. 'It may not come in our time, but come it will, and if you do not want to earn the curses of your grandchildren, or your grandchildren's grandchildren, you will pay heed to the world you leave them.

'What good will heirlooms be to them, if their land is barren? What use will treasure be, if they have no food?'

Somewhere in the crowd a baby whimpered, and began to howl. Its mother hushed it, and gave it her breast.

'Look!' cried the wizard, pointing. 'Is that not a touching sight? See how gently she holds her baby, nourishing it with milk and with love! She might as well dash out its brains on the ground as give no thought to the world it must live in after she has gone.

'Fallond is dying. You know it, if you think about it. How long is it since a trading ship last came? Ten years? Twenty? How long since any, friend or foe, have come to seek us out? The North is falling under a mantle of ice. This is a dwindling race in a lost land. Fallond is dying. You must return to Ilyriand.'

For a while there was total silence. Too stunned even to register their surprise, the audience stared at him, baffled.

At last Emerick broke the spell. 'Do you mean we are all to get up—men, women, children, the old, the sick—and walk blindly into the wilderness?'

'It is not for me to tell you how to do things, only what must be done. My part is wisdom, King. I am not your steward, to make arrangements for you.' The wizard remained serene, as if this concerned him hardly at all.

Emerick glared.

'That is no answer to give to your King,' snapped Conrad.

'He will get no other at your bidding,' said the wizard tranquilly.

6

Conrad's jaw tightened. 'You are impertinent as well as foolish, old man.'

'And you are a liar—of the worst sort, one who deceives himself.'

'I do not lie,' said Conrad, furious.

'Precisely.'

Conrad flushed, then relaxed into a contemptuous smile. 'All this is beside the point, wise man. You will have to tell us the way to this land—*we* do not know where it is.'

'Oh but we do.'

Everyone—except the wizard—stared in astonishment, not only at the statement, but at its source. Ferdy was a vague, fuzzy-featured boy who, being extremely shy, rarely spoke at all except when he talked too much. He knew something of herbs: apart from that, no-one ever took any notice of him. He blushed hotly and plunged on. 'I—I found a m-map in the library . . . It was wedged at the back of a shelf, fallen down behind some old scripts. It's a bit blurred, and the words are in the old language, but I can make out some of it. It was made by Tancred's scribe. It's a map of their journey here from Ilyriand. Shall I get it?'

'Yes,' said Ronan.

Ferdy ran off and returned a few minutes later carrying a rather tattered parchment. Conrad moved forward to take it from him, and passed it to the King.

Emerick stared at it. A long silence ensued, broken when Conrad noticed the wizard heading towards the door. 'Where are you going?' he called.

'I have said what I came to say,' replied the wizard, and went on walking.

'Helpful as always,' murmured the dragon. 'Still,' he went on with a yawn, 'at least with a wise man like that the King doesn't need to keep a fool.'

The wizard, by the door, turned. His eyes glittered. 'One piece of advice I will give you, Emerick: whoever else you send to find Ilyriand—send the dragon.'

'Hey, I'm not going anywhere!' cried Prothero.

'What, take that pestilential overgrown lizard?' exclaimed Conrad.

But the wizard was gone.

The King was looking at the map, aware that everyone else was looking at him. The longer he sat there the less he could think of anything to say. His eyes were old, the light was dim, and he had never been very sure about maps. Was he even holding it the right way up? The rough markings meant nothing to him, except that he must make a decision. At his time of life he wanted to be past making decisions, especially for other people. Why wouldn't they be content to sit by the fireside in peace? His eyes slid from the map to the flames now burning low in the hearth. He could crumple up this horrid parchment, pronounce it rubbish and throw it on the fire. Some might blame him, but at least it would be an end of the matter. He sighed. The lifelong habit of responsibility re-asserted itself.

'I shall need to consider this further,' he declared. 'I shall retire.' He rose, pulling his shawl around his shoulders. Bent but dignified he walked slowly from the room.

CHAPTER 2

THE HARBOUR nestled in a deep inlet a mile or so from the sea. Above it the cliff rose steeply, topped by the castle of Fallond, its back to the snowy mountains, seeming almost to have grown out of the crag to which it clung. But for those who sheltered within its walls it was no more than a toehold in a barren and inhospitable land. The castle was decaying, its edges blurred by time, its people dwindling, too few now to fill the rooms. Whole corridors lay abandoned to rats scrabbling and spiders slowly spinning.

The mountain tops had for days past been shrouded in drifting cloud, and now the mist came rolling up from the sea, blotting out the land in a clammy chill. Conrad stood watching from the tower as the fog closed in, his face as cheerless as the day.

His features could have been finely carved from stone, so unresponsive were they. His hair was black, his face pale, dominated by dark and heavy eyes, which, like his whole body, seemed clamped in an unyielding rigidity. His clothes too were black, but these, despite the drab colour, had a certain elegance that came less from vanity than from fastidiousness. He looked very handsome, but quite untouchable.

The tower had been built to command a wide view all round, in the days when attack might come. For years past it had been unnecessary; none came to challenge their ownership of this bleak land.

North and east, the mountains: stark, forbidding, ice-capped even in summer. Each year the ice crept closer, the valleys were green for a shorter span.

West and south, the sea.

He had known it for a long time now, without ever putting it into words, even to himself. The land was changing, as if

9

gradually the covering of green was being scraped from the granite beneath. The trees were dying. Each year the water invaded more of the land. The melted snow stagnated and the trees stood on; gaunt ghosts, flowered only with the spectral fantasies of lichen, the bloated creep of fungi.

A gull drifted past on flickering wings, wailing mournfully. While the world shrivelled about them, they went on about their petty concerns as if there were no tomorrow.

'Beg your pardon, Sire.' A nervous voice broke in on his brooding. Quailing under Conrad's unwelcoming glare, Ferdy stuttered, 'The King requests your presence in his apartments. They're talking about Ilyriand.'

Ronan watched from the window of his tower room.

All morning the Prince had been waiting for a summons which hadn't come.

He had risen soon after dawn and dressed carefully in his newest clothes—he had been growing so fast lately that most of his clothes were too short. Too excited to eat, he prowled restlessly around the room, not daring to go elsewhere in case he missed the call when it came.

The hours crawled by. He had to allow time for Emerick to wake, dress, breakfast . . . but surely he had been waiting long enough?

A cold suspicion began to trickle into the back of his brain. Surely they couldn't ignore him? He dismissed the thought. He was old enough, they couldn't still treat him as a child. Soon he would be king, when his grandfather died. And now they were deciding the whole future of his people. They couldn't leave him out. He gripped the sides of the window, his knuckles whitening.

At last there was a little flurry of activity about Emerick's apartments, people coming and going. Ronan sat down facing the door, trying to look unconcerned, expecting the knock.

None came. He flung himself back to the window in time to see his uncle cross the courtyard with Ferdy at his heels. The door closed behind them.

Rage surged up inside him till he thought he would explode.

He grabbed a chair and smashed it against the floor. A leg splintered.

Humiliated, close to tears, he threw himself on the bed and buried his face in his arms.

The heat struck Conrad like a blast from an oven, and the musty smell caught him at the back of his throat. Mastering an impulse to throw open the windows, he sat very upright on a wooden bench. Ferdy slithered in beside him.

The King sat, wrapped in furs, by the fire. Nearby, Thayer lounged at his ease. Senior captain and assured in his rank, he smiled peacefully. His jerkin gaped over the beginnings of a paunch.

Emerick passed Conrad the map. 'I want your opinion on whether I should send an expedition to seek Ilyriand. Young Ferdinand sees no problem in it—Thayer sees quite a few.'

'With your permission, Sire,' said Thayer. 'As I see it the problem is this. We have for a guide a map made some five hundred years ago ... '

'Five or six,' interrupted Ferdy.

' ... Some five *or six* hundred years ago,' resumed Thayer. 'A little worn in places, illegible in others, and much of it incomprehensible, but never mind. With this guide we have first to sail an unspecified distance over unknown seas, to land on a strange shore, no doubt populated and probably unwelcoming. We then have to walk some vast distance into the territory of people who, when last we met, practically wiped us out. When we have found their fortress—without their finding us—we look for a key which nobody could find some five—or six— hundred years ago. Having located this key, we then walk another vast distance through trackless wastes in search of a country which, if it ever existed, and if it was as good as repute would have it, has no doubt been taken over long ago by some discerning tribe. Having found it and removed the inhabitants, we then walk all the way back to the coast, find our ship and sail home, where our loved ones will doubtless be enchanted to hear of our exploits but will be able to make nothing of them, for how we are then to convey our whole people to this mythical

11

land I cannot begin to imagine.'

Ferdy looked somewhat daunted, but Conrad, glancing up from the map, merely raised an eyebrow. His voice expressed only disdain. 'Thayer speaks as a man who has spent too long in the bosom of his family.'

'At least I have a family,' replied Thayer, nettled. 'And it's no part of my duty to them to go wandering off into the unknown on a wild goose chase.'

'Each to his own,' replied Conrad indifferently. 'I have never refused a challenge. If you feel it's beyond your powers . . . ' He shrugged.

'No one has ever accused me of cowardice,' stated Thayer. He glared at Conrad, fuming. Conrad was so convinced he judged right, and did right; he had no room for human frailties, but stood always aloof and ready to condemn. Thayer knew that if he lost his temper he would regret it. For a moment he was tempted nonetheless. Then the lifelong habit of comfortable caution reasserted itself. 'The idea is absurd, suicidal.'

'Enough,' said Emerick. 'I have not yet decided whether anyone should go.'

'I want to go,' said Conrad.

'I daresay you do,' said his father. 'So would I have done, forty years ago. It comes a little late for me. We were a great people once, you know, filled this vast castle. Now what are we? A mere handful, skulking in a barren waste, a shrivelled kernel rattling in a shell too big for it . . . I remember the tales they used to tell of Ilyriand . . . A warm land of eternal summer, where the trees are always in fruit, where sun and soft rain come in equal measure, where on the shores of a great lake the sand sparkles like silver and the water like gold. There is wealth, all the riches man could ever desire! What I should give just to feel warm again!'

His glance fell on the fire, which was beginning to smoke. 'Mend that, will you,' he said irritably. 'All a load of poppycock, no doubt,' he went on. 'Stories to befuddle men's brains and teach them discontent. Isn't that what Osric was saying last night—that you should stay where you're well off, not go wandering somewhere that's bound to be worse?'

12

'But,' said Conrad carefully, poking at the fire, 'we are not well off here.'

'Hmm. You're a cold customer, Conrad. I've never known what to make of you. Not like your brother. I always knew where I was with Ingram.' The old man's face puckered with an unforgotten sorrow.

'You would rather it had been me who died?'

'Did I say so?' Emerick glared malevolently at his son's unresponsive back, still stooped over the fire, and went on pettishly, 'Why I should trust you I'm sure I don't know.'

'I have never been disloyal.'

Emerick snorted. 'So you say. I've seen you. Ever since Ingram was killed, watching me, waiting for me to die so you could have my throne. Well you've missed your chance, haven't you? Ronan will soon be grown up now. You'll never be king, for all your fine ways. What do you say to that, eh?'

The fire spat in the sudden silence.

'Say something, will you!' cried Emerick. 'Oh, why isn't Ingram here? I could trust him.' His voice was that of an old man, weak and afraid.

'Trust me,' said Conrad.

'You? Trust you? I've never trusted you. Not since Ingram died. The two of you went hunting and only you came back. How could I trust you?'

Conrad straightened, his back taut, the poker still in his hand.

Emerick quailed, frightened of his own words. 'No. No, I didn't mean it. Ronan is what we've made him, a namby-pamby weakling and I'm a foolish old man who'd be better off in his grave. Is that right?' His eyes glittered as Conrad finally turned round, his face wooden. 'You want a throne, Conrad? Go find yourself one in Cloud-Cuckoo-Land. You have my permission!'

'Thank you. I will.'

'Can I come?' Ferdy burst in eagerly.

Conrad looked at him. He was too young and probably lacked courage.

'I—I can read the map—well, most of it—and I know a bit of the old language—and I've read all the histories—and I'm quite good with herbs . . . '

13

Thayer snorted with laughter. 'A worthy volunteer. And don't forget you have to take the dragon!'

Conrad's lips tightened. 'I don't want any useless encumbrances.'

'Volunteers should not be gainsaid,' mumbled Emerick vaguely. He had an idea he had said that—or heard it said—a long time ago when it had seemed to mean something. 'As for the dragon,' he added, pulling himself together, 'I think you should take the wizard's advice. He's almost as old and stupid as I am, but still he is a wizard.'

'I've never known whether he's a magician or a madman,' yawned Thayer, stretching his legs out towards the fire.

'The one does not exclude the other,' observed Conrad drily. 'I will need a crew for the boat,' he went on. 'They will return here and come back for me in the autumn. I will take only a small party —we will need to travel quickly, not attract attention . . .'

The talk went on. Emerick lost the thread, and began to doze. The fire burned low.

It just happened—or so Wescott said—that he was passing the King's apartments that afternoon. Pausing to take a pebble from his shoe, he explained, he chanced to hear some of the conversation within. At first he could make out little, but then a word caught his ear. 'Silver' he heard, and 'gold'. And then a phrase which rang in his head like a bell: 'All the riches man could ever desire.' His nose quivered, as always when he had unearthed some secret plot. He hurried off to find Gardol.

He found him in his little tower room, high above the damp sea airs and carefully curtained against draughts. Gardol was knitting a muffler. The two friends made an odd contrast: Wescott was small and thin, Gardol big and fat. Both, though, were light on their feet; one did not always hear them coming.

'I don't know,' said Gardol, shaking his head dubiously, when he had heard what Wescott had to say.

'But don't you *want* to be rich?' demanded Wescott.

'That's as may be. There's no saying but what it might be nice to be rich. But it sounds dangerous to me. One can't be too careful with strange lands. Full of foreigners, as like as not.'

14

'Ah, but don't you see? That's what they'll *say*,' explained Wescott craftily, rubbing his nose. 'They're bound to tell us it's dangerous. They'll think if they scare us off they can keep all the treasure to themselves. But we're too clever for them. If we help to sail the ship they'll have to cut us in . . . '

Wescott rambled on, but Gardol had stopped listening. His knitting lay forgotten on his lap: there was a queer look in his eyes, and his mind was already far away.

Gardol believed in looking after himself, in taking care. But although he had elevated the avoidance of risk into a fine art, there was a sneaking little corner of his brain which thrilled to the thought of excitement and adventure. Ever since he was a child he had listened with a trembling anguish to the exploits of heroes of the old days, nursing an image of himself setting out one morning, a pack on his back, on a quest for unknown lands and sights unseen.

He became aware that Wescott had stopped talking, was waiting for an answer. 'Um. Of course, Wescott. Anything you say.' He took up his knitting again. He would need socks, gloves, hats, scarves, and it was always better to wear wool next to the skin . . .

The news of the expedition spread without ever being officially announced. By evening, as Conrad and Thayer left the King's apartments, everyone in the castle seemed to know.

Derwin was one of the first at the scene. 'You can count me in,' he said. 'I've been working on a design for the boat . . . '

Conrad looked at him thoughtfully. With his curly hair, the colour of sunshine, and his guileless blue eyes, Derwin stood out among this dark-haired, dark-eyed people. In looks he took after his grandfather, sole survivor of a ship which sailed out of the west to wreck on Fallond's rocky shores. The foreigner had told strange tales, of floating islands, of mountains rising suddenly in the sea to spout fire and stain all the sky with black clouds of stinking vapours. Though he had learnt their language and married one of their women, he was never really accepted by the Fallonders.

Some said Derwin resembled his grandfather in more than

15

looks. He had a sideways manner of looking at things: original, said some; irresponsible, said others. His parents had died when he was a small child and he had been brought up by an uncle and aunt, fond enough of him, but already overrun with children of their own, and rather daunted by this cuckoo in the nest. He was always taking things apart to see how they worked, and putting them together differently to make them work better. His aunt, despairing over her re-designed loom and constantly changing kitchen, was unrelievedly glad when he grew old enough to join the fishing fleet.

'All right,' said Conrad, making up his mind. 'You can come. As for the boat—you can show me the plans later.'

The next volunteers—Wescott and Gardol—were more unexpected.

'Is this a portent?' said Thayer, marvelling.

Conrad made no objection. They were good enough seamen, if stupid, and their motives did not concern him. Later he was to regret he had not enquired more deeply; but as it was he had too many other things to think about.

Suddenly, scattering the crowd like a whirlwind, a small figure hurtled at Thayer and clasped him remorselessly around the waist. 'You will take me to Ilyriand won't you? Say you will, please, father, you must!'

'Behave yourself, Brinny,' said Thayer, smiling although his voice was stern.

Abruptly she released him, and made a mock curtsey, grinning. 'Begging your pardon, *Sire*—but you will take me, won't you?'

'I'm sorry, child, but I can't—for the simple reason I'm not going myself.'

'*Not going?* But why not?'

'It is only to be a small expedition—and my part is here—'

'But *someone's* going! And I'm going with them!'

'No, Brinny, I'm afraid you're too young.'

'I'm not! I'm nearly fifteen!'

'Thirteen, as I remember.'

'But anyway—' Brinny launched into a list of all the reasons why she should have her way. Arguing, she considered, was one of the things she did best. Short, plump, fierce and determined, the dimples which she hated flashing in her cheeks, she stood her ground and talked. At one point she tried to include Conrad in the argument, but meeting his sardonic eye she wisely decided to concentrate on her father.

At last she paused to catch her breath. 'Hush!' begged Thayer. 'I still say you are too young and—quiet, Brinny!—in any case it's not my decision. The Lord Conrad will decide who accompanies him.'

'Then—' she looked up at Conrad, putting on her most winning smile. 'Please?'

'No,' said Conrad briefly, speaking to Thayer. 'You are right. Brianna is too young.' So saying, he swung on his heel and walked off.

'Oh!' gasped Brinny, indignant, glaring after him. 'Oh—just you *wait*!'

Aloof from all the excitement, perched on his favourite isolated pinnacle, Ronan sat brooding. He did a lot of brooding these days. He didn't seem to fit inside his skin; his body felt unfamiliar, as if it ought to belong to someone else. His thoughts would plunge into another world from which he would wake with a feeling that something thrilling had happened, only to find with a shock of disappointment that everything was just as usual.

He was tall for his age, and thin. His face was long and thin, almost triangular, with a narrow nose and large, dreamy eyes. His brown hair curled slightly, and stuck out at odd angles around his ears.

Hunched in his cloak, he watched the streamers of cloud, tattered by the wind, whipping across the face of the moon. His mind was already half a world away, in search of Ilyriand. Pictures of daring deeds, of red-eyed Axemen, of vast sea monsters and magic palaces, surged before his eyes.

Suddenly a tremendous blow knocked him from his perch. Two large feet pinned his shoulders to the ground, and warm breath fanned his cheek as the panting dragon laughed in his face.

'Grrrr,' said Prothero.

'Get off, you great brute!'

'I scared you! Admit I scared you!'

'No you didn't! I'm not afraid of anything!'

Prothero looked sceptical, but made no comment as he rolled over and settled down, his chin resting on the battlements. In spite of his size—he measured fully twenty feet of scaly russet coil—he seemed only half-grown still. His over-large paws gave him an unfinished appearance, although it was nearly thirty years since the wizard had found a female dragon, dead, lying across her clutch of eggs, and had rescued one which he hatched in the warmth of his breast. Reared in the castle, never seeing another dragon, Prothero had adopted the ways of people. He liked his creature comforts: his food well cooked, and something soft to lie on. Occasionally he made a token gesture towards behaving in a dragonish manner, but he had only fireside tales to go by, and really he had no wish to slay maidens and lie on hoards of mounded treasure—most uncomfortable, he thought.

'Listen!' cried Ronan suddenly, jumping up. 'Do you hear that?' A wild honking clamour swept overhead, borne on the wailing wind. 'Geese. Going south. Oh, if only I could fly with them!'

'Well, I'm glad I can't. Nasty dangerous things, wings—can land you in all sorts of trouble.'

'But to be free like them—to soar on the wind—to seek adventure . . .'

'All sounds very disagreeable if you ask me.'

'But you're *going*!' cried Ronan, desperately.

'Going where?'

'*Ilyriand!*'

'Not if I can help it.'

Ronan stared at him, perplexed. 'Don't you *want* to go?'

'Not in the least. There are always fools who want to die like heroes, but I don't see why I should be one of them.'

'I'd rather die a hero than live in chains!'

Prothero winced, his aesthetic sense offended. 'If you're going to be emotional you might try not to be banal,' he said. 'And inaccurate. You can hardly claim to be particularly fettered. Heir to the throne, your every whim considered . . .'

'You don't *understand*,' wailed Ronan. 'They never let me *do* anything. I *must* go on this journey. I feel—mock if you like!—I feel my destiny lies in the south.'

'Hmm. Well I feel my destiny lies by the fireside, and if you'll excuse me, my paws are getting cold.'

The dragon heaved himself up and wound off to find a warm spot, while Ronan fixed his eyes on the clouds scudding across the moon, his ears ringing with the calling of wild geese.

CHAPTER 3

IT WAS next morning. Outside the sun was shining. Inside the King's apartments it was fusty as usual. Ronan's mother sat, her hands folded demurely in her lap, while Emerick explained to her about the expedition. Widowed six months before her son was born, Alina had remained so, accepting without complaint her role as mother to the heir and watching quietly enough as life passed her by. She made a good listener, and was Emerick's chief confidante, adept at handling his shifting moods.

As he outlined his hopes and fears a wistful note crept into his voice. If only he were thirty years younger, he confessed, nothing could have prevented him from going. Such opportunities for adventure—and such an adventure—came too rarely.

Nodding sagely, Alina agreed. 'I would like to go myself,' she murmured.

'You! Nonsense!' cried Emerick, scandalized. 'You're a woman. Your place is at home.'

'Naturally,' she agreed, unsurprised. 'But if the thought of this quest can stir even my feeble woman's heart—' May I be forgiven for talking such balderdash, she thought crossly, but sighed sedately as she paused, '—you may judge what it does to my son.'

Emerick eyed her warily. 'He is far too young.'

'I think he is only young because we have kept him so, cossetting him, keeping him safe from dangers. Consider, he is nearly sixteen—it's time he tested himself if he is to become a worthy king.'

'Perhaps I should allow him a little more scope,' agreed Emerick reluctantly. 'But not to go on this expedition—it's far too dangerous.'

'Conrad would like him to go,' said Alina, keeping her fingers crossed.

'He would?' The King paused, startled. 'No,' he said, giving way to a sudden burst of moist-eyed sentiment. 'He is my only grandchild. I love him too much to let him go.'

'And I love him too much to prevent him. To see him chafe like a bird in a cage fluttering at the bars while its fellows fly south to the sun. He needs this experience. Too soon he will be bound by responsibilities and duties, the things required of him by custom and convention. You would go if you could. Let him.'

'I—I will think about it,' said Emerick testily.

Alina said nothing, knowing she had won. The victory was not sweet, but it was all she had. She looked across the room to where the stone window barred the sunlight which fell just beyond her reach.

'You wanted to see me?' Conrad's voice cut in as Alina sat musing over her embroidery.

He was towering above her, seeming in her chamber much larger and more daunting than usual.

She laid her embroidery by carefully, refusing to be intimidated. 'Would you leave us, please?' she asked her companion. 'We have something to discuss.'

'Have we?' enquired Conrad, raising an eyebrow.

'Would you sit?' she requested. She could manage him better if he were nearer her level. Only now she couldn't think how to start. It had seemed easy when first she decided to send for him.

She kept her voice carefully neutral, detached. 'My son wishes to join you on your journey,' she began at last.

'I want no infants with me.'

'He is nearly sixteen.'

'He is a child.'

She paused, considering Conrad. She had known him all her life yet still he was alien: big, aggressive, male. And he still hadn't sat down. She stood up, walked to the window and looked out. She spoke without looking round. 'What were you doing when you were sixteen?'

'I—don't remember.'

'I do. When you were sixteen you were spending every day hunting. You would have resented greatly being called a child.'

'Ronan is a dreamer. He would be no help, only a hindrance. I should be forever rescuing him from some silly fantasy.'

'Yes, he dreams—and if he's not allowed to live out his dreams he'll never become the king he should be.'

'The risks are too great.' Conrad spoke with an air of finality, moving towards the door.

Alina turned. 'The King wants him to go.'

Conrad stared at her. 'He said nothing of it to me.'

'But that is his wish. He told me so this morning.' She met his eyes squarely. His were the first to drop.

'Then there is nothing more to be said. By your leave, I have work to do.' He nodded curtly and strode out.

Alina's grateful smile shrivelled as the door closed behind him. She took three slow steps, turned, and kicked her embroidery violently across the room.

They gathered that afternoon in Conrad's quarters, which were secluded but cold. Conrad looked round the room and sighed. Ronan was too inexperienced, too eager, and likely to lead them into all sorts of trouble. And Ferdy: his skills at doctoring and at map-reading might be useful, but he was so short-sighted that if it came to a fight he would be as likely to kill his friends as his foes. Derwin at least had ingenuity, if not size and strength— although some of his ideas were crack-brained enough to invite disaster. Prothero had refused to go until, infuriated by Conrad's description of him as a useless encumbrance, he had insisted on going out of sheer perversity. Such was the gallant band he was supposed to lead through hostile and alien lands. Gardol and Wescott were already complaining about the draughts. Still, at least their part was only to sail the boat. Half an hour of their company had already proved rather too much.

Derwin was outlining his design for the ship, basically a larger version of the fishing boats, high at the prow and the stern, with a deck fore and aft and a central hold for stores.

'And,' he said triumphantly, 'in the stern a second mast. We can double the amount of sail, and she'll go much faster.'

Gardol drew in his breath sharply, 'I shouldn't do that,' he said, shaking his head. 'I don't hold with going too fast. Before

22

you knew where you were you could be sailing off the edge of the world.'

'That is, if she didn't heel over with all that extra weight at the stern,' agreed Wescott.

'Well, you could have three masts, one forrard as well,' offered Derwin, amending his sketch. 'She'd go even faster then, but I might need to change the proportions of the hull—and then it might be a bit much for you two to handle on the way back. What do you think?'

'I think,' said Wescott sharply, 'that she'd be bound to sink on the way there so there's not much point in bothering about how we'd get back.'

'Perhaps,' interrupted Conrad, 'since we shan't have much time for sea trials, we should stick to one mast. I want to set off in early spring, as soon as the sea is clear, not waste the good weather playing with boats.'

'A pity,' said Ferdy, peering at the drawing. 'She looks awfully pretty.'

'I don't mind,' put in Prothero, 'so long as there's enough room for me to lie down under cover. Dragons suffer dreadfully from the cold.'

'I couldn't agree more,' said Gardol. 'And cold and wet together make a lethal combination. I remember . . .'

'All we require,' said Conrad, his voice icy, 'is a simple boat which can be sailed by two men, and carry six men, a dragon, and enough stores for three months. We will need to take some food to keep us going for the first part of our journey on land. We will be travelling through the land of the Axemen, and it would be better not to have to spend time hunting. Prothero can carry it,' he added indifferently.

'Why me?' demanded the dragon.

'You want to be of *some* use, don't you?'

'Yes—no—I mean of course I'll be of use. I'm a ferocious dragon, I'll terrify all our enemies.'

'You are a cowardly hulk of useless blubber and you couldn't terrify a rabbit. You can carry the baggage.'

Ronan, sitting in the corner, sighed. It didn't seem like the dawn of a great adventure. His thoughts drifted away . . .

23

The geese Ronan had heard were the forerunners of the autumn migration. For days the sky over Fallond was noisy with birds and the moon darkened with flickering wings. Out of the north they came, in an urgent, endless stream, and the south swallowed them up. Then, suddenly, one morning they were gone. The empty sky glimmered. And it began to snow: hard specks at first, scudding on a chill wind.

Derwin was out late that day, helping to lay in supplies of firewood. As he returned from one last, lone trip it began to snow in real earnest.

He could hardly carry his load: there was something compulsive about picking up sticks, it was difficult to know when to stop. Bent double, and half-blinded with snow, he almost missed it. Then he saw the shape move.

It was a grey goose, huddled pathetically with feathers fluffed out. Derwin set down his sack. 'Hello,' he said, surprised. 'You should have gone.'

The bird made no move, its eyes dull and sad.

'Are you hurt? It's all right, I'll help you. It's all right . . .'

His voice was gentle, reassuring, and the bird too weak to struggle. Only it hopped once, toppled, used its wings to regain its balance, and was still.

'Have you hurt your leg? You poor old thing, no wonder you got left behind. Here . . .'

Very gently he gathered the bird up into his arms. Resigning itself, the goose made no attempt to peck. Forgetting his load of wood, Derwin hurried back to the castle.

In the tiny room that served him as bedroom, workroom and store for his herbal remedies, Ferdy sat poring over the map with Conrad. Ferdy's knowledge of the old language was, to say the least of it, patchy: he had tried to piece it together from long studying of old writings, a feeling for the shape of words, and much guesswork. He could decipher a good deal of the map, but some things remained obscure, especially distances. A number seven and a squiggle might mean miles, or days, or months.

Conrad was torn between respect for the boy's endeavours, and irritation at his vagueness. Maps had not come much in his way before, so this one seemed all the more important.

The door opened and Derwin walked in carrying a goose. 'Ferdy, can you help? She's hurt her leg.'

'Then wring its neck,' said Conrad. 'And take it to the kitchens.'

'I can't do that!' cried Derwin, scandalized. 'She trusts me.'

'Tuck her under your arm so she can't flap her wings,' said Ferdy. 'Conrad, you hold her beak . . .'

Conrad found himself holding the bird's head, fingers clasped round the tooth-edged beak. He looked at the goose. She looked back at him. He shifted his grip slightly, so the bird could breathe freely. 'This is ridiculous,' he muttered.

Gently, Ferdy ran his fingers down the damaged leg. 'It's broken. A clean break. It might mend. If she doesn't die of shock.' He cut splints from a piece of wood, very carefully teased the broken bone together, and bound it in place. He topped the dressing with a piece of smooth leather stuck down with glue. 'I hope she won't be able to get that off. She'll try, of course. But if it stays on the leg should mend. Now she needs rest, and warmth, and quiet.'

'Thank you,' said Derwin. 'I'll find her a nice secluded spot.' He crept out, the bird in his arms.

'Crazy,' muttered Conrad. 'Crazy.'

But next morning he found himself going to enquire after the invalid.

'Emma?—She's fine,' said Derwin. 'Look, she can hop around a bit, and she's eaten some grain.'

'You should have wrung its neck. If it lives you can't let it go. Even if the leg mends well enough for it to fly—which it probably won't—it's too late for it to migrate. And you're surely not expecting to keep it eating its head off all winter?'

'Why not?'

'Because there's barely enough for us to eat, that's why.'

'Well, she can have some of mine. I don't eat much.'

'You'll be lucky if you're eating at all by the time this winter ends.'

The goose, recognizing a friend, honked musically, hopping and flapping across the room to settle on Conrad's boot. She did

25

look a lot better—her eyes bright, her feathers groomed. The neat ruffles on her neck fascinated him; he bent and ran his fingers down them. She felt soft, firm and warm.

'Well,' he said straightening, 'just keep her out of the way—or someone will have her for dinner.'

CHAPTER 4

IT SNOWED for days and for weeks, as if the sky were bent on smothering the earth. The sea froze, and the boats lay idle on the shore, disappearing beneath the snow which fell and fell and, caught up by the wind, rose to fall again in vast drifts, drowning the shape of the land.

It was the worst winter anyone could remember. They were prisoners in the castle; cold, bored and hungry. Food was kept under guard. Some of the old, too tired, and some of the very young, too weak, died. Their bodies could not be buried.

Plans for the journey went on, and Derwin spent most of his time in the wood store, working on the ship. He had occasional help, but preferred to work on his own, feeling with his fingers the shape growing out of the timbers. Nearby, Emma spent her convalescence comfortably cushioned on a pile of wood shavings. The pile of finished timbers grew and grew while man and goose shared a companionable silence broken only by the clunk and hiss of tools on wood.

Derwin was probably the only person in the castle to whom the winter did not seem long: he had the keel, stem and stern to fashion, the ribs, crossbeams, strakes, mast, rudder ... He was glad of some help with the floorboards and the vast quantities of wooden rivets. There were no oar-holes; the ship was too big, its crew too small. She would carry a large area of sail, but could easily be worked by a crew of two. He had worked out some ingenious devices to make tacking easier; the mainsail could be brailed in, instead of lowered, and the angle of the yard could be adjusted by ropes through a succession of pulleys. And with a fair wind she would kiss through the water ...

Perched on a pile of rigging, Morgan stitched lugubriously. For sixty years he had been expecting the worst to happen. If it hadn't happened yet, well then the worst was still to come. He

27

was probably the best sailor in the fleet, he could plot a course by the whiskers on his nose, but he could never leave harbour without anticipating disaster. Now, as his fingers moved nimbly over the sailcloth, he was convinced that the whole enterprise was doomed. 'I don't hold with these new-fangled ideas,' he said. 'If you ever get it launched, it'll sink.'

Derwin laughed. 'So why are you sewing the sails?'

'Oh well—just to help out a friend, you know.'

Smiling, Derwin went back to his planing. 'I think we should call her the *Return*,' he said suddenly.

Morgan snorted.

Brinny spent the winter practising. Always honest, she had to admit that apart from brains and heroism she had little to offer the expedition in the way of practical skills.

Her first move was to take a bow and some arrows from the armoury—without asking, although it wasn't stealing as she would of course return them. Except that when they saw how well she could shoot, they would beg her to keep the weapons and put them to use.

In the mean time she found a secluded cellar, used as a grain store, for some quiet practice. She heaved some of the sacks to one side, chalked a target on the wall and started shooting.

Brinny's mother was considerably surprised, but rather touched, by her sudden request to learn how to darn things. 'That's very thoughtful of you, dear,' she said. Brinny smiled amiably. Mending the sacks would be good practice for repairing clothes on the journey.

Down in the courtyard, children were fighting snow battles. His face close to the frosty window, Ronan watched them with a mixture of scorn and longing. 'I wish there was something to do,' he muttered.

Alina, her fingers busy with her weaving, gazed thoughtfully at her son's back. She knew better than to offer suggestions to him in this mood. The silence persisted, broken only by the clatter of the loom and the children's distant cries.

'I wonder how they're getting on with the boat?' she said

28

eventually. 'It must be nearly finished by now. Ah—bother, the shuttle's caught.'

'I'll do it.' Ronan knelt and deftly straightened the tangle. 'There you are.'

'Thank you.' For a moment their eyes met in a smile.

'And I'll find out about the boat for you.' He rose, kissed his fingers to her, and was gone in a swirl of hangings.

He found Derwin busy on the boat, with Morgan and the goose for company. 'I want to see what you're doing,' he stated, breaking in on their conversation.

Derwin willingly put down his plane. 'Come aboard.'

Morgan, shaking his head indulgently, went on stitching.

'Of course she'll look much better when she's finished. But I'm glad you've come now, I can show you how the steering system works. It's my own design.' Derwin scrambled around the boat, pointing out its original features.

Ronan sat on the side. 'It's very small. Where are my quarters?'

'Your quarters? Well—you can sleep on the deck if it's fine. If it's wet there should be a bit of room in the hold.'

'In the *hold*! You can't mean it!' Ronan leapt up, eyes blazing.

Derwin opened his mouth to say something, took a step back, and tipped head over heels down into empty space. The thud as he landed was drowned out by Ronan's crack of laughter.

With a turn of speed surprising for his age and bulk, Morgan swarmed up the side and down into the hold. 'My dear fellow, are you all right?'

Crumpled in a heap, Derwin clutched at his hand, teeth clenched.

Ronan's head appeared looking down. He gasped.

'I'll—I'll—be—all right—in a minute,' murmured Derwin.

'Sit here . . . come on . . . can you manage?' Morgan coaxed him up on to a step.

Anxiously they watched, one on either side, as Derwin's face turned from pale to ashen. 'I'm fine,' he said, and fainted.

'He's gone!' wailed Morgan.

'Dead?' cried Ronan.

Emma flapped her wings and set up a clamorous honking.

Derwin's eyes remained closed. 'Could someone please,' he murmured, 'fetch Ferdy?'

'I'll go.' Ronan tripped over the goose in his haste. She pecked him. Swearing, he ran out.

Apart from bruises, Derwin's only injury was to his right hand, which appeared to be broken. Ferdy strapped it up, tied it into a sling, and ordered him not to use it.

'How long for? What about the boat?' Derwin was appalled.

'As long as it takes,' said Ferdy severely. 'The boat will have to wait.'

'I'll help with the boat,' said Ronan. A prince should not work with his hands. Still, he had an uneasy feeling he had been responsible for the accident—and then it would be something to do—

'And I will,' said Morgan. 'You just tell us what to do, young 'un, and we'll do it.'

So, as the winter stretched on, Ronan and Morgan worked side by side. Derwin supervised, assisted by Emma, who seemed to have her own ideas on things. Brinny too came to help, and struck up a friendship with Morgan. 'Nice little thing,' he said of her. 'So eager to please. She's making herself quite indispensable.'

Brinny, overhearing, grinned to herself.

Slowly the boat took shape. She had beautiful lines. Morgan, appreciating her with a sailor's eye, gradually stopped referring to 'your journey' and began to talk of 'our boat'. Without it ever being discussed, everyone came to assume he would travel on her.

Outside, the snow continued to fall.

From deep within a dreamless sleep Ronan became aware of someone shaking him. 'Go away,' he mumbled.

'Sire! Sire, wake up!'

'What is it? Go away, let me sleep.'

'Prince, you must wake up. You must come, now!'

'Why, what's happening?' Awake now, Ronan sat up.

30

'Come where?' he demanded.

'To the King's apartments.'

'But it's the middle of the night,' protested Ronan. 'What *is* going on?'

'I don't know, Sire.'

Either the man didn't know or he wasn't going to say. 'All right,' sighed Ronan. Bleary-eyed, he dragged on a cloak and shoes.

The torches flared and guttered as they hurried along the passage. The wind howled, lifting the hangings. Outside Emerick's room people clustered, talking in hushed voices. Ronan brushed past them and opened the door.

The room was full of people. Alina turned and beckoned him to the bedside.

At first he thought the King was dead, and himself King. Emerick lay deathly still, his eyes vacant, his face twisted. Then the old man's chest heaved as he took a harsh, rattling breath.

'What is it?' asked Ronan.

'A seizure,' said Alina. 'He is very ill.'

Ronan stared, fascinated, at the contorted mask which had been his grandfather's face. 'Can—can anything be done?'

'We have done all that is possible.'

It was his uncle's voice. Conrad stood at the far side of the bed, staring down.

Ronan suddenly felt very hot, with the press of people and the fire roaring in the hearth. He let the cloak slip to the floor. 'What should I do?' he asked.

Alina's hand clasped his shoulder. 'Nothing. Only wait.'

All that night they sat, in a silence broken only by that irregular, rasping breath and the spit and crackle of the fire: Ronan, with Alina at his side, and opposite, Conrad.

For a while all Ronan's thoughts were taken up with listening to his grandfather's breathing, frightened that each breath might be the last. Death seemed to hover like a great moth, fluttering just above their heads, ready at any moment to settle, smothering, choking, blotting out . . . His throat convulsed, he could hardly breathe, no longer sure whether it were

Emerick or himself who was dying.

Ronan clenched his fists, his nails digging into his palms, willing his heart to stop pounding, the blood to stop drumming in his ears. He could not show himself a coward, not in front of Conrad . . .

Eventually he won back control of his body and found the courage to look up. No one seemed to have noticed his panic. As time went by his fear quietened.

If Emerick died, Ronan would be king. If Conrad let him.

His uncle's shadow lay across the bed. Silhouetted against the torches on the wall behind, Conrad's face was hardly discernible. Impossible to tell what he was thinking. But then he was always like that. Always remote.

When I was little, thought Ronan, I was scared of him but I thought he was wonderful. So tall and strong and powerful. And his clothes . . . I wanted to be able to dress like that, and to hunt like him. I was always trying to please him, but I could never get close. He was always making me look a fool . . . Every time I tried to show him how well I could do something he could do it better. Just because he's older. But I'll show him yet. He's always looking down on me and what makes him better than me anyway? I'm the one who'll be king . . .

Ronan jerked back to the present, remembering that before he could be king, Emerick must die. He was old, but he had always been kind . . . The Prince's eyes filled with tears.

'Go to bed,' said Conrad.

'No,' said Ronan, 'I want to stay.'

'Come Ronan,' said his mother. 'Conrad is right. You go and get some rest. We will call you if there is any change.'

Dismissed Ronan walked reluctantly to the door, then turned back to see his uncle's dark, brooding figure still hunched over the bed.

Two days later, Conrad met Alina as she left the King's room.

'No change?' he asked.

'None. Nor will be, I think. I don't believe he will fully wake again, but yet he does not die.'

Conrad looked at her, pale in the cold morning light, noting

32

for the first time the threads of silver in her black hair. 'I should not go on this journey,' he said.

'You must. It is as the wizard said, we have no choice. You must go, Conrad, but come back quickly. I do not like to think what would become of our people if we had to face another such winter here.'

'But how will you manage? Emerick cannot rule.'

'Then I shall rule in his name. We shall make ready while you are away, build enough ships to carry all our people. As soon as you return to show us the way, we shall set sail for Ilyriand.'

Conrad raised his eyebrows. 'You have great faith in my success.'

'I trust you,' said Alina. 'I have to.' She looked up at him, seemed about to speak, then changed her mind. She turned, pulled back a window hanging. A blast of chill air and a wan light entered the passage. Outside was a frozen world, snow upon ice upon snow.

'How many have died, these last weeks?' She spoke low, staring out at the bitter cold. 'How many more will die before winter ends? As soon as the ice breaks you must set sail, and you must return before the winter comes again. Before it does we shall be ready to leave Fallond. It is home for us no longer. If you delay we shall leave anyway and trust to chance that we find somewhere to go.' She turned to face him. 'I will not stay here to freeze to death. We can at least die warm!'

'I shall have very little time,' said Conrad. 'And there is no telling what I shall find . . .'

'I know. Go soon, come back quickly.' She tried to smile. 'I trust you, Conrad,' she said again.

Frowning, Conrad watched her go.

They woke one morning to the sound of water dripping. The wind had slackened and veered to the west; in the warmer air the thaw began. Streams flowed again, first in trickles, then torrents, then floods. As the waters subsided, colour returned: blue in the sky, green on the earth. The fishing boats set sail once more.

One evening Conrad met Derwin as he walked up the winding

track from the harbour, Emma as usual hobbling at his heels. Now out of splints, her leg had mended reasonably well, as had Derwin's hand.

'The ship's nearly finished,' Derwin announced. 'We'll be able to launch her in a couple of days.'

'Good.' Conrad bent to greet the goose, then paused as a thought occurred to him. 'You're not thinking we can take the goose with us, are you?'

'Why not?'

'I already seem to be taking with me on what should be a very important enterprise all the lame ducks of Fallond—I don't see why I should be encumbered with a lame goose as well.'

'Oh, I don't know, it seems appropriate,' grinned Derwin.

Conrad looked at him, clenched his lips tight, and strode off. As he turned a bend in the path, an arrow hissed past inches from his face and thudded, quivering, into a tree at his side.

He whipped round, crouched, ready to spring before his assailant could draw again—and saw Brinny, bow in hand, grinning at him.

'How about that for shooting?' she said. 'I can do even better than that. Shall I show you? You'll have to take me with you now.'

Speechless, Conrad slowly advanced on her.

Brinny's smile wavered. For a moment she hesitated then, reading the look of murderous rage in Conrad's eyes, she turned and fled.

Prothero, perched on a rock, an interested spectator, sniggered. 'Tut, tut, Conrad,' he called. 'Why don't you pick on someone your own size?'

On the eve of their departure, Alina called the travellers together to wish them well. They met in the great hall so that Prothero too could attend. Even Emma the goose was there.

'I am sorry,' said Alina, 'that the King cannot be here to wish you farewell. I speak on his behalf. But I am sure you don't want to spend your last evening listening to long speeches. All I shall say is, I wish you every good fortune, a speedy voyage, a successful outcome, and a safe return. The future of our people

34

depends on you. I know we can rely on you. Now raise your cups and let us drink to Ilyriand!'

'To Ilyriand!' cried Ronan fervently.

'Can we have a bit less enthusiasm, please?' said Prothero, looking pained. 'We may be sent on a fool's errand but we don't have to pretend to enjoy it.'

'It's not a fool's errand!' Ronan was scandalized. 'You heard what my mother said. Our whole future depends on it.'

The dragon snorted. 'I tell you it's a wild goose chase.' He licked his lips, looking sideways at Emma.

'Come on, Prothero, you know you'll enjoy it,' said Derwin. 'Look at you all! Why so miserable? And what's wrong with you, Ferdy?'

'I wish I wasn't going,' said Ferdy. 'I'm not brave—and I get seasick.'

'You can't possibly go on being seasick for the whole of the voyage.'

'I can,' said Ferdy simply.

'Oh, do cheer up. Shall I play something?' Derwin got out his flute.

It was a beautiful instrument, mellow and true, its music haunting, evocative, impossible to listen to unmoved. Derwin played serenely on, oblivious to all but the music he was making, as the melody slipped from melancholy to sighing.

Glancing round, Conrad saw that Morgan's eyes were wet with tears. Embarrassed he looked towards Alina. Her eyes were stony, her fingers writhing in the folds of her dress.

'Can't you play something more cheerful?' Conrad demanded abruptly.

'What? Oh, sorry. How about this?' Derwin broke into a catchy jig.

'I liked the other tune better,' said Ronan.

'That is because you are young,' said a new voice. 'And sadness is still a game for you.' The wizard stood framed in the doorway.

'I thought you were dead,' cried Conrad, startled.

'Thank you for your concern. With your permission . . .' He inclined his head towards Alina, and lowered himself on to a

35

stool. He looked thinner than ever, frail, as if a wind might blow right through him.

Ronan, annoyed at the suggestion that he had not known suffering, but too much in awe of the wizard to contradict him, seethed inwardly.

'Have you come to wish us well?' enquired Conrad, his voice edged with sarcasm.

'That—and for a cup of ale. *Is* all well?'

The two men's eyes met and held.

'Well enough,' said Conrad indifferently, looking away.

'I wonder.'

Derwin brought the wizard a drink. 'Have you seen the ship?' he asked.

'Yes. I admired her very much. You have worked hard.'

'Mmm—though I still think I could improve the rigging. It would only take a couple of days. If I were to . . .'

The conversation, and the argument, became general. The wizard sipped his ale and listened. The candles burned low. Prothero fell asleep.

'And have you thought,' asked the wizard at last, 'what you will do if ever you find Ilyriand?'

'Of course I have,' cried Ronan. 'I shall make my people great again. We'll get there, I know we will. It's just sitting there waiting for us, with everything we need. I shall build a palace— or several, one for every week of the year!' he added with a laugh.

The wizard looked at him. 'Think,' he said, 'of a world without men. A world where the sun shines, and the rain falls. Where grass grows, nibbled by deer in the early morning. Where the unwary deer is pounced on by the wolf. Where the wolf, when it dies in turn, is swallowed up by the earth. And where its body lies the grass grows thicker . . . There is a balance in the natural world that no other creature can upset. But you, you have that power. Power, endless power: but not the wisdom to know where it will lead. You can reach out your hand and change the world. Change one thing, and that may change another unforeseen, and that another, and another, until the world lies about you in ruins and you stand alone in the desert

36

wind of your shattered dreams.'

An uneasy silence followed this speech, broken by a rumbling snore from Prothero. 'Encouraging as usual, aren't you?' remarked Conrad.

'I speak the truth. I hope that those who listen are wise enough to learn.'

'Well it's my land and I'll do what I like with it,' Ronan muttered crossly, but he said it to himself.

'It's very late,' said Alina. 'And we should be in our beds.'

'Of course,' said the wizard. 'I wish you well with your journey. But don't forget what I said!'

CHAPTER 5

IT WAS a fine morning. The whole of Fallond had turned out to see them off. The dragon had, with some difficulty, been manœuvred on board and now lay complaining about the lack of space. Emma sat sedately in the bows, Conrad pretending not to notice her. At least she was one problem which could if necessary be eaten.

'Where's Brinny?' asked Morgan. 'She'd like to see us off.'

'I haven't seen her since yesterday,' said Ronan.

'Perhaps it was too painful for her,' sighed Morgan. Thayer looked suspicious but said nothing.

A few minutes later there was a piercing scream. Conrad appeared from the hold, a struggling figure pinned under one arm.

'We have a stowaway,' he announced.

'Let me down!' yelled Brinny. 'You big bully!'

'What you need,' said Conrad, 'is a good hiding.' He carried her, still kicking and screaming, down the gangplank, and dumped her unceremoniously at her father's feet.

'Just you wait!' she stormed. '*Just you wait!*'

Ferdy would gladly have changed places with her. He huddled miserably in the stern, trying not to get in the way as people scurried around him shouting cryptic commands and doing inexplicable things with ropes. As if by magic sails appeared. The bow swung away from the quayside, the sail flapped, then filled with a crack and the land was slipping away from them. Appalled, Ferdy felt the deck heaving beneath him. He swallowed, closed his eyes, felt worse, opened them again, saw the crowd of wellwishers waving goodbye. He closed his eyes once more . . .

The deck was rising and his stomach was sinking. Or was it the other way round? Both heaved together. He felt himself

being dragged across the deck. 'Never be sick to leeward,' said
Conrad. 'Oh, find him a bucket somebody!'

Ronan stood in the bows looking back to where the figures of
his mother, Thayer, and the rest were dwindling into a blur. The
small one still waving must be Brinny.

He turned to look forwards where the bows surged towards
the unknown. The wind whipped through his hair. He stretched
up his arms, gripped the ropes on either side and laughed aloud.

For many days the wind hardly varied and the ship scudded
south under a cloudless sky. Life fell into a tranquil pattern.
They all took turns to steer, keep watch, trim the sails—all, that
is, except Ferdy. He did eventually stop feeling sick, much to his
surprise and some time after he felt he had died of it. But he
could never understand what he was supposed to do. For him
innocent ropes took on a life of their own, twisting out of his
hands, tripping him up, unaccountably lengthening when they
were supposed to get shorter. Things came to a head when,
trying to coil up a rope in a high wind, Ferdy lost control of it
and it flew from his hands over the stern. He was standing on
the other end and fell over as it wrapped itself round his ankle.
At least he caught the end of the rope and stopped it
disappearing altogether. But suddenly the ship was bucketing
round in circles and everyone was shouting and running, except
for Morgan, who came aft, his grey hair streaming in the wind
but his balance not at all thrown out by the wild cavorting of the
deck. He looked glumly over the stern.

'What—what's the matter?' gasped Ferdy, still on hands and
knees.

As the sails slithered down the mast the crazy plunging
ceased. The *Return* still went round in circles, but quietly.

'The rope's fouled the rudder,' said Morgan.

Ferdy picked himself up and staggered over to the rail. 'Will
we sink?' he asked anxiously.

Morgan sucked at a tooth. His long face lengthened.
'Probably,' he said. 'I expect the rudder will break off and we'll
be doomed to drift until we founder.'

'Rubbish,' said Derwin, clapping Ferdy on the shoulder. 'Of

course we won't sink. All we have to do is unravel the rope, then we'll be under way again.'

'Right then,' said Conrad. 'In the water with you.'

Derwin looked dismayed. 'Er—I can't swim.'

But Conrad was already kicking off his boots. He tied Ferdy's end of the rope to the mast and, knife in hand, went over the side. The ship was tossing up and down in the waves, as well as continuing to spin. Ferdy, peering over the stern, couldn't think how Conrad could ever get hold of the rudder long enough to free the rope.

'I expect he'll drown,' said Morgan, sniffing. 'Misfortunes never come singly.'

'I should have made the rudder so we could lift it on board if it fouled,' remarked Derwin thoughtfully. 'If I'd had more time . . .'

'The saddest words in all the world,' lamented Morgan. 'It might have been . . .'

'Good old Morgan,' grinned Derwin. 'What would we do without you to cheer us up?'

'Well, I do try to look on the bright side,' said Morgan bravely.

The ship stopped its circling motion and settled to sloshing up and down in the waves. Ferdy closed his eyes and breathed deeply, waiting for his stomach to return to its proper place. When he opened his eyes again, Conrad was looming over him, dark and damp, but still elegant.

'In future,' he stated, 'you will kindly confine yourself to swabbing the decks. If you wish to have a future.'

Ferdy winced. Derwin gave him a sympathetic smile and a mop.

After that, Ferdy kept very quiet, devoting himself to cleaning up and to trying not to get in anybody's way. Life settled back into the shipboard routine.

Morgan spent much of his time fishing, both for fish and, by way of variety, for fulmars. These would fight viciously for bait trailed on a line then, as the victor was still pluming itself on its good lunch, Morgan would haul it up and hit it on the head. After a while the remaining birds would grow cautious and keep their distance; but they always, eventually, came back. There were good pickings to be had from the ship, and the inedible remains of their dead companions were squabbled over as eagerly as the rest of the rubbish.

Derwin played his flute, or carved small pieces of wood into intricate shapes. Emma took occasional short flights around the ship, but for the most part sat on the deck, preening, or slumbering with her head tucked under one wing. She spent the nights asleep in the crook of Derwin's knees, a warm and comfortable presence; but she had an unfortunate habit of waking just before dawn, and waking everyone else as well with a loud honking. Even Ferdy, bad-tempered in the mornings, began to talk about goose stew.

Gardol and Wescott spent much of their time in the hold, muttering. They stopped talking if anyone else came near.

Conrad kept his own counsel.

Prothero slept.

Ronan wasn't certain how he felt. His first excitement died down and he took refuge once more in day-dreams. From these he would wake with a thrill to realize he was already in an adventure; but then he would grow bored again. He enjoyed the comradeship, but resented the lack of privacy. He was not used to being on such close terms with others; he wanted to keep his distance, but he wanted to make friends. He was never quite sure how to react, particularly to Conrad, whose silent assumption of authority both irritated and impressed him. His uncle's brooding presence filled him with a mixture of fear, admiration, envy and resentment—and something else: a craving for affection.

It was another bright and peaceful morning.

'Sail ho,' remarked Prothero in conversational tones. 'Port— or do I mean starboard? Over there, anyway.'

They all crowded to the rail, screwing up their eyes to make out the tiny shape. In all this vast ocean, to meet other humans seemed something wonderful. They stood and watched for a while. Gradually it became apparent that the ship, though still far distant, was on a converging course. Eventually they returned to their usual occupations, only glancing occasionally towards the horizon, where the shape grew very slowly larger and more distinct. Only Conrad remained at the rail, a tiny crease between his brows.

Ferdy went back to his chores, tending the fire and, armed with bucket and mop, swabbing out below decks. He could never think where the dirt came from all the time. No matter how often he cleaned, it always seemed to need doing again. When he climbed back on deck, Prothero and Ronan had joined Conrad at the rail. The other ship was much closer.

'It's no good,' Conrad said. 'We can't fool ourselves any longer. Those sails are black.'

'What of it?' asked Ferdy, but suddenly everyone was busy shouting, changing course, cramming on more sail.

'What's the matter? What are we doing?' Ferdy asked in vain until, as the *Return* settled to her new course, running straight before the wind at a new and hideous speed, Derwin took pity on him.

'Only pirates have black sails,' he explained.

Ferdy blenched. Pirates were a legend, a rumour of horror and death lurking in the open sea. No-one had ever been captured by them and lived to tell the tale. 'What are we going to do?' he asked faintly.

'Run,' said Derwin. 'We can't fight them, we'll just have to hope we can keep out of their reach until sunset. After dark we should be able to lose them.'

'Do you think—*can* we outrun them?'

'I don't know. That ship is very fast. But so are we!' He grinned.

There was nothing to do but wait, as the *Return* hissed through the waves and the pirate ship followed after. Wait, and look from the ship, to the sun, to the sea. The sun was still high, and the pirates came ever closer.

Hours passed. The ship, the sun, the sea . . . Nobody moved, except occasionally to make a slight adjustment to the sails. Even Morgan, steering, had stopped lamenting and only gazed dumbly along the same inexorable triangle.

The ship, the sun, the sea . . . Conrad caught Derwin's eye.

The two of them huddled together, whispering.

The ship, the sun, the sea . . . 'I wish they'd hurry up!' Ronan's voice cracked unsteadily, his face white and taut.

Conrad looked at him, then said, 'Come and help, Ronan. We're trying to think what's best to do.'

Derwin raised his eyebrows, then shrugged, and began explaining to Ronan.

Ferdy picked up his bucket and mop and started to wash the deck. He had to wash round Prothero: the dragon, eyes closed, refused to move.

Morgan sucked at a hole in a tooth.

Conrad jumped down into the hold and started to sort out some non-essentials, which he tossed overboard. 'My clothes! You can't do that!' wailed Gardol, emerging for the first time from his hiding-place.

'Any arguments and I'll throw *you* overboard. That would lighten the load considerably.'

The day dragged on. The sun burned hotter. Prothero still lay, apparently asleep, snoring gently.

'I don't know how he can sleep at a time like this,' muttered Ferdy, angling his body into the largest patch of shade he could find.

When he woke it was immediately obvious that they had lost the race. Although the sun was now dipping towards the water, the pirate ship was so close that he could make out figures with flashing swords lining her side.

'Get down,' hissed Ronan.

Obediently, Ferdy crouched down again. Prothero lay in the bows, still as a figurehead. Ronan knelt beside him. Morgan was at the tiller, his face fixed in an expression of profoundest gloom. Derwin and Conrad were squatting in the galley. Wescott and Gardol were almost invisible in the darkest recess of the hold, a blanket clutched over their heads. Ferdy thought of going to join them, but decided he would rather die in the open air.

Nobody moved. The gap was narrowing rapidly now. *Return*'s sails flapped and sagged as the pirate ship robbed her of the wind. Peering over the side, Ferdy saw the attackers poised, some with grappling ropes, all with swords. There was just a little sea between them, and now, too late, the sun flared orange behind the masts.

Twenty yards, fifteen, ten . . .

'Now!' cried Conrad.

Prothero twisted suddenly to life, vast and terrifying, shooting out a great gust of blue flame towards their assailants. Ronan lit an arrow at the flame, then shot it spiralling towards the black sails. Conrad and Derwin too were shooting burning arrows, lit at the galley fire: always at the rigging; and now the black sails were flaming red. Some of the pirates were turning, running for buckets, hacking at burning ropes. Others, still bent on boarding, prepared to jump.

Suddenly there was a new danger as the wind caught the flames, and sparks showered the deck of the *Return*. There was Ronan, running with a boathook. There was the goose, flapping and honking. Arrows hissed and thudded. A pirate leapt, landed on the rail, eyes white, glaring, sword burning with reflected red. Ferdy threw a bucket at him: he toppled over backwards and vanished with a muffled shriek. Prothero, unrecognizable, spouted flame and fury. There was fire all around.

Ronan clutched his last arrow, determined to make it count. He singled out his quarry, a big man yelling orders. Carefully he fitted the arrow to the string, waited for the ship to settle at the top of the rise. They were so close he could see the streak of grey in the man's hair, the gap in his teeth that showed as he shouted. It's only like shooting at a target, Ronan told himself, drawing back the string. He hesitated.

Then, abruptly, it was over. Their sails, bellying once more with the wind, lifted them away. The black and flaming masts fell back into the orange sunset. As they watched, the burning sails, cut away, finally fell hissing into the sea. The red sun etched the outline of what was now a pitiful, dismasted hulk.

'You know, I rather enjoyed that,' remarked Prothero.

'You did well,' said Conrad.

Prothero poked a claw in his ear and shook his head. 'My hearing seems to be going funny. Must have been all the noise.'

Tears pricked at Ronan's eyes. He had failed. Just when it

mattered he had lacked the courage to shoot.

'Well done, Prince,' said Conrad.

'I didn't kill him,' said Ronan.

'Quite right. There was no need.'

Ferdy felt quite amazingly happy. 'What will happen to them now?' he asked, grinning. 'Will they sink?'

'Oh no,' answered Derwin. 'But they won't be able to go anywhere in a hurry. Although of course where there's one pirate ship there may be others . . .'

Taking no chances, they altered course and continued to scud along as fast as they dared in the moonlight. They all remained on deck, not feeling like sleep.

'Did we kill many?' asked Wescott.

Conrad's lips twitched. Wescott and Gardol had been cowering out of sight throughout the battle. 'No,' he answered. 'I wouldn't give much for the chances of the man Ferdy knocked overboard, but I didn't see anyone else in real danger.'

'But I only threw a bucket at him,' objected Ferdy.

'Yes, but you knocked him down between the ships—if he didn't get crushed he probably drowned.' Conrad could still hear the man's cry, see the terror in his eyes as he dropped.

'Well I didn't mean to—I think,' said Ferdy, unsure.

'Ah well,' began Prothero. 'I always remember the wizard saying that a sneeze in the wrong place might start an avalanche that might bury a town.'

'What a discouraging thought,' said Derwin.

'If you believed that you'd never do anything,' said Ronan.

'I believe it,' said Prothero.

'Which is why you never do anything,' said Conrad.

'Excess of thought, not absence of energy. I have hidden depths.' The dragon yawned and composed himself for sleep.

'Of course,' said Ferdy thoughtfully, 'if you look at it like that it's probably just as dangerous to do nothing.'

'Indeed,' Morgan agreed. 'I've heard it said that living can be fatal.'

Derwin looked at him narrowly, suspecting a joke.

'Still,' said Ronan, 'those pirates did deserve to die, didn't they?'

45

'Why?' asked Morgan. 'If we killed them we'd be no better than they are.'

'But they're *evil*,' protested Ronan.

'I don't know,' yawned Prothero, opening an eye. 'At home with their families they're probably nice peace-loving folks, fond of flowers and kind to animals.'

'And the sooner they're safe at home and far away from us, the better I'll be pleased,' added Conrad.

CHAPTER 6

NEXT DAY dawned sweet and soft, the horizon as clear as the azure sky. A warm breeze filled the sails, the ship slid through a tranquil sea. After an anxious night on watch, Conrad felt he could finally relax. Stretching out in the warm sun, he settled down to sleep.

Which was soon interrupted as a shadow blotted out the sun. Through eyes narrowed against the glare he saw Wescott, arms akimbo, scowling down at him. The light edged the little man's graceless silhouette with a quite inappropriate radiance. Gardol, as usual, wallowed at his elbow.

'Now look here,' began Wescott belligerently.

'But I *am* looking,' complained Conrad.

'It's not good enough. Pirates and such. Nobody said anything to us about pirates. Just sail the ship, you said. Nothing about going in peril of our lives.'

'You knew it would be dangerous.'

'Ah, well you were bound to *say* that,' said Wescott cunningly.

Conrad closed his eyes and breathed hard. 'What do you expect us to do about it?' he enquired. 'Turn round and go home? The pirates are behind us now.'

'That's as may be,' answered Wescott darkly. 'What we're saying is, the price has gone up.'

'What price?' demanded Conrad, sitting up. 'What are you talking about?'

'Oh that's nice, that is.' Wescott turned to address Gardol, who shook his head in sad agreement. 'Risk our lives for them we do and they try to swindle us. Well, we're not going to be bamboozled. You can't pull the wool over *my* eyes,' he added, warming up. 'I know your little game. Think you'll keep all the treasure to yourself, do you? Well, you're very much mistaken. A third share, that's what we want, and that's what we'll have.'

'Look, you poor misguided dimwit,' cried Conrad. 'I don't know where you got that idiotic notion, but you'd better forget it. There *is* no treasure.'

'Don't give me that! I heard the King tell you about the silver and gold. You're no better than a thief, that's what, and if we don't get our just deserts you'll be sorry you were ever born.'

Conrad slumped back against the mast, his lips curling in a smile. 'I hope,' he said, very quietly, 'very much, that you do get your just deserts. And you are very welcome to a third share of all the gold and silver I am seeking. No, I'll be generous. You can have it all. And now, you pair of addle-pated, dunder-headed nincompoops, get out of the sun and let me sleep!'

Wescott and Gardol retreated, muttering darkly. Prothero, who had been an interested listener, yawned. 'Yet another ticklish situation handled with Conrad's usual tact and diplomacy,' he remarked. 'What a happy little band we are to be sure.'

'And you can keep quiet,' snarled Conrad. 'It's time you learnt your place.'

'Which is?' asked Prothero sweetly.

'You are the baggage-animal. At present you are useless. You don't sail the ship, you don't clean, you can't even get your own food!'

'And if one does all the work and another lies around and is waited on, which is the master and which the servant?'

'Be very careful, dragon. I might just cut you open to find out what makes you so superior.'

'Promises, promises,' murmured Prothero.

Derwin had invented several games played with small pieces of wood, either tossed in the air, or moved on squares marked on the deck. One such game was in progress, accompanied by shouts and roars of laughter as the wholly imaginary stakes of ships, mountains and castles in the air changed hands.

'You owe me two castles, Ferdy,' said Ronan, taking the dice. 'And I owe Morgan a mountain . . .'

Conrad sat at the tiller; Prothero at his usual place in the bows.

Wescott and Gardol nursed their grievances in the hold. Most of their anger was directed at Conrad, who was clearly responsible for everything.

'It's not right,' said Gardol.

'Shouldn't be allowed,' agreed Wescott.

'Threw half my clothes overboard, he did . . .'

'Trying to cheat us out of our rights . . .'

'What I say is, they were *my* clothes . . .'

'Thinks he can outsmart me, does he. Well, we'll soon see about that . . .'

'He'd no right to throw them overboard . . .'

'He didn't say anything about us having to go in peril of our lives.'

'That's right, he didn't,' agreed Gardol. 'And what's more,' he added, glancing over his shoulder, 'it wasn't right to let the Prince run such risks. Conrad should have kept him out of danger.'

'Didn't though, did he? Thrust him right into it, didn't he? Mark my words—' Wescott's voice sank to a sepulchral whisper. 'Mark my words, Ronan won't survive this voyage. If he was dead, who'd be the heir?'

Gardol's eyes opened wide. 'Why, Conrad! He—'

His speech ended in a strangled gasp. Conrad was standing in front of him, his eyes glittering, a knife in his hand.

'You need a wash, fat man. Would you like to take it now?' He stepped forward till the knife tip poked Gardol's belly. Gardol gulped, opening and closing his mouth like a landed fish. He felt the ladder behind him and went up it backwards, his eyes glued to the knife. Conrad followed after, prodding with the dagger as Gardol backed away.

'You're carrying too much blubber, fat man. Shall I cut some off for you?' Conrad's voice had sunk to a velvet purr.

Gardol felt the rail hard at his back. Rigid with terror, he stared as the knife point caressed gentle circles around his belly.

Suddenly Conrad snorted in disgust. 'It wouldn't be fair,' he said. 'You'd poison the fish.'

He turned, gave one contemptuous look at Wescott, then sheathed the knife and walked off. Gardol slithered to the deck in a palpitating heap.

'Just you wait, Conrad,' muttered Wescott as he hurried—cautiously—to his friend's aid. 'Just you wait . . .'

The weather changed next day. The wind veered to the south, so that they had to tack constantly in order to progress at all. And it began to rain; a hard, driving drizzle which did nothing to improve anyone's temper.

With the uneven sea chopping at the sides of the ship, Ferdy began to feel queasy again. Emma, pining presumably for green grass, marched irritably round the deck, hissing if anyone came near her. Wescott and Gardol hardly spoke to anyone, and to Conrad not at all. While Ronan expanded and relaxed in the enforced intimacy of shipboard life, Conrad found it irksome. He was accustomed to receive as of right the respect due to the King's son in Fallond; on ship it was impossible to keep his distance, to fend off unwanted familiarity.

Then, through an uncertain haze of rain, they caught sight of land. They altered course towards it. Any diversion would be a relief.

The land proved to be a group of small, low islands, bare and rocky. Only a few, the largest, had any covering of green. For the rest they were grey stone, blotched yellow with lichen and spattered white, rank-smelling, with the droppings of countless birds.

As very cautiously they circled the islands, kittiwakes burst over them in screaming clouds. Black cormorants stood on the crags, motionless.

A larger island loomed up through a spatter of rain. 'Make for that bay,' called Conrad. 'It looks as good a place as any to land.'

Morgan, sucking dubiously at his teeth, reluctantly put the tiller over. Derwin, in the bows, took soundings. Suddenly Ferdy screamed.

'There's a man looking at us!'

'Idiot,' said Derwin amiably. 'It's a seal.'

The seal bobbed down into the water, then surfaced again, its great black eyes still fixed on the ship. Ferdy realized that what he had taken for partly submerged rocks or weed was a great many seals with whiskery faces, all watching him.

'Port!' yelled Derwin, but Morgan had already altered course. The reef slipped safely past.

Gradually, zigzag, they nosed into the bay. The rain stopped and a silver glint flickered in the drifting clouds.

The anchor hissed into the water. *Return* tugged, swung, then stilled, bobbing gently.

The island sat grey between the leaden sea and the disintegrating sky. Waves sucked and gurgled at black-weeded rocks. The wind hovered. A gull flew overhead, regarding them from a yellow eye, cawed briefly and fouled the deck.

'Well, we got here,' said Morgan, in some surprise.

'Yes,' said Prothero. 'Can someone tell me why we bothered?'

'Gardol and I will volunteer to stay on guard,' stated Wescott, very dignified.

'But—' began Gardol. Wescott nudged him smartly in the ribs.

Conrad stared at them suspiciously, then shrugged: the chance of being relieved of their company for a few hours was too good to be missed.

'Water,' said Prothero, eyeing the distance from ship to shore, 'is bad for dragons . . .'

'Why?' asked Derwin, grinning. 'Does it make them shrink?'

'. . . So I shall take a little rest.'

'For a change,' added Conrad.

Gardol watched wistfully as the dinghy slipped away towards the island.

'Now's our chance!' Wescott hissed in his ear.

Gardol jumped. 'Don't do that!' he cried, his heart lurching. 'And why did you make me stay on board?'

Wescott smiled genially at this further proof of his superior intelligence. He glanced round at Prothero, who was lying with his chin on his paws, eyes closed and snoring gently. 'Don't you see,' he explained patiently. 'Now's our chance to get our own

51

back on them. All we have to do is set sail and leave them here. We can be back in Fallond in a month.'

Gardol looked at him blankly.

'Do what?' he said.

Wescott sighed. 'We go,' he said. 'Maroon them. When we get home, we say we've taken them to the land of the Axemen. We'll be heroes and can claim our reward.'

'But—but what if we meet the pirates?' protested Gardol, taking the largest objection first.

'Ah—I thought of that.' Wescott looked very cunning. 'If we *should* meet them, we say let us go and we'll tell you where to find the Prince of Fallond and his henchmen, the villains who attacked the pirate ship.'

Gardol, brows furrowed, peered at him unhappily. 'I wish I'd never come,' he lamented.

'Nonsense,' said Wescott bracingly. 'Look, even if we go on, we'll still have to sail back to Fallond on our own. And what I say is, the sooner the better. And this way we get our revenge on Conrad. Look at how he attacked you the other day—why, it's simple self-defence to cut and run while we've got the chance!'

'Ye-es—but what if they build a ship and come after us?'

'What with? They've no tools bigger than a hunting knife.'

'And then we're expected to go and look for them in the autumn.'

'So we don't have to *find* them, do we?'

'Oh . . .' Gardol looked around miserably for some escape. He'd never liked making decisions. He felt as if he were trapped in a quaking bog, not knowing which way to turn lest he be swallowed up . . . 'I wish I'd never come,' he said again. Then he noticed Prothero, fast asleep. 'You've forgotten something,' he said, pointing.

Wescott glanced round. 'Oh, him. We'll dispose of him.'

'But—*how*?'

'Quite simple. We cut his throat. All right?' He smiled sweetly. 'I've never liked him. On my word, prepare to make sail!'

He drew his dagger. The long narrow blade glinted in the sun as softly, tiptoeing, Wescott crept down on the sleeping dragon.

Ronan leapt out of the boat and pulled it up on the beach. There was no sign of human habitation. The only prints in the sand were those of birds. The sea hissed and the wind blew.

'It looks quiet enough,' said Conrad.

Morgan yawned. 'I'll look after the boat,' he said, lowering himself to the sand.

'I'll take Emma for a walk,' said Derwin. 'Find her some nice grass and fresh water.'

'There're some very interesting-looking plants . . .' murmured Ferdy, already drifting off.

'Get back here before sunset,' called Conrad. He took his bow and arrows from the boat. 'I'll see what I can get to vary our diet a bit . . .'

Ronan headed inland. It was good to feel firm earth beneath his feet again, although now, after so long aboard ship, it was the ground that seemed to rock and swell like the sea.

The wind sang in his ears, and in its shadows the yammering of kittiwakes. He was climbing steadily uphill. Occasionally he paused to get his bearings: the island was larger than he had expected. The sea-sounds faded gradually, and left him with the sighing wind and rustling grasses, and the churring, buzzing flitter of a myriad insects.

The sun was out fully now, warm on his back. He yawned sleepily and, like a bee drugged with nectar, drowsed on. Butterflies rose in clouds. The vegetation grew more and more dense, broken only by occasional rocky outcrops.

The rocks, mottled with lichens and partly hidden in the tall grass, grew larger as he went along, until he realized he was following a trail marked with standing stones. Soon they were taller than he, stark against the sky, casting deep shadows. And then, abruptly, they ended where a great slab of stone arched over the ground. The blackness beneath it was lit by a curious gleam.

Puzzled, Ronan crawled under, and found that the glow came from some bloated, paunchy toadstools which shone with a sickly pallor. Both intrigued and repelled, he held up a hand to one and saw all the colour drained from the flesh. It was almost as if he could see the white bones beneath the skin.

It was then that he noticed that the cavern was the mouth of a tunnel. A rock which had closed the entrance had fallen to one side, and peering round it he found himself staring into a passage with smooth walls and a beaten floor. He cast around for a suitable stick, and set to work with his tinder-box. Soon the torch was lit, and he made his way down into the darkness.

It was deathly cold after the bright sunshine outside; chill seeped into his bones. The walls glistened like a slug's trail on wet earth. Water dripped.

In places great stone slabs lined the tunnel, carved with strange patterns of lines and concentric circles. Ronan could make nothing of them, except that one pattern was repeated many times: a circle and, inside it, a sign like a snake.

The tunnel led downwards, then twisted. At the bend one wall was cut away to form a cavern. Ronan, lifting his torch, stepped into it. The flame spurted, and sent shadows dancing around where, stretched out, lay the figure of a man. All the flesh was gone, though gold wreathed the whitened bones and jewels glistened between the sunken ribs. A crown had fallen down across what had been the face.

Swallowing hard, Ronan wiped the chill sweat from his forehead. Almost he retreated to the open air, but, lured on despite himself, he went on down the tunnel. It turned this way and that, but always downwards. More carvings lined the walls. At each bend was a chamber; in each, another royal burial. One was the body of a child, only two or three years old, but still the white bones were studded with the dull gleam of gold.

Even deeper led the tunnel, and now there were no side-chambers, only a darkness still more intense and a silence that throbbed against his ears.

The passage ended in a wide cavern, in the middle of which, by the glimmer of the torch grown suddenly more feeble, Ronan made out a dark shape like a throne. He had a horrifying conviction that he was not alone. He spun round. The darkness shifted. A rustling whisper scraped through his brain.

He swallowed, closed his eyes for a moment. The darkness settled. The throne was a high table on which were set out weapons and cups all studded with jewels. Ronan stretched out his hand. His fingers closed on a torque bearing a curious device. The shadows leapt forward once more.

The knife was heavy in Wescott's hand as he sidled towards the sleeping dragon. Already he could feel the blade slide into the soft place beneath the jaw and see the sudden spurt of blood.

Closer and closer he crept. He knelt, and pulled back his hand to strike.

Prothero opened his eyes, yawned, stretched, and sat up. 'I must have dozed off,' he said, 'with the sun being so warm. Turned out nice today, hasn't it?' He glanced at Wescott who was sprawled on the deck, a glazed look in his eyes. 'I could just fancy something to eat. You wouldn't like to fetch me a little snack?'

Wescott fled. Gardol joined him in the galley.

'He heard everything!' wailed Gardol. 'I know he did. He was lying there listening to everything we said and when the others come back he'll tell them and they'll kill us!'

'N-nonsense!' said Wescott. 'He was asleep. He never heard a thing—didn't even see the knife.' He peered up at the deck, where Prothero was unconcernedly licking at a flaking scale. 'You see?' He filled a bowl with fish and biscuits, and carried it almost jauntily to the dragon.

'Something to keep you going,' he said, with an ingratiating smile.

'Ah, thank you, my dear chap,' murmured Prothero. 'So kind . . .'

But Gardol, peering from the galley, was almost sure he saw a dark gleam in the yellow eyes.

Derwin set off along the beach in search of a stream. Emma waddled behind him, stopping sometimes to peck at some grass, then taking a flying run over the sand to catch up. There were many smaller birds around, waders mainly, with long bills and piping cries. Most had chicks, balls of fluff on long legs that twinkled as they fled along the shore then plumped down to blend instantly into the background.

The bay curved round to a rocky spit pocked with pools,

lumpy with limpets and mussels. Derwin scrambled over it into the next bay. Emma flew over, circled, then skidded to a halt in a shower of sand. Honking protestingly, she hobbled over to Derwin and sat on his feet.

'Are you tired of walking? All right, I'll carry you.' He hoisted her up into his arms and went on. The goose looked round, bright-eyed.

Half-way round the second bay they came to a stream, fresh and sparkling as it spilled down over the sand. Derwin waded up it, between grassy banks, until it opened into a silver lake, edged with reeds. A moorhen dabbled among lily-pads followed by a scurry of black chicks. Water splashed as a fish jumped. Dragonflies whirred.

'This looks a nice place,' said Derwin. 'Fancy a swim?' He set Emma down on the bank and rubbed his tired arm muscles. The goose waddled towards the water, then turned to look at him. 'No, I can't swim. You go.'

She pecked at the grass at the water's edge, then stepped delicately down through the reeds.

Derwin lay on the bank among king-cups and columbines. The sky was blue now, and quiet. A bug walked up a grass stalk. Grasshoppers chirped, and the moorhen's trill rang across the water. He lay watching the patterns of leaves against the sky.

After his meal Prothero gave himself a thorough grooming, graciously accepted a drink of water from Wescott, then composed himself once more for sleep.

Wescott took his boots off. He always trod lightly: barefooted on the wooden boards his padding steps made no sound at all. Stealthily, very stealthily, he inched forward.

Prothero slept on.

The rippling sea slapped against the sides of the ship. A seagull cried. The dragon snored.

Three more steps and he'd be there. Wescott paused, all his attention focused on that tender spot at the corner of the jaw . . . He realized he was holding his breath. Now . . .

The dragon sat up and belched. A small spout of blue flame flickered at his nostrils.

Wescott bolted.

Prothero yawned and settled down again.

'I'll get you!' screamed Wescott in an hysterical whisper. 'Just you wait! I'll get you!'

Ferdy was standing close to the entrance of the tunnel, calling.

'Oh, there you are!' he said, relieved. 'I saw you coming this way, then you disappeared. I couldn't think where you'd gone—What's the matter? You look as if you've seen a ghost.'

Ronan was taking deep lungfuls of the sunny air. 'I think I did.'

Ferdy stared at him curiously. 'What's that round your neck?'

Ronan pulled it off and held it glittering in the sunlight. The torque was wreathed with weird patterns and bore at the centre a circle, within it the sign like a snake. 'I found it,' he said, and suddenly grinned. 'I'm not sure what happened—but I won!'

First at a brisk walk, then at a run, he fled back the way he had come, and to Ferdy's questions he answered not at all.

It was cooler now, the sun dipping towards the sea.

Wescott sauntered along, hands casually behind his back, his dagger in his hand.

Prothero opened one eye and grinned amiably.

Wescott passed on, whistling nonchalantly.

'I'll get him,' he muttered savagely to Gardol, lurking in the hold. 'I'll get him if it's the last thing I do.'

'I feel sick,' said Gardol.

Conrad jumped down the rocks on to the beach. It had been a successful hunt.

Morgan was still sitting where they had left him. Ronan was shying pebbles into the water.

'All quiet?' asked Conrad, looking out to where the *Return* swung at her moorings.

'A nice peaceful day,' said Morgan. 'Really it's been very pleasant,' he admitted. 'Derwin and Ferdy are just fetching some firewood. Yes, really a very peaceful day . . .'

'Here's something for you to cook,' said Conrad. 'I'll keep

one of the hares. It's my turn to stand guard tonight. I'll go and relieve our two staunch comrades over there.'

'I'll come with you,' said Ronan.

'There's no need.'

'I'd like to.'

'Then we'll keep two hares. Oh—and something for the dragon.'

'He's coming!' Gardol whispered frantically.

'Who?'

'Conrad—and Ronan.'

'Oh, are they?' asked Prothero, sitting up. 'I wonder if they've brought something nice for my dinner?'

Wescott and Gardol stood watching dumbly as the boat came slowly nearer.

'A good day's hunting?' asked Prothero hopefully, as Conrad came up the side.

'Good enough. And have you had a good rest?'

'Good enough,' said the dragon.

'Here, you two,' called Conrad. 'Your turn to go on shore.'

With a turn of speed surprising in one of his bulk, Gardol slithered down into the dinghy, beating Wescott by a whisker.

Wescott had had a long hot day, by turns infuriating and frustrating. He rowed slowly, his mind busy with its festering injuries. Of course the dragon hadn't heard, or he would have said . . . Wouldn't he? Of course. He'd have told Conrad straight away.

That Conrad, always throwing his weight around. Not even a word of thanks for looking after the ship all day. And the others just as bad. They thought they could push him around, make him do all the chores, run all the risks, then treat him like dirt. He—Wescott! Well, if they thought they could get away with that sort of thing, they were very much mistaken. As they'd find out to their cost. He'd teach them. He owed them no loyalty, not after the way they'd treated him. Thought they could get away with murder, they did. Well, it amounted to murder. Exposing him to bloodthirsty pirates—and all sorts of other dangers to come, no doubt. Threatening him—and poor old Gardol—with

58

a knife, just for speaking their minds. He had a right—no, he had a duty, a duty to protect himself. Self-defence, no one would ever say different. Not that anyone need know . . . He could trust Gardol, and there'd be no other witnesses.

He'd have to get Conrad first. He was the dangerous one, the others were fools . . . Gradually a plan began to take shape.

'You're rowing round in circles,' complained Gardol, coming out of a stupor to wonder why they were taking so long to get to the shore.

'Listen,' hissed Wescott, shipping the oars and leaning forward. Gleefully he outlined his plan.

He was disappointed in his friend's reaction. Gardol thought any such idea was far too dangerous, and when it was pointed out to him that not to do anything was in the circumstances equally dangerous, he showed an irritating tendency to put his hands over his ears and refuse to come out.

At last, by bludgeoning and persuasion, Wescott brought him round to listen to the details of his plan, to which he was adding all the time new and yet more brilliant refinements.

'We do it next time Conrad's on the night watch,' explained Wescott. 'We wait for the darkest part of the night, then tiptoe up to the man at the tiller. Just as he starts to say hello we stab him in the back and one, two, over the side with him. The look-out wonders what's happening, comes to investigate, before he knows where he is he's in the water with his throat cut, and we're back in bed all snug and tight. Now—this is the really cunning part—when questions is asked we say we saw the dragon prowling around and he must have eaten them. It all comes of trusting wild beasts, we say, and we'll have to do away with him. So they chuck *him* over the side, and they're lulled into a sense of security 'cause they think they've got rid of the culprit. And that's only three of them left. And if we can't get rid of them three all unsuspecting then my name's not Wescott!'

He finished on a note of triumph and paused in silent contemplation of his genius. Then he looked over to Gardol and asked eagerly, 'Well, what do you think?'

But Gardol was crouched in frozen misery, paralysed and dumb.

Wescott regarded him sadly. As a conspirator he left a lot to be desired.

'Ah well,' said Prothero. 'I've had a tiring day. I think I'll take a little nap before supper.'

'Do that,' said Conrad cordially. 'Conserve your strength.' Taking out his knife, he picked up a hare and started to skin it.

As he dropped the neat pink carcass into a pot he became aware of Ronan watching him. He looked up enquiringly.

Ronan flushed. 'Is—is that difficult?' he asked.

'You want to try?'

'I don't mind.' The boy took the knife and a second hare and looked perplexedly from one to the other. Abruptly he stabbed down.

'I should keep your eyes open,' advised Conrad. 'Otherwise it won't be the hare you'll skin.'

Ronan shifted his grip on the knife and attacked the animal with more deliberation, sawing a long slit down its belly. The limbs fell open, defenceless. The head jigged around, flop-eared, sunken-eyed. Frowning determinedly, Ronan hacked at the carcass, his fingers twitching in disgust. It had looked so easy when Conrad was doing it: the fur and the guts just fell away. But the hare was still warm, and slippery, and jerked the wrong way as if it were still alive. Desperately he changed tack and tried to cut off its head. He couldn't stand the sight of those furry blood-stained ears. The carcass leapt under the knife and shot out of his hands on to the deck. Torn between laughter and revulsion, Ronan started to giggle. 'It's so slimy,' he said. 'And so pathetic, and so—so *bloody*.'

'Give it here,' said Conrad, grinning. In a few deft movements he finished it off and dropped the mutilated corpse into the pot.

Ronan contemplated his outstretched hands, sticky and smelly with blood. 'Conrad,' he said suddenly. 'Have you killed many people?'

Conrad stared at him. 'What makes you think I've killed any?'

'Oh—well, I thought—the barbarians, you know.'

Conrad relaxed into a laugh. 'How old do you think I am?

60

The last time Fallond was attacked was—what—twenty years ago?'

'Oh, I thought—you seemed so confident when the pirates attacked us, I thought you must be used to killing people.'

'Hares, yes—people, no,' Conrad answered drily.

'And didn't you even see the barbarians?'

'See them?' said Conrad slowly, speaking as if from far away. 'Yes, I saw them. I was supposed to stay in the nursery, but I wanted to see my father slay the monsters . . .'

'And did you?' asked Ronan, after a pause.

'No. They weren't monsters. They looked quite ordinary, except their clothes were odd. There was one quite close, had a white shirt, he got a spear in his belly and lay there looking so surprised, twitching and plucking at the spear while the blood seeped out . . .' Conrad glanced down at his hands, red with hare's blood, and stood up. 'Time I got on with the cooking,' he said. 'Or we'll be having supper for breakfast.'

CHAPTER 7

THE MOON rose, full, pale and putrid. The trickle of silver light made the water seem even blacker. Gardol gazed vaguely at it from the bottom of a well of misery. He longed to join the others in the hold, to pull his blankets over his head and find oblivion.

His watch tonight. Tomorrow night, Conrad. And Wescott expecting him to ... No, he couldn't even think about it.

He had a pain in his chest. Perhaps he was dying. All this stress and worry lately, a strain on his heart ... They'd be sorry if they found him dead in the morning, his empty eyes staring at the sky. He shuddered, then belched. Supper had disagreed with him, was lying heavy on his stomach. Maybe he could wake Ferdy and ask him for a remedy. But then he might disturb the others and they'd be angry with him.

Looking aft, he could just make out the shape of Wescott hunched over the tiller. Beyond, nothing but black sea and chill stars. Why had he ever come? He didn't even want to be rich. He'd been quite happy in his little room in Fallond, with everything he needed. He should have known better, he should have known he'd never be a hero striding the world in search of fame and fortune. He was big and fat and a coward. And he was so cold, so uncomfortable, so scared ... Tears suddenly stung his eyes and his vision blurred.

It was then that he saw it, through a film of tears. Its head was as big as a boat, reared up on a vast and scaly neck. Its teeth were jagged cliffs and the stars were in its eyes. Silently it reared up, silently stooped over Wescott who dozed on unsuspecting.

Gardol tried to shout a warning, but no sound came. For one long moment he stood paralysed, then, catching up a boathook, he ran.

There was no one to see as Gardol, brandishing the boat-hook, his mouth gaping in a soundless shriek, hurtled forward to protect his friend.

Then the scream came, wailing from the sea to the stars, and suddenly ended.

The scream woke them in time to see the monster's huge head vanishing beneath the waves. Of Wescott and Gardol there was no sign: only the abandoned tiller, swinging.

Morgan hurried to get the ship back on course. The others clustered on deck. No one suggested going back to sleep. Conrad fetched his bow, though he realized it would be a very inadequate defence should the sea serpent return—as at any moment it might.

But dawn rose on a quiet sea.

'Well, what are you all looking so glum about?' asked Prothero over breakfast, a subdued meal. 'None of you liked them.'

'But it's such a horrible way to die,' protested Ronan. 'Eaten alive!'

'Well?' enquired the dragon, chewing on a hunk of meat. 'Everyone has to eat.'

'How can you be so callous? They were *men*.'

'So what's so special about men? Why shouldn't I take the sea serpent's side? After all, we're probably related.'

There was a short silence, broken by Derwin. 'Tell me, Prothero, if you were really hungry would you eat us?'

A slow smile spread over the dragon's face. 'Wouldn't you like to know?' he said.

'I suppose,' Derwin remarked later, unenthusiastically, 'I suppose we ought to sort out their things.'

An expression of acute distaste flitted across Conrad's face. 'Good idea,' he said with assumed vigour. 'Carry on.'

'Well—someone—Ferdy, will you help?'

'Must we?' he asked.

'Of course we must,' said Morgan. 'We may find something which will be of comfort to their grieving families.'

'They didn't have any families.'

'Nevertheless,' asserted Morgan, raising a finger, 'we should do our best to comfort the afflicted. I would do it myself only I'm steering the ship.'

Down in the hold, Derwin and Ferdy broke open Gardol's pack and gazed at the contents with something like awe. Lengthily, they counted.

'I say, Ronan,' called Derwin, his head appearing on deck. 'Gardol had forty-three pairs of socks.'

'No—really?'

'Look.' Spilled out on the deck the socks lay, twisted, voluminous, and infinitely pathetic. They were beautifully knitted, with neatly turned heels and elegant stripes. They were also, just a little, smelly.

'Heavens,' said Ronan, holding one up. 'Aren't they *huge*!'

'Do you think they'd fit me?' asked Prothero. 'I do get a trifle chilly around the talons and of course I'd need two pairs at once.'

'If you think I'll tolerate the spectacle of a dragon in striped socks padding around the ship—' began Conrad.

'This is not seemly,' interrupted Morgan. 'A little respect for the dead, if you please.'

'I don't see why,' said Prothero. 'We never showed them any while they were alive. Why should we start now?'

'I don't know,' said Derwin. 'I have a lot of respect for anyone who could knit that many socks.'

Ronan giggled. Conrad, straight-faced, fixed him with a stern eye. 'Enough of this frivolous badinage,' he said grandly.

'Frivolous what?' asked Prothero.

'Badinage,' repeated Derwin. 'It means . . . I'm not quite sure what it means.'

'If no one has a better suggestion,' continued Conrad ruthlessly, 'I propose we throw this garbage overboard.'

'It seems a bit heartless,' Ronan demurred.

'Do you want them?' Conrad demanded.

'Well—no.'

'Then . . .'

Solemnly Derwin scooped up the armfuls of forlorn footwear and stepped aft. One by one he tossed them on to the quiet sea. They strung out behind, coloured streamers bobbing on the waves, till slowly they filled and gloomily sank.

CHAPTER 8

FOR TWO days they made good progress, running before a fair wind, the ocean empty of all but a distant school of whales, and dolphins that leapt and played around them.

'How marvellous,' said Derwin, watching a dolphin shoot out of the water, arc through the air, and plunge back, twisting its tail to hit the surface a resounding smack. 'I wish I could swim.'

'Do you?' said Conrad, a curious expression on his face; and when by the following day the wind had died to a flat calm, he reminded him of it.

'You did say you'd like to learn to swim. Now's your chance.'

'What do you mean?'

'It's a lovely warm day, the ship's going nowhere, and I'm going to tie a rope round you and throw you overboard.'

'Oh no you're not.'

'It's the quickest way to learn to swim. Swim like a dolphin, you said.'

'Just an idle fancy,' said Derwin, backing away nervously.

Conrad looked on with sour satisfaction: it was pleasing to find something Derwin wasn't good at.

'Sea water makes me sneeze,' said Derwin. 'It gets in my ears, it—' He turned and bolted.

But Ronan and Ferdy barred his way. Rope in hand, they pounced.

Conrad was less ruthless than he had threatened. He dived in beside Derwin, and proved to be a surprisingly good teacher.

It became very hot as the sun climbed towards noon. One by one they all stripped and jumped into the water. All, except Prothero.

By mid-afternoon, Derwin had achieved a reasonably effective dog-paddle, and was cruising around the ship, very pleased with himself. Until, lifting his head from the water, he found himself looking into a giant eye.

'The monster!' he thought, and slipped under the water.

The whale broached with a snort like a giant bellows.

No one had seen it coming. It was just, suddenly, there—immense. Derwin, floundering back to the surface, realized his mistake. He reached out to touch its skin, found himself trapped by a flipper. The whale dived. Derwin hurtled down, bubbles bursting past his ears, into the green depths, whirled away by the animal's endless, effortless strength. Almost he was drowning, almost it seemed worth it; then the whale turned slowly, dreamily, and he spun back to the surface, the light exploding in a shower of spray.

Conrad was there, and caught him. ' "Like a dolphin," we said. Take your time, and work up to whales!'

Ferdy opened his eyes on an empty sky. He yawned and stirred, feeling the wooden planks hot on his naked skin. Sun-drowsed, he blinked, dozed, and woke again, deciding to take just one more swim to refresh himself before supper. He rose to his feet, stretched, and a great coil of rope was thrust into his arms.

He stared at it, bewildered, then looked round. Everyone seemed to be frantically, incomprehensibly, busy. 'What am I supposed to do with this?' he asked plaintively.

Morgan, hurrying past, muttered something about securing stores.

'I thought I'd have another swim.'

'Don't be daft,' said Derwin. 'Can't you see there's a storm coming?'

Ferdy inspected the sea. Apart from a sort of circular swell it was as tranquil as it had been all day. True, the sky to the west was a rather funny colour, but there was no sign of an approaching storm.

Not liking to argue, he climbed down into the hold, found some boxes, and started to tie them together. The rope, as usual, had a will of its own, and either the knots were too loose or he got his fingers caught in them. But eventually he achieved what he felt was a very creditable effect. He stood back to admire it, and even pointed it out to Derwin.

Derwin contemplated it in silence, then tugged thoughtfully at a knot. The edifice wobbled, swayed, disintegrated. Still without a word, Derwin re-stacked the boxes, covered them with a cloth, and began expertly to lash them down.

Ferdy withdrew to the galley where he gave vent to his feelings by making batter. He had mastered the art of shipboard pancakes, overcoming the lack of fresh ingredients with extra energetic beating and skilful use of the fork. It was a soothing occupation.

'What are you doing?' asked Conrad.

'Making pancakes,' answered Ferdy defensively.

'Good idea. It might be a while before we get another meal. Do some fish as well.'

He disappeared again.

Ferdy looked up at the sky. It reminded him of the inside of a brazen helmet, won in some forgotten battle, which now gathered dust in the library at Fallond.

He went back to his cooking.

Two hours later he was regretting the pancakes. The storm had hit them like a cliff flying. In seconds the world had turned into a shrieking, gyrating darkness where directions, dimensions, elements whirled in a chaotic unreason.

Hardly had the ship wallowed into the trough of one wave before she was hurtling up the next; and though her mast was bare except for the tiny triangle of the storm sail, the wind howled about her until her timbers seemed to come alive, shaking and wailing in anguished fury.

While the others were wrestling with the ship, Ferdy was miserably aware of failure. He'd been congratulating himself on getting his sea-legs at last: now, when it really mattered, all he could do was vomit. Again and again his stomach heaved and turned itself inside out.

After one such shuddering spasm had died down, Ferdy staggered to his feet and up on deck with some vague idea of helping. He lurched as the wind hit him, then a great wall of water reared up, exploded on the deck, and falling back took him with it. I'm overboard, he thought, I'm drowning—but the line round his waist held firm and the next wave dashed him back on to the ship.

Conrad grabbed him and pushed him back below, shouting to the dragon, 'Can't you hold him down?'

'I might, if I knew which way was up,' wailed Prothero. But his words were lost in the wind.

Ronan struggled towards the tiller. The storm had grown yet wilder and he knew the ship could not survive. The waves rose like mountains of fire tumbling down to crush her. Black against the luminous dark he saw the ship fall from the wave, tip, and topple, engulfed, down where the storm was a mere shaking thunder.

He shook his head to clear it as the *Return* thudded against the next wave, hit the wind, and with a splintering crack the mast snapped, and fell. As Ronan looked up it struck him hard on the temple, bearing him down to the deck in a welter of wood and cordage. Water washed over him.

The ship lurched as the weight of the mast dragged at her side, threatening to capsize her. Conrad ran to free her, hacking feverishly at the wet ropes.

A wave crashed over them: Derwin was torn from the tiller like a straw in the wind. Morgan lost his footing but hung grimly to the tiller as it swung and the ship yawed out of control. The next wave would end it.

Then as the last rope parted, the mast fell instantly away. Morgan fought back the tiller, the wave crashed harmlessly by and the ship lived on. Conrad caught up Ronan's inert body, unsure even whether the boy was alive or dead and with no time to find out. 'Look after him!' he shouted, dumping the body unceremoniously into the hold.

Dawn. The storm had passed. The *Return*, a battered hulk, wallowed in the heavy swell.

They were all cut and bruised, but still alive. But the ship was sinking. They had been bailing for hours, and the water was gaining on them, seeping through the opened seams. And the dinghy had been washed away.

'I've failed you,' said Derwin miserably. 'I should have—oh

never mind.' Emma rubbed her head against his knee and looked sympathetic.

'At least,' said Morgan, as he heaved another bucket of water over the side, 'there's one comfort. Since we're all going to drown it doesn't matter that we're lost.'

'Have you any idea where we are?' asked Conrad.

Morgan sucked his teeth. 'Can't really say. We were blown east, but how far there's no way of telling.'

Ronan joined them. He had been sleeping; his head was swathed in a bloodstained bandage. 'Can I help?'

'Do you feel up to it?' asked Conrad.

'Of course.'

Conrad passed him a bucket, smiled briefly.

'Are we going to drown?' Ronan asked.

'Probably.'

Ferdy scooped up yet another bucket of water and passed it to Morgan. Morgan wasn't there. They were none of them there. 'I suppose this is it,' he thought. 'This is when we sink.'

He climbed out of the hold, still clutching his bucket.

They were all crowded in the bows, talking about birds. I don't believe this, thought Ferdy. We're drowning and they go to look at birds.

He emptied his bucket over the side. 'Isn't anyone else bailing?' he asked plaintively.

Derwin came up grinning. 'There's a lot of birds over there,' he said.

'Yes, I *know*. I like birds too, but is this the time?'

'That means there's land not far away. Come on, you've stopped bailing!'

As the sun set they stood on a rocky shore surrounded by such stores as they had been able to salvage, watching as the waves crashed over what remained of the *Return*, grounded on a reef. Soon the ship vanished beneath the rising tide.

'Well, at least we're here,' said Derwin. 'Wherever here is.'

CHAPTER 9

CONRAD WOKE with the first hint of dawn. It was low tide. The
ship had vanished from the rocks. He left the others still sleeping
where they had dropped, exhausted.

The cliffs rose steeply from the little rocky cove, but at one
point, where there had been a rockfall, it was an easy enough
climb. From the grassy cliff-top Conrad looked around. It was a
grey day. On either side the land wound through a succession of
rocky promontories and narrow inlets. There was no sign of any
people, only a few wind-stunted hawthorns and, scattered
around, some great grey stones. He shared the solitude with the
wheeling birds and the sound of the sea.

But although he headed inland the sound of waves crashing
did not diminish: after a while it seemed even to grow louder.
Dismayed, he found out why.

The ground fell away at his feet. Below, at the bottom of a
sheer cliff, the sea roared and spat in a narrow passage. He was
on an island. Before him, the mainland spread out, forty feet
away, as inaccessible as the moon.

'It really is an island?' asked Derwin. 'There isn't anywhere it
joins up?'

'No,' said Conrad, swallowing a mouthful of breakfast. 'I
walked all round. Some places the gap is narrower, but there
isn't anywhere we could cross.'

'Can't we swim?' suggested Ronan.

'It may have to come to that. But it would be very difficult.'
Privately Conrad thought that he himself would be the only one
with any chance of surviving such an attempt, but he didn't say
so. 'The problem is, the cliffs are so steep on the side facing the
mainland. And then the channel is very narrow—the sea runs
through it with tremendous force.'

'Some of the wood from the ship has been washed up already,' began Derwin. 'We could build a raft, we've got plenty of rope . . .' He looked dubiously at Prothero.

'Why don't you say it?' asked the latter irritably. 'Dragons don't swim, or ride little rafts, or climb vertical cliffs. Has it not occurred to you that we might as well give up? Even if we ever found this promised land we couldn't go back and tell them about it, not without a boat.'

'But we can't just give up!' cried Ronan.

'You are both right,' said Conrad. 'It looks as if we have already failed, but we have to go on.'

'Of course we do,' agreed Derwin. 'Something will turn up. What we could do, we could use the rope and the wood to build a bridge. Then all we need is to get one of us across carrying one end of a rope, the other end is attached to the bridge and he pulls it across.'

'I still think we should just stay here,' said Prothero plaintively.

'There's nothing to eat here,' Derwin pointed out. 'Except each other . . .' He grinned an apology for the feeble joke.

'Well, you'd last me a while,' said the dragon thoughtfully.

More wreckage came in on the next tide, including the beautifully carved stern post. 'Ah well,' said Derwin, looking at it ruefully. 'It'll come in useful, a good bit of wood like that.'

Prothero, who could in fact climb quite well, got himself up the cliff, and, after a good deal of grumbling, even helped to carry the stores across the island.

They set up camp at the spot where the channel between island and mainland was at its narrowest: twenty feet of dizzy, spume-spitting abyss. They had some food, one cask of not very fresh water, most of their spare clothing and an assortment of planks, ropes and other debris from the wreck. There was an astonishing amount of rope. 'It always comes in useful,' said Derwin. At any rate they had enough to make a bridge. There remained the problem of how to get it across the gap.

'If only you weren't such a *bird-brain!*' cried Derwin, giving up at last the attempt to make Emma fly with the rope. The goose, alarmed, took off and flew to the opposite cliff, where she preened her tail feathers with an offended air. 'If only she'd take the confounded rope with her,' wailed Derwin. 'And tie it securely to a handy rock,' he added.

'Get her to carry you over,' suggested Morgan with heavy irony.

'Now that's an idea,' said Derwin, and leaving the others still working on the bridge he disappeared towards the cove.

Conrad prowled along the cliff-top, looking for the least impossible spot to cross to the mainland. Getting down would not be difficult, they had ropes; but he would then need to cross to the opposite cliff and climb up it. Even at low tide it didn't look very hopeful.

They were eating another cold and uninspiring meal when Derwin came into view carrying something on his back.

'There,' he said triumphantly, depositing his burden. 'What do you think?'

They looked at it doubtfully. 'What is it?' asked Conrad.

'It's a flying machine.'

'A what?'

'Look, the channel's only twenty feet wide here. It would be a very short flight.'

'It would need to be,' said Conrad.

'No, really, it's quite simple. You tie this round your waist . . .'

'I do?'

'Then *this* round your arms, and that spreads out the wings. I knew that spare sail would come in useful. Then you pull on the rope to get some lift. The only trouble is, *I* can't work it. My hand—where I broke it—just isn't strong enough. But I know it will work. Trust me.'

'There are two pairs of wings,' Ronan pointed out.

'Well, yes, obviously it needs two people to work it. You need a bigger area of wing than one man could manage, to get enough lift to cope with the weight.'

'No,' said Conrad.

'No what?'

'No, I am not going to tie myself up in knots and throw myself over the cliff.'

'I don't know,' said Morgan. 'If you want to kill yourself it's as good a way as any.'

'At least you can't ask me,' said Prothero.

Derwin's face fell. He looked sadly at his invention and stirred it with his foot.

'I'll try it,' said Ronan.

'You will not,' said his uncle.

Ronan ignored him. 'Show me how it works, Derwin.'

Derwin willingly spread the contraption out on the ground and began to demonstrate its use.

'I've always wanted to fly.' Ronan laughed as he tried to strap himself in, then, as the harness tangled, tripped and landed on the ground in a welter of ropes and flapping canvas.

Conrad watched with a sardonic smile. 'You're wasting your time. No one will go with you.'

'I will,' said Ferdy, and instantly regretted it. Terror engulfed him as he realized what he had let himself in for. People were talking at him from a long way off, telling him to change his mind. But he couldn't back out now. He felt sick. He grinned vaguely and stared at the ground.

Derwin, full of excitement, harnessed up his two volunteers. They practised, running down the slope towards the sea, pulling on the ropes so that the wings flapped. At one point, when a gust of wind took them, they almost became airborne. Ronan laughed exultantly. 'This is wonderful!' he cried, leaping into the air.

Conrad tried several times to intervene, ordering them to stop. But Ronan refused to listen, calling instead to Ferdy, running, laughing.

With an exclamation of impatience, Conrad strode off.

At last Derwin was satisfied. 'Good. Very good! Now we just have to finish the bridge . . .' It was nearing completion. Methodically Derwin checked each knot.

'You know it really doesn't look very strong,' worried

Morgan. 'Although I don't suppose we'll get to use it anyway . . .'

'Oh yes we will,' said Ronan.

Conrad loomed up. 'Leave that, I want to talk to you.'

Ronan straightened up reluctantly. 'What is it?'

'There's something I want to show you.' Without waiting for
a reply Conrad strode off along the cliff-top.

After a moment Ronan shrugged and followed, plunging his
hands in his pockets and enjoying the walk. A brisk breeze blew
through his hair and the smell of the sea blended with the scents
of flowers.

'Here,' said Conrad. He threw himself down on the ground,
then wriggled forward till he could see over the edge. Ronan
copied him. 'What am I supposed to be looking at?'

'Can you see, in the middle of the channel, where the waves
are breaking over rocks?'

'Yes. What of it?'

'At low tide those rocks are exposed. All I have to do is climb
down, get onto and over the rocks, off the far side and up the far
cliff. I take a rope with me and pull the bridge over.'

Ronan stared at the seething channel, and across at the sheer
rock face, its outlines misty behind gusts of spray. 'That's all?'

'I admit there are risks. There is no course open to us which
does not have risks. Imagining that a few pieces of rope and
sailcloth will turn you into a bird does not seem to me to be the
saner option.'

Ronan looked at him, bright-eyed. 'All right. You think you
can climb the unclimbable and swim the unswimmable. I think I
can fly. We all have our little fancies.'

'I will grant you this much. If I make the attempt and fail, then
you may try your flying machine.'

'Meaning that you will die in the attempt, and in that
event . . .'

'Possibly. But until then I forbid you—'

'Forbid!' Ronan jumped up and started to walk away. 'See if
you can stop me!'

Conrad overtook him in a few strides. 'You may defy me to
the extent of killing yourself if you wish, but you can't take

74

Ferdy. He's terrified out of his mind.'

Ronan's mouth set in an obstinate line. 'Ferdy wants to come. He offered. He believes in me.'

'Ask him again!' snapped Conrad.

'I will. You'll see . . .'

Ferdy was still sitting in the same position, looking at nothing. Ronan dropped down in front of him. 'Ferdy—do you want to change your mind? Do you want to back out?' But Ferdy just looked vague and said nothing.

'You don't have to do it,' said Conrad. 'No one will blame you . . .'

But Ferdy shook his head. 'It's all right,' he muttered.

Conrad turned his back.

At last everything was ready. The bridge was finished. One end of a rope was tied to the bridge, the other to the flying machine. Morgan embraced Ronan, tears running down his face. 'Do I have to watch this?' asked Prothero.

Ferdy groped his way with hands that didn't quite belong to him. Things were happening either very fast, or very slowly. Or both at the same time. If only he could wake up. People were mumbling at him. There was a roaring in his ears. Somebody shouted. They were running towards the cliff. His eyes closed tight, he pulled frantically at the rope.

The land ended and his feet floundered over emptiness.

The others forgot to breathe, could hardly bear to watch. The wings spread wide. The line snaked out behind. It was just a narrow gap, if only . . . Something snapped. The wings folded up like a hanging bat. The machine plunged, down and sideways, round a corner of the cliff, still falling, out of sight.

Emma took off in a flurry of wings. Conrad pulled at the line. It came too easily. He hauled it up until he held the frayed and broken end.

The goose flew past again and again, calling, a high keening wail. There was no other sound but the crash of the sea on the rocks.

They searched, without hope, for the wreckage. Further along the cliffs had been worn into weird shapes, leaving black gaping

75

fissures where the debris or the bodies might lie invisible. And below, the rising tide boiled angrily over the rocks. And still Emma flew up and down, wailing that shrill unbirdlike howl.

Morgan was too distraught, Derwin too shocked, Prothero too lumbering, to be very effective. Conrad was in a raging temper: he found himself wishing he could come upon Ronan safe and well so that he could throttle him. Pictures of this pleasing revenge coursed through his mind, interspersed with images of falling, falling through the wind, and the rocks leaping up to tear and crush . . .

Night fell. They had found nothing.

CHAPTER 10

'TIME TO move,' said Conrad, shaking them out of a night of little sleep.

'What?'

'Where to?'

'Why?'

'I intend to climb across to the mainland at low tide. We'll move the baggage now. Then I shall need a long rope and something to tie it to. Prothero seems the obvious choice.'

'Excellent,' grinned the dragon. 'Then I'll have you at my mercy.'

'I don't know how you can,' lamented Morgan. 'When I think of those poor young things . . .' His voice choked with emotion.

'It's my fault,' said Derwin. 'I know what happened now. I forgot—when I added extra wings to give extra lift, I forgot the extra weight. Otherwise I'm sure it would have worked. But I'm to blame. I as good as killed them. If only I could have gone myself!' He stared over the cliff-edge, his blue eyes clouded.

Conrad, walking off with his arms full, turned and looked bleakly back at him. 'They were a pair of crack-brained idiots. My only regret is that I failed to put a stop to their folly, and yours. Meantime we have a mission. I suggest we get on with it!'

'If people were meant to fly, they would be born with wings,' declared Prothero.

'Oh shut up!' said Derwin. He started tying baggage on to the dragon's back.

Conrad lay sprawled on his stomach, taking one last careful look at the route he had worked out down the cliff.

The land could have been hacked through by a blunt axe. The cliff fell away sheer beneath him and the opposite cliff rose just as precipitiously. But in between, appearing at high tide as only a few jagged splinters pounded and lashed by spray, was an outcrop of rock battered by the sea into unlikely, distorted shapes. Now, with the tide just before the ebb, it looked black, treacherous, slippery with weed and altogether uninviting; but there were no other options, except slow death by starvation. And he was not going to accept failure. He had lost the ship and four of those he led—but surely he couldn't be held responsible for sea serpents and storms and idiots who threw themselves over cliffs?

Conrad got to his feet, checked the rope one last time, then, padding it with sailcloth, tied it round Prothero where his waist would have been if he'd had one. Morgan fussed over the knot, sighing. 'So soon after the other two . . . such a pity . . . all so young . . .'

The sun went behind a cloud. It looked as if it might rain.

Conrad took up the coil of rope, wound it over his right shoulder, between his legs, and up over the left shoulder. Then, letting it out bit by bit, he backed towards the cliff.

Poised at the edge, he hesitated. It was against nature to lean back, out into nothingness. But any other way would be disastrous. With his heart in his mouth he went over the edge.

Once started it was easier. Leaning back, braced against the cliff, he kicked out and slid rapidly downwards. Only the rope hurt where it chafed his body and burned his hands.

'Ouch,' said Prothero. 'This rope hurts. I'll be cut in half soon at this rate.'

Derwin found he was holding his breath. Cautiously he let it out. The cliff was slightly undercut, and to see Conrad now he had to hang right over the edge. His head swam as if the slightest movement might send him plunging into the abyss.

'That's just how it was,' said Morgan reminiscently, 'when that lad—what was his name now? Kelby? Kelsey?—anyway, he was climbing down the cliffs just the same way. After gulls' eggs, he was. But he ran out of rope and he hadn't knotted the end. Came off the end, he did, and the sea swallowed him up. Dashed to pieces before he had time to drown, I shouldn't wonder,' he concluded with gloomy satisfaction.

'No consideration,' said Prothero bitterly. 'No thought for

78

others. Only, here's a rope and no tree to tie it to, let's tie it to Prothero, he doesn't have feelings. He's only a dragon, doesn't matter if he gets cut in half—ooh—ouch—oof!' He let out a long sigh of relief as the strain went off the rope. Conrad had reached the foot of the cliff.

Gradually getting his breath, Conrad turned to study the way ahead. From now on the rope which had been his lifeline would become a hindrance. There were too many places where it might snag and pull him off balance.

The sea surged and boiled around the rocks, at times covering them completely, slapping upwards in a fury of spray, then sucking down as if to swallow the stone into its own limitless depths.

So far as he could judge this was the tide's lowest ebb: it was now or never. The ledge on which he crouched would not remain a haven for long. He waited for a wave to pass, then stepped across on to the rocks.

It was a wild scramble, a desperate clinging with fingers and toes as the water constantly heaved up and crashed down around him, tugging with nearly irresistible strength. He had little time to choose his way, could only flail from one precarious hold to the next, his eyes stinging, his hands growing numb with the cold. Twice the rope snagged, and he had to return to free it. But he was making progress. Twisting round a spur of rock he paused to catch his breath, and found that the far cliff was now the nearer one. He went on with more confidence: only to find defeat staring him in the face.

The rocks ended several feet short of the cliff. Between, the sea roared black and violent.

But he couldn't give up. There was no other way. He wiped his eyes, smarting from the salt spray, and peered at the cliff. There was a ledge, some four feet down and slightly to the left. If he could jump across to it, if he could find handholds, there was a vertical crack which might offer enough purchase for him to climb back up out of reach of the sea.

He waited for a wave to strike and begin to sink, then he jumped. His feet hit the ledge, his fingers scrabbled desperately for the crack, but there was no time. The sea came and took him. The water boiled and thundered in his ears as he was sucked down and down . . .

Derwin gasped, and, craning forward for a better look, almost overbalanced. Morgan caught at his ankles, trying to pull him back.

'He's been washed away!' choked Derwin. 'Oh, where is he?'

'I can't say I'm surprised,' said Morgan. 'But do come back from the edge. I know it's only a matter of time for us all, but . . .'

Derwin leapt to his feet and ran back to the dragon. 'Prothero! Wake up! Move! Pull on the rope!'

'What? Why? Oh, all right.' The dragon lumbered to his feet.

'He's back on the rocks,' called Morgan.

'Prothero, don't move!' shrieked Derwin.

'Make up your mind,' grumbled the dragon.

'Drowned, though,' added Morgan.

Derwin was once more spread-eagled on the cliff edge. 'Where? Oh—but he's not moving—no, he's all right, he's hanging on. But he's got it all to do again!'

'I daresay,' said Morgan. 'But you won't help by falling off yourself. I promised your aunt I'd look after you.'

Reluctantly Derwin moved back a few inches, as down below the whole struggle began again. He could hardly bear to look, but couldn't tear his eyes away. His body shuddered and cringed in sympathy as now more frequently the waves dashed over Conrad, lashing him with cold clutching tentacles, snatching at his frail grasp, raining down, all about, hurtling up from below. It seemed impossible anyone could continue the fight—Derwin felt he could die from just watching—but very gradually the tiny figure crawled on, sometimes forward, sometimes casting back, until, after an eternity, Conrad reached the last rock. 'He's going to jump,' wailed Derwin. 'I can't look . . .' But he continued to stare down, unconscious of the growing numbness from where Morgan, eyes averted, sat firmly on his feet.

Prothero, eyes closed, snored.

The tide was rising fast now. The jump was yet more difficult, and this had to be the last chance. Hands clenched, nails biting into his palms, Derwin willed Conrad across the gulf. At the last moment he closed his eyes.

When he opened them again, Conrad was clinging to the far cliff.

'He's done it! He's done it!' Wriggling back from the edge, Derwin hugged Morgan for sheer joy.

'Well, well, well, who would have thought it?' said Morgan, peering nervously downwards. 'Mind you, he's still got to climb the other cliff.'

'Oh, he'll manage that,' said Derwin. 'I should think . . .'

At that moment Conrad could do nothing at all. He clung desperately to his perch, waiting for the breath to come back to his body while the sea sucked and plucked at his legs, seeking to pull him back.

Close to, the cliff looked different. The previous day Conrad had spent hours staring, tracing a route, picking out holds. A chimney first. Then, as it petered out, an exposed sheet of rock which he would have to traverse somehow to a vertical crack. Fifty feet up the crack. Then what looked like an easy bit, with ledges where he could rest. The last stretch looked the worst—a wall of rock about twice his height with hardly a hold to be seen. By that time it would be too late to worry. If he fell then it would be two hundred feet into the foaming rage of rock and sea.

Now, half drowned, battered and bruised, he knew it was impossible. Through a mist of spray the cliff soared sheer out of sight.

Everything depended on this. On the rope, snaking down from the top of the cliff opposite, hung the hopes of all his people.

A great wave smashed through the channel, soaking him afresh. He took a deep breath and started to climb.

The chimney was wet and treacherous, slimy with weed, rough with barnacles. Conrad wedged his body across and by pushing hard with his legs, forced himself upwards. All the time the sea was beating up at him, trying to snatch him back, like a hound snapping at his heels.

By the time the chimney ended the rock was dry. He quelled the temptation to hug the cliff and, both hands securely latched, leaned out and looked round. The rope arced from his waist across the void to the top of the far cliff, where he could just make out a watching figure. Derwin had been taking in the slack on the rope. It hung, neither a help nor a hindrance now, but it might yet be a lifeline. Upwards the cliff reared uncompromising, ominous. Conrad did not look down.

The crack was some twenty feet to his left. There were a few faint holds: a chance.

Cautiously he began to sidle across the hostile cliff. Hand, hand, foot. Pause, while his other foot groped for purchase. Hand, elbow, knee. The rock was swelling out, nudging him away. His back felt desperately exposed. The cliff was fighting him, punishing his presumption. It would kill him if it could. No holds. Back. Down, losing precious height. Across. Stop again. Nowhere to go. And then a gift: a stout pinnacle.

He pulled on the rope, coiling up the slack. He could just feel the presence on the far end, letting it out.

Conrad looped the rope around the pinnacle. It slipped. Again. Tug. It seemed firm. Anchored, he slid his left foot out, stretched out his left arm, groping for a hold. It was inches out of reach. No way to get there securely. He lunged. Caught it, just as his sideways momentum gave out.

He wound himself into the crack and let his heart slow, then twisted back to unhitch the rope. It swung free and the slack was taken up again.

The crack seemed more forgiving. That was his undoing. He moved quickly, becoming confident. Too confident. As he heaved up on his right foot the rock gave way. He was slipping, falling, out of control. *No!* A moment of furious anger. He crashed into a ledge, teetering, fighting for balance.

He clung. If he moved it would upset his fragile equilibrium. If he did not move he would slip anyway.

Slowly, cautiously, he stretched out one hand, took hold. Then the other. Pull. On his feet. Secure, for a moment.

He began to shake, all over, uncontrollably. I shouldn't have done this, he thought, I'm going to die. Still he shuddered, knowing that he had to stop shaking, or fall.

He unclenched his teeth, willed his hands to relax, breathed slowly. The stone before his eyes was bright, flecks of mica sparkling in the sun.

The crack was petering out, the holds becoming more and more precarious. He was climbing with all his body, clinging almost with his teeth and nails. He wouldn't have thought it could be done, but he was doing it. Handholds high up, nothing for his feet. He heaved upwards, taking all his weight on his arms, found a ledge. Good. Very good.

He was smiling. He had taken on the cliff and he was winning. With death always a hairsbreadth away he felt vibrantly alive. He paused to wipe the sweat from his face.

Such a little way to go now, but with the last of his strength. Clamped on two precarious holds, his left leg and right hand swinging free, he hung over the abyss.

There were no holds above that he could see. No way to get up those last few feet. But it was too late to seek another route. If he didn't move now he would fall.

With one last despairing effort he threw himself upwards.

CHAPTER 11

THE GULL sailed past, very leisured, but upside-down. It was followed by two others, also upside-down. The fact that their feet were sticking up in the air seemed less odd than that their wings should be arched the wrong way. Derwin would be able to explain it . . . The thought jerked him to full consciousness, and to remembering.

The harness had caught round a jagged edge of rock: Ferdy was suspended head down over the roaring sea.

Reason said that he should climb very slowly and carefully up the harness, lest he dislodge it. Reason failed to make much impression. He lunged up the rope in a wild and undignified scramble, arriving perched on the pinnacle breathless and shaking.

When the blood had returned to his feet, and his heartbeat to something like normal, he plucked up the courage to look around. He was on a ledge, half-way down the cliff. Further down the ledge was a still shape. Ronan. He lay sprawled on his back, totally still, his face waxen. His tunic had torn at the neck; a dark trickle of blood ran from his forehead, round the swell of his throat, beading the gold of the torque he was still wearing.

Cautiously Ferdy crawled along the ledge and knelt by his side. Ronan opened his eyes.

'Here,' said Ferdy, 'let me look at that cut on your head—are you hurt anywhere else?'

Ronan sat up, slowly. 'I don't think so.' He blinked, trying to bring the world back into focus.

'You know, we were very lucky,' said Ferdy, bandaging the gash on Ronan's forehead with a strip torn from his shirt. 'No serious injuries, I mean.'

'And we did make it across. All we have to do now is get up the cliff.' Ronan pulled himself to his feet and stared upwards.

His spirits sank. There was no way they could climb that.

'It's getting dark,' said Ferdy.

'Let's move along a bit. The ledge seems to get wider further down and we need more space to sleep. Dropping off here could prove fatal!'

Ronan led the way, leaning against the cliff face as he sidled along the crack. Ferdy kept his eyes on the rock, taking it one slow step at a time. When he looked up he was alone. 'Ronan!' he squawked.

'Here.'

'Where?'

Ronan's face appeared from under a shelf of rock at the back of the ledge. 'I've found a cave. It seems to be quite deep. There may even be water at the back.'

Carefully Ferdy squeezed in through the entrance, into the dark.

'I don't think there is a back,' remarked a disembodied voice. 'It's not a cave, it's a tunnel. I wonder where it leads?'

'Ronan, it's dark.'

'What?' The voice was faint and indistinct.

'I said it's *dark*!' Ferdy fought against a rising tide of panic. Suddenly Ronan was beside him again.

'Yes, we need a torch. Have you got your tinder-box?'

'I don't know . . .' Ferdy fumbled in his pouch. 'Yes, here it is.'

'Good.' Ronan ducked out under the ledge, and re-appeared carrying a piece of the wood which had been used to brace the wings. 'This should do.'

But the feeble light shed by the torch did little to restore Ferdy's confidence. He felt reluctant to approach the tunnel, as if some secret brooding menace lurked there in the dark, waiting . . .

'Come on, then,' said Ronan.

'No,' said Ferdy. 'It's—it's dangerous.'

'Of course it is. But it must be better than sitting half-way down a cliff waiting to starve to death. Come on, things can't get any worse.'

'No—but—I'm scared. I can feel something down there, something awful at the end of the tunnel.'

Ronan wasn't going to admit he was frightened. Knowing that Ferdy was relying on him to lead gave him courage. 'It'll be all right. Follow me.'

Clutching the torch, he plunged down the tunnel. Ferdy followed, muttering darkly. Before long his teeth were chattering. It might have been from the cold. The tunnel was damp as well. Moisture ran down the walls, and as they went on, and down, they began to splash through puddles.

Here and there were spiky protrusions, some sticking up from the ground, threatening to trip him up; others projecting from the roof in a treacherous attempt to knock his head off. They gleamed squelchily, like something going rotten. Sometimes caverns opened up on either side, contorted shapes jagged with mysteries. Beyond the torchlight, darkness lurked.

Still the tunnel wound onwards, and ever downwards. Ferdy tried not to think of the weight overhead, the mountain pressing down on him . . .

Water seeped through cracks in the rock and pattered down the chilly walls. Now they were wading along a stream. The cold water oozed into their boots and into the marrow of their bones.

Still Ferdy followed as Ronan's shadow danced before him. Other images flickered in his eyes: swollen rivers, mountains crumbling, a mighty weight of grinding water, cold stone . . . Suddenly he felt he had to hear a human voice or go mad. 'You will be careful, won't you?' he said inanely. 'Don't drop the torch.'

'What's that?' Ronan half-turned to catch Ferdy's words, distorted in the dead air.

'I said—'

Ronan stumbled. As he tried to get his balance the torch flew away in a blazing arc, hit the ground, sizzled and went out. There was a chaotic, flailing time while they sought each other in the blind and total darkness. Then Ronan found Ferdy, then the torch, soaked through. 'We'll never get that lit again, not unless we can dry it out.' He pushed it down the front of his tunic. 'What was that you were saying?' he asked.

Ferdy spoke in very controlled tones. 'I *said*, "Don't drop the torch." '

'Oh. Well, it's a bit late now. Still, things can't get any worse.'

'You said that before,' Ferdy pointed out sourly.

But when they picked themselves up and went on, curiously enough he felt more composed and less inclined to worry about lurking perils. He could imagine nothing worse than to be lost in the bowels of the earth, in total darkness, and doomed to die of hunger if he didn't first die of the damp and cold. The worst must have already happened.

Ronan led the way, but now with arms outstretched and probing feet. Ferdy clung to Ronan's belt and shuffled along with his eyes closed. It seemed less dark that way.

Ronan went as fast as he could, as fast as he dared. His eyes stared wide into the nothingness of the dark, terrified of the emptiness, terrified that at any moment it might be empty no more. His hands groped for something to cling to, shrank from what they might find. The thudding of his heart was pursuing feet. Only the clutch of Ferdy's hand in his belt drove him on. Ferdy needed him. Ferdy was afraid. Ronan was a prince and could not show his fear.

Gradually the tunnel became narrower, till Ronan could feel the walls on either side. And the stream became deeper, now swirling around their ankles. Sometimes, icily, their feet strayed into holes and they plunged in up to their knees. Then they found the roof was getting lower. Soon they had to walk bent double.

Ronan stopped. The water now was waist deep. His probing fingers felt where the tunnel roof dropped suddenly under the surface of the stream. Why wasn't Conrad here? He would have known what to do. Ronan was close to tears, close to giving up. But if he had to die, he could at least die well. Even if Conrad never knew.

Awkwardly Ronan felt for Ferdy's hand as if to give comfort, in reality seeking it. 'Can you let go of me for a moment?'

Reluctantly Ferdy released his grasp. Then, abruptly, he was alone. His groping hands met nothing but solid rock and the stream going into it. Ronan had vanished.

'But things couldn't get any worse,' he thought, dazed.

Then, splashing and gasping, Ronan was beside him again.

'It's all right. We can get through. You can swim underwater, can't you?'

'Like a fish,' said Ferdy, with a certain lack of conviction.

'Good. Just follow me.' Ronan took a deep breath and once more was gone.

Ferdy felt his way down into the icy water. 'Things really can't get any worse than this,' he muttered.

The water closed over his head.

After that things became rather confused. There was darkness, and water, and cold, scratched hands, bruised knees and bumps on the head. There was crawling, and swimming, and sometimes walking almost upright, but Ferdy went through it all in a blurred unreality in which his only, growing, and overwhelming desire was for rest. Finally he sank to the ground and refused to move.

Fortunately they were in a dryish part of the tunnel. Ronan slithered down beside him, saying, 'We mustn't stop for long. It's too cold.'

They sat, shoulder to shoulder, the silence broken only by their uneasy breathing and the quiet splash of the stream as it trickled by their feet.

Ronan was almost happy. He felt he was doing well. Conrad would have to admit it. If he ever knew.

'I'm so sleepy,' murmured Ferdy.

'We mustn't sleep. We're too wet and cold. We'd never wake up again.'

'I don't think I want to. And it must be night-time by now.'

'It doesn't make any difference here.'

Ferdy opened his eyes, shuddered, and closed them again. 'I was always afraid of the dark. Right from a child.'

'I know what you mean. If you can't see, you don't know what might be there—'

'Don't!'

'Sorry.'

There was a pause. Ferdy's head began to nod. Ronan tugged at the bandage on his forehead. 'Can you feel to tighten this a bit?'

There was no reply.

'Ferdy. Ferdy, wake up!'

'What you want?' asked Ferdy sleepily.

'You must stay awake!'

'Keep me awake, then.'

'*How?*'

'I dunno. It's you wants to stop me sleeping.'

'If we sleep now we'll die. *Listen!*' Ferdy's head was beginning to loll again. 'Listen to me! Look, I'll tell you a story.'

'All right. I like stories.' Ferdy yawned, made himself sit upright.

Ronan, staring into nothing, plucked inspiration from the dark.

'Once long ago in the dream time the world was always dark. There were no birds but owls, no insects but moths, and the lynx and the wolf prowled secretly and unseen.

'It so happened that the lynx was out hunting when he came across a cave blocked by a great boulder. The lynx sniffed around it in case there was something good to eat sheltering there. Then his fur stood all on end, for a voice spoke from inside the cave.

' "Let me out," said the voice.

' "Who are you?" asked the lynx.

' "Let me out," the voice said again.

' "What will you give me if I do?" asked the lynx.

'But all the voice said was, "Let me out."

'The lynx sat down, and licked his paw, and washed his face. He was curious to know who the voice belonged to, but the boulder looked very heavy and difficult to move.

' "Let me out," said the voice again.

'The lynx got up, put his nose under the boulder, and pushed hard. The great rock rolled away from the cave.

'Out roared the sun.

'The lynx fell flat on the ground with his paws over his eyes. His whiskers were singed as the sun flamed by, braying and trumpeting into all the corners of the world.

'The dark was terrified. Fleeing before the sun it went to hide in the deepest hole it could find . . . Are you still awake, Ferdy?'

Ferdy smothered a yawn. 'I'm awake.'

'Then it was always light. The sun brought with it new creatures with bright colours, singing birds and gaudy butterflies that fluttered and danced.

'The lynx narrowed his eyes to tiny slits and slunk from tree to tree.

'Then the sun, enthroned in the sky, looked down on the world and smiled. "Ah, my children," he said. "This is good. Now I will hold my court, to receive praise and hear petitions."

'The first petitioner was an owl. Hooting sadly, his feathered eyelids fast closed, he said, "Mighty sun, your brightness is too great for me. I cannot open my eyes. I cannot see to hunt, and I must starve."

'The sun laughed. "Then you must learn to hunt with your eyes closed," it said. "My swallows burn blue, flashing in the light. Their flight pleases me more than your sad gliding."

'The next petitioner was a moth, beating desperate wings and crying, "Mercy. Give us back the darkness. I must die in the light!"

'But the sun only laughed again. "See my butterflies that sparkle as they dance! Their bright colours please me more than your drab hues. Die if you must."

'The third petitioner was the lynx. "Great sun," he said, shielding his slit eyes with one great furry paw. "It was I who released you from your captivity. Grant me a favour in return, give us back some corner of darkness. For in the dark I take my prey unawares and they die unknowing. But in your great light the small creatures can see me hunting them, and they flee. Yet there is no dark place for them to hide, and the chase goes on for ever. So will they die of always being hunted and I of always hunting."

'A third time the sun just laughed. "Friend lynx," it said. "You released me of your own free will. You will have to learn to control your curiosity if you cannot abide the consequences."

'Then there came before the sun a bright yellow butterfly, fluttering like part of the sun's own rays.

'"Well, little butterfly," said the sun. "Have you come to dance in praise of my radiance?"

'But the butterfly was weak, and landed trembling on a

flower. "Great sun," she began in a feeble voice. "Butterflies must dance. We live to dance and mate and dance together so long as your brightness shines down upon us. While it is light we must dance. There is no rest. Great sun, give us rest. I have danced too long." And the butterfly folded her wings and died, dropping to the ground like last summer's leaf.

'The sun wept two great scalding tears that sizzled when they hit the earth. Then he called the lynx and said, "Go, seek out the dark. Tell him henceforth time shall be divided between the day, when I shall reign, and the night, which shall be his."

'So that is what they did,' ended Ronan. 'When the sun dips into the sea, out creeps the dark. And this, Ferdy, this is the hole where the darkness lives—Ferdy?'

But Ferdy was fast asleep.

It felt to Ferdy as if he had hardly closed his eyes when Ronan was shaking him awake, saying, 'Come on. We must keep moving.'

'Why?' asked Ferdy resentfully, but allowed himself to be hauled to his feet.

The stumbling in the dark went on.

And on.

And on.

Ronan still led, and Ferdy, still with his hand clasped firmly in Ronan's belt and his eyes tight closed, followed on behind.

Then for the millionth time he stumbled, and instinctively opened his eyes. He gasped.

'What is it?' asked Ronan.

'A light. At least—' He rubbed his eyes. '—It's just a sort of redness. I don't think it was there last time I looked.'

'I can't see anything.'

They went on, then after a while: 'I think you're right,' said Ronan. 'Red, like fire. Perhaps we're coming to the centre of the earth, where volcanoes spawn and dragons breed.'

'That's a cheerful prospect.'

'I wish Prothero was here.'

'I wish Prothero was here and we were where he is.'

They went on.

There was a light. A red light.

91

'You remember,' said Ferdy, 'when I said I thought there was something awful waiting for us.'

'Mmm.'

Ferdy swallowed. 'I think it's just down there,' he said in a small voice.

They turned a corner and saw where the passage ended.

It ended in a cavern lit by fire. The immense black shadow of a giant bearing sword and spear fell across the opening.

Ferdy clutched at Ronan, though no longer for fear of losing him in the dark.

Very, very slowly they went forward. The giant shadow dwindled to become only that of a very large warrior. To compensate they could now see further into the cavern. It was full of very large warriors.

'I thought you said things couldn't get any worse,' muttered Ferdy.

'They *may* be friendly.'

'They don't look it.'

Their whispering caught the attention of the guard, who turned and peered suspiciously into the darkness. Ronan swallowed hard. He had brought Ferdy this far. To what? But they had no choice. Resolutely he stepped forward.

Instantly they were surrounded. The warriors, all with swords at the ready, did not look any more friendly at close quarters. The nearest was the largest, and the one with the longest sword. The chief, presumably. His eyes were black and glittered.

'I said there was something nasty down here,' murmured Ferdy.

'It's all right,' said Ronan. 'Things *can't* get any worse.'

The chief took another slow, deliberate step towards them. Ferdy fell to his knees. Ronan's pride wavered. Caution, or sense, won. He too knelt.

Ferdy closed his eyes, waiting for the end. Ronan watched in fascinated horror as the chief raised his sword. He was dreadfully aware of his naked chest where his shirt had torn. Slowly, very slowly, the sword tip approached. Gently it brushed the torque around Ronan's neck.

Suddenly the warrior whirled around, lifted up his sword and cried out. The echoes of his cry met an answering chorus from

92

his followers. One hand to their hearts, the other to their swords, they dropped to their knees.

'This is ridiculous,' murmured Ronan. 'We can't all kneel.'

Ferdy opened his eyes. 'What are they kneeling for, anyway?'

'Something to do with this torque, I think.'

Ronan stood. Slowly he pulled the torque from his neck and held it out.

The chief surged to his feet like a broaching whale and clasped him in a huge embrace. Taking the torque he raised it to the ceiling, cried out, then solemnly placed it round his own neck. Again he spoke, in a language of which Ronan and Ferdy understood not a word. But the tone at least was clear.

There was another roar of approval. Then Ferdy found the warriors were all looking at him expectantly. He shot an anguished look at Ronan.

'Well,' said the latter. 'Go on—do something!'

'What?' wailed Ferdy.

'I don't know—improvise!'

Ferdy rose to his feet, coughed, bowed to the chief and launched into a lengthy speech. Made bolder by the fact that his audience could obviously understand nothing of what he said, he became quite eloquent, throwing in random snatches from nursery rhymes and old stories whenever his inspiration began to flag.

At last he finished, bowed solemnly once more to the chief, again to the warriors.

The chief, smiling, embraced him, then roared out a command.

'I wonder why the torque made such a good impression,' said Ronan.

Ferdy shrugged. 'I've no idea. But I'm not complaining.'

He broke off as a man approached with a pile of dry clothes and gestured to them to change out of their wet things. Gratefully they did so. By the time they had found their way into the unfamiliar (and rather too large) costumes, food had been prepared.

While they ate, Ferdy, sitting next to the chief, did his best to sustain a conversation with him. This was not easy as the warriors' language seemed to consist mostly of grunts. Ronan, on his other side, kept giggling and was of little help. However, they succeeded in exchanging names: the warrior chief was called Ugug, with the stress on the first syllable. All the warriors seemed to have similar names, with only slight differences in emphasis or pitch. It was, thought Ferdy, a language full of pitfalls for the unwary. He eyed the warriors' massive frames, hoping they were not quick to take offence.

Ugug took a last gnaw at a bone, then cleared a patch of the sandy floor. Using the end of the bone he began to draw. He pointed at a squiggle and grunted. Then, talking rapidly, he jabbed at some circles and dots.

Ferdy felt his head swimming and his eyelids getting heavy. The food and the warmth were proving too much for him. Smothering a yawn he glanced round at Ronan, only to discover that the Prince had snuggled down on the ground and was fast asleep.

Ferdy turned back to the chief, smiled apologetically, and followed suit.

CHAPTER 12

'THERE WERE moments,' confessed Derwin, 'when I didn't think you'd make it.'

'Really?' said Conrad.

The bridge had been an almost complete success. Once Conrad had made it to the top of the cliff, he and Derwin had walked along opposite sides of the gap to a place where jutting rocks on either side offered a safe anchorage. Conrad had then pulled across the rope, and the bridge. It was just long enough. The bridge was secured, and Derwin walked across.

'But then I said to Morgan, "He'll do it."'

Morgan had groped his way across with his eyes shut. Then Conrad and Derwin carried across the baggage. 'We'll get the useful things over first,' said Conrad, 'before we let the dragon cross.' He could not have said anything better calculated to make Prothero trust his bulk to a flimsy contraption of rope and twine. Tail stretched out behind him, he reached from end to end. Conrad watched. The bridge held almost to the last moment. Just as Prothero put one foot on land the rock on the far cliff shifted, slipped, slid over the brink. Gracefully the bridge swung downwards. Less gracefully the dragon scrabbled, scrambled and hauled himself to safety.

There was a splash far below as the rock hit the sea.

'It's a good thing we brought the baggage first,' remarked Conrad.

'I'm quite all right, thank you for enquiring,' said Prothero.

Conrad smiled sweetly at him. 'Of course. We couldn't do without you, could we?'

By the time they had eaten, the sun had set. 'I think,' said Conrad, yawning, 'that we'd better keep watch. There are paths on the cliffs not made by rabbits.'

'You mean we might be attacked?' asked Morgan, horrified.

'It's possible.'

'But that's dreadful. Unpleasant people prowling about—oh dear, I shan't be able to sleep a wink.'

'Then you might as well take first watch.'

'Very well. Only if we're all murdered in our beds, don't blame me!'

There was a full moon rising, huge and pale, streaked with cloud. A dull light glimmered from the sea. Morgan sat, feeling very much alone. Derwin and Conrad were sleeping; Prothero, after shifting restlessly for a while, had moved off in search of a larger area of flat ground. Morgan shivered resentfully. At his time of life he should be tucked up in a warm bed, not sitting up all night on a draughty cliff. The shadows behind the rocks shifted: at any moment they might turn into creeping Axemen with bright eyes and shining blades. He wouldn't even be able to run away, not with his bad knee. On the whole he'd rather have his throat cut while he slept. At least he wouldn't know anything about it. But he had promised to keep awake . . . Glumly he watched the moon track upwards across the sky.

His snores mingled with the sigh of the wind and the distant surge of the sea.

They didn't stand a chance. They were all sleeping quietly when finally the shadows woke, grew, swarmed about them. Before they knew what was happening they were trussed like deer for the spit.

Derwin was dumped unceremoniously on the ground. The last stretch of a nightmare journey through which he had been half dragged, half carried, had been underground. He was in a cave ill-lit by flickering torches, filled with the massy silhouettes of his captors. Beside him lay Conrad, his eyes closed, blood on his face.

'It's all my fault,' said a voice behind him. 'I should have kept awake. I'm sorry, lad.'

Derwin twisted round to see Morgan, who lay in a heap, his face raddled with misery. 'Oh well, I expect they'd have got us anyway,' he said comfortingly. 'There are too many of them to fight.'

'Nice of you to say so,' said Morgan. 'Though it might have been all over by now. I wonder how they'll kill us?'

'Perhaps they won't.'

Morgan nodded towards their captors, who had moved away and were talking earnestly. 'Bound to. I expect that's what they're talking about. How to do it, I mean. Whether to throttle us, or cut our hearts out, or just leave us here to starve. Or perhaps they're going to eat us,' he added, struck by a sudden thought.

'Stop blathering, man.' Conrad had woken up.

'Oh dear—it's all my fault. It's just—oh dear . . .' Morgan's voice trailed away.

'Turn over, Derwin, back to back. We'll get these ropes untied for a start.'

Derwin kept an eye on their captors while Conrad, behind his back, tugged at the bonds on his wrists. After an eternity the first knots parted; the rest were easier. With a quick wriggle Derwin loosened the ropes around his arms and chest.

'Still!' hissed Conrad.

Two of their captors approached with slow, swinging strides.

Derwin closed his eyes, tried to breathe.

The men walked past and disappeared into a passageway.

A few minutes later they were all free. 'I don't know why you're bothering,' grumbled Morgan. 'We'll never get out of here alive.'

'Lie down and keep quiet,' snapped Conrad, then shouted: 'Here!'

One of the guards broke away from the group and walked up. With a sudden, convulsive movement Conrad caught him by the ankle, jerking him off balance and throwing him to the ground, snatched his knife and held it to his throat. The man, feeling the blade touch his skin, lay still. His companions, who had rushed forward, now halted at a little distance.

'Let us go,' said Conrad. 'Or I'll kill this man.'

There was a long silence. Nobody moved. A torch flared and hissed.

'Let us go,' repeated Conrad. A trickle of blood appeared where his knife rested on the man's throat.

Morgan let out a wail.

'Quiet!' There was a hint now of desperation in Conrad's voice. There were more people coming into the cave. 'Let us go! Don't you *understand*?'

'It's all right. We're all friends here really.'

'*Ronan!*'

'Let the poor man go. You're frightening him.' Ronan was enjoying himself.

Conrad rose bewildered to his knees, relinquishing his captive, and passed his hands over his eyes. 'Is this a dream or a nightmare?'

'Neither. We came in at the back door, as it were, and have been enjoying these good people's hospitality.'

'They make very good soup,' added Ferdy.

Conrad buried his head in his hands.

Ugug hurried forward, inspected the new arrivals and grunted to Ferdy. The other warriors, losing interest, began to drift off. Conrad hesitated, then returned the knife to its owner, remembering that he had promised himself the luxury of throttling Ronan if he ever saw him again. Later. His head hurt.

Suddenly a great bellow thundered out and the vast bulk of a dragon filled the cave entrance, blotting out the light of dawn. A warrior screamed, trapped between the dragon's claws as blue flame flickered about his head.

'Prothero! Put him down at once,' commanded Ronan.

'Can't I eat him?'

'No!'

'Not even a little bit?'

'Not even a nibble!'

Prothero let the man go, sighing plaintively. 'I'm hungry.'

'How about some soup?' suggested Ferdy.

Later that day they collected together their baggage and prepared for a long walk. They found the warriors' hospitality rather oppressive and did not feel disposed to linger. It was then that Conrad noticed Derwin was missing.

'Where's Derwin?' he demanded.

'Oh . . .' Ferdy looked embarrassed. 'Gone for a walk, I expect. Excuse me, I must just—um—' He busied himself with his pack.

Derwin, meanwhile, was looking for Emma. He had managed to recruit one of the younger warriors, Gurug by name, as guide, by taking him into a corner and drawing him pictures in the sand. Among a tall people Gurug was one of the tallest, and correspondingly massive. He would have made two of Derwin, with some to spare. But he seemed interested. Derwin sketched the outline of a goose, then some wriggly lines for the sea, and pointed in the direction from which he hoped they had come. Gurug nodded eagerly and went to fetch his spear, a weapon the size of a young tree. Shaking his head, Derwin pointed to the picture of Emma, then to his own heart, linked his forefingers together and tugged. Gurug stared at him, baffled. Sighing, Derwin gave up further attempts at explanation. Perhaps the warrior's aim would be poor.

Outside the cave it was cold and bright. Gurug strode steadily along, his giant spear clasped in his enormous fist. Derwin stepped rapidly to keep pace. What if Emma had gone? Flown away? He would miss her. Especially at night, snuggled in the crook of his knees. Waking in the early morning, waddling up to his pillow and tweaking at his hair until he turned onto his back so that she could settle on his chest, crooning gently . . .

And now perhaps she would have flown away, thinking he had abandoned her.

The sky was bare, empty of clouds.

Derwin glanced up at Gurug, whose big red face gleamed with anticipation. No doubt he was thinking of goose stew. But she's *my* goose. My own particular goose . . .

They heard the sea before they saw it, the cliffs a green sweep against a clean blue sky. And out of the sky, arrowing down towards them and honking with joy, came Emma. Gurug drew back his spear, ready to throw, and in the same moment Derwin caught his arm and tugged the spear towards the ground. With a clatter of wings Emma landed and Derwin gathered her up in his arms. Gurug stared in anger and amazement, then meeting

99

Derwin's smile, slowly grinned. Laying down his spear, he ran his huge hand gently down the feathers of Emma's soft throat and beamed with delight. Emma nestled against Derwin's neck, cackled, and pulled lovingly at his hair.

It was getting dark when they returned to the cave. Conrad was stretched out by the fire, apparently dozing.

'I had to fetch Emma,' said Derwin.

'But naturally.'

'You didn't mind?'

'*Mind?* Why should I *mind?*'

'Oh good. Only—'

'Only this.' Conrad spoke very slowly, very deliberately. 'If once more, just once, you disobey me, you will regret it.'

Derwin encountered a glare of such furious and implacable rage that he swallowed, and fled.

CHAPTER 13

IN THE morning, early, they started on the next stage of their journey. Emma was comfortably ensconced amongst the baggage on Prothero's back.

'Packed lunch, I see,' said the dragon, eyeing her. 'Well, I do like my meat fresh.'

Their hosts walked with them as far as the brow of a hill, where they waved farewell. Gurug offered Emma some green blades of grass, which she nibbled graciously. The chief, wearing the golden torque that Ronan once had worn, raised his spear in salute.

The travellers set off south-west. They had no clear idea of where they were going. They were off the map, and all they could do was to head in the direction which they hoped would bring them eventually to the land of the Axemen. And then, with luck, back onto the map.

Once away from the coast, they found themselves in an apparently endless forest of birch and pine. They saw no sign of people. Sometimes there were faint paths made by animals, but mostly they picked their way between the trees and through an undergrowth of bilberries and heather, starred with pale flowers. Conrad had no need to see the sky to carry a direction in his head, and he led them unerringly. It was good to be back on land again.

But Morgan, out of sound of the sea for the first time in his life, became increasingly depressed, muttering that he didn't want to go, he wasn't supposed to, he should be going home to Fallond.

'You can swim if you like,' said Conrad blightingly.

The hunting was good: each morning Conrad was up first, to return as the others were stirring, with rabbits, pigeons, sometimes deer. The others took these daily provisions for granted—except for Ronan, who looked on Conrad's skill with a mixture of admiration and jealousy, and tried in vain, day after day, to wake up early enough to accompany him.

Finally one morning he was woken by a shower of rain. It was still dark and he almost turned over in his warm bed, reluctant to leave a comfortable dream. Then, resolutely, he put his head out of his blanket and let the rain splash on his face. And, as Conrad set off, bow in hand, Ronan fell in behind him. Conrad glanced round briefly, but said nothing.

They followed a faint track which wound downhill through the sleeping forest. Try as he would, Ronan could not equal the heavy man's silent tread. Just as he thought he was going really quietly, a twig would snap under his feet: he felt the disapproving tension in the other's back. At last Conrad turned, put his finger to his lips and strung an arrow to his bow. Nervous, on tiptoe, hardly daring to breathe, Ronan followed.

They rounded a corner. Before them, a lake, gleaming in the first light of dawn. There was a sudden flurry, then Ronan saw a deer lying by the water, an arrow in its throat. He gasped. 'You were so quick! I didn't even see it!'

'A matter of practice,' said Conrad, hoisting the deer onto his shoulders.

'But how did you know where to find it?' asked Ronan.

Conrad paused, considering. 'Partly the lie of the land and the smell of the air. Most creatures go to drink in the early morning. And the tracks.' He began to point out to Ronan the things which to him seemed so obvious: chewed branches, hoofprints, a pile of dung. Soon Ronan too began to see the signs. Together they pored over the muddy banks of a stream, detecting the tracks of a wild cat, the rock which an otter had marked with its spraint.

There was a bird singing. Ronan looked up and spotted it: a robin, prominent on a high branch of a birch tree.

'It's a good way to fight a war,' said Conrad, cocking his head towards the bird.

Ronan looked puzzled. 'What do you mean?'

'Listen.'

They stopped under the tree. The robin kept one eye on them

but went on singing. Gradually Ronan became aware that what he had taken for a single bird's song was a medley of many: as one paused, answering echoes came from neighbouring trees. So sweet a sound, but with a chilly edge.

'There he stands,' said Conrad, 'wearing his flag on his front and shouting defiance for all he's worth. And his enemy perches three trees away and shouts back. The one with the best and loudest song wins the largest area to live in.'

'Can I come again tomorrow?' asked Ronan as they walked back into camp.

'If you like,' said his uncle.

So they fell into a new pattern, where Ronan accompanied Conrad each morning. If the hunting took a little longer, Conrad made no complaint.

Ronan learned to tell the tracks of a fox, a beaver and a bear; to distinguish an elk wallow from that of boar; to find on trees the marks left by cats honing their claws and deer fraying the velvet from their antlers; to tell whether a pine cone had been handled by a squirrel or a mouse; to read in the muddy ground the story of a hunting lynx and the death of a vole. From piles of empty nutshells, the pellets of owls, and drifts of feathers, he began to see that the forest, apparently occupied only by a few fleeting birds, was in fact teeming with creatures to which his coming was the signal for a silent vanishing.

And he learned to move more quietly, and to be still, and to watch. There were few animals that Ronan had ever seen alive before, and to gaze on them at peace in their own world was a breath-quivering enchantment. He saw an elk strip the leaves from a slender sapling with one rasp of its tongue; he saw squirrels playing tag like flames along the branches; a fox leaping, all four feet in the air, snapping at a butterfly; rabbits nibbling, bright-eyed, noses twitching, hopping where the dawn light cast long shadows on the dewy grass.

He felt happier than he had ever done. At last he could do things, nobody told him to wrap himself up warm, to come in out of the cold night air. And if his uncle was still a better hunter than he was, well it was only a matter of practice—Conrad had said that—and he'd soon be as good. Or better.

103

After supper they would sit around the fire and talk, remembering Fallond, imagining Ilyriand. They would tell stories, and Derwin would play his flute, jaunty tunes that set their feet tapping. The noise they made spread far beyond the pool of light around the fire. The forest seemed tranquil. They saw no one, so there was no one there. They talked and laughed and took no account of listening ears.

In the still dark before dawn Conrad shook Ronan awake, and then led the way across the wet grass and into the deeper darkness of the trees.

There was a warm, damp smell of toadstools in the forest; Ronan could see them gleaming palely all around. An old dead tree stump was covered with fungus, big as dinner-plates. Conrad snapped one off and slipped it into a bag. 'Good to eat,' he whispered.

It grew lighter as they went, and shafts of early sunshine fell through the trees. A pigeon began to coo, ruffled its feathers and relapsed into silence.

Suddenly Conrad stiffened, then, half crouching, slipped to the edge of a clearing, and knelt. Ronan dropped down behind him. On the far side of the clearing was a herd of stags, out of bowshot for the moment. They settled down to wait.

The early morning sun was sucking up long skeins of mist and sparkling on dewy cobwebs. It was very still. The sound of the deer tearing at the grass came distinctly across the clearing, and the reedy whistle of a robin floated on the air.

It was also cold. Ronan felt the chill permeating his bones. He could see Conrad kneeling in front, bow in one hand, arrow in the other, motionless as the trunk of the tree that sheltered him. Ronan looked at Conrad's dark profile, and wondered, not for the first time, what he was thinking.

There was a barking cough from the deer. For a moment they stopped feeding, heads alert, ready to flee; then they relaxed, and one by one began again to pull at the grass. They were nearer now. Ronan noticed how the stags seemed to take it in turns to watch for danger. It was not yet the mating time, but already there was some sparring among the herd, a little short jostling for superiority. One very fine buck raised his head and snorted: he would obviously have many wives. Pettishly he crowded an old stag out of the way. The thin old stag limped aside, and nosed wearily at the grass. He would get no wives this year, nor ever again. And with his strength he seemed to have lost all zest and will. He looked ready to die, thought Ronan. Then he began to wonder which deer Conrad would take. It was dreadful to have to kill one of these lovely creatures, plump and glistening with health. Still, they had to eat. The nearest was a young buck, sleek, rounded, self-assured. No, thought Ronan, I'd rather eat nuts and berries all my life. For a moment he was tempted to clap his hands and frighten them all away.

Conrad never took his eyes off the approaching deer. He could feel a twig digging into his knee, but he never moved. He was aware of Ronan crouching behind him. Perhaps he should let him try a shot—but if he missed they'd go hungry. It was difficult, this business of looking after the youth. The deer were getting close. He watched the old stag, jostled again, limp aside. For a moment he saw the world through its eyes, tired, worn out.

The young buck was now only a few yards away. Slowly, silently, Conrad fitted the arrow to the bow, pulled back the string.

The sun was getting stronger now.

There was a hiss, a thud; and a deer fell. The herd fled. Ronan started up, stared in surprise. The old buck lay dead on the ground.

'They'll grumble,' said Conrad. 'The meat will be tough.'

Ronan started to sing as they walked back to the camp. After a moment Conrad joined in. A squirrel leaned down and scolded them from an overhanging branch.

'Look! Strawberries!' cried Ronan, dropping to the ground.

The strawberries nestled like jewels in the grass, half hidden by trailing brambles. They were piercingly sweet, exploding on the tongue. Though tiny, there were enough to eat by the handful. Then Conrad, reaching for an elusive clump, found himself inextricably entwined in a bramble. 'This takes me back,' he remarked, munching more berries as Ronan tried to unravel him. 'It's years since I ate strawberries . . .' He grinned as he stepped away from the brambles.

'Conrad,' said Ronan.

'What?'

'Oh—nothing,' said Ronan; but smiled.

The others were up when they got back, and rather cross at being kept waiting. Nor were they very pleased when, that evening, the deer was cooked.

'This meat's tough,' grumbled Morgan. 'Is this the best you could do?'

'All I could get,' answered Conrad briefly.

Ronan grinned.

Next day Conrad let Ronan take the lead. Ronan moved differently now, steadily, confidently and quietly. He was still heavy-footed, and no doubt always would be, but he was much improved. He was filling out: more muscles and fewer loose ends. The journey was doing him good.

'Look!' cried Ronan, pointing. He knelt down, peering at some tracks in the earth. 'Look, here's where a mouse was walking, and *here*, a scuff mark and two drops of blood—it must have been killed by a bird, there aren't any other tracks. I saw that first,' he finished proudly.

Conrad assented, seeing in his mind's eye the owl drifting silently, searching with its golden feathered eyes, the mouse pattering, whiskers twitching, suddenly hunching in panic as it sensed the killer swooping, claws snapping in the mouse's neck.

Ronan led on and, surprising some pigeons on a branch, killed them as they slept. Carrying them back in triumph he said, 'I wish they'd let me go hunting before. It's much better than fishing.'

'Your mother would not thank me for teaching you,' said Conrad.

'But why not? They're always saying I mustn't do things, but they never say *why*.'

'Because your father was killed while hunting.'

'Is that all? One can be killed falling off a rock or die of a fever sitting at home. Conrad—tell me about my father. I don't remember him you know, and Mother won't talk about him, and all Grandfather says is how I'm not a patch on what my father was.'

Conrad paused, said, 'Ingram was always your grandfather's favourite.'

'But what was he like?'

'I'm not the right person to ask.'

'Why not? He was your brother.'

'Leave it. You would do well to learn to curb your curiosity about things that don't concern you.' He quickened his pace.

Ronan glowered at his back. 'Well I shan't leave it,' he muttered under his breath.

He waited until, later that day, they were travelling through a fairly open patch of woodland. Conrad, as usual, was up ahead, leading the way. After him, the ponderous bulk of Prothero, and then Ferdy. Ronan fell into step beside Derwin and asked abruptly, 'Why won't Conrad talk about my father? What's all the mystery? Why won't anyone tell me anything?'

'Oh, I don't know. There was some old scandal, I think, but I was only a kid. Morgan, do you remember?'

'Remember what?' asked Morgan, roused from sad consideration of how much his feet hurt.

Ronan repeated his question.

'Ingram? Now that takes me back . . . A lovely lad he was. Mind you, I always said no good would come of it . . .' Morgan relapsed into silence.

With a considerable effort Ronan curbed his impatience, assumed his most winning smile, and said beguilingly, 'Of course I never knew him. But you remember him, don't you. Won't you tell me about him? Please?'

Morgan looked at him, a disconcertingly perceptive stare. 'Right now you've a real look of him. Charm the birds off the trees he could. He and Conrad were always together when they were boys—well, brothers, so they would be, wouldn't they? Though Ingram was much older and he was always the leader. Into all sorts of mischief he was, but he could always sweet-talk his way out of it. And Conrad would trot around after him— Ingram used to call him his dog.' He paused, remembering the laughing prince, feckless, arrogant, slightly malicious and

107

always sure he could get away with anything; the younger boy, admiring, eager to please. All so long ago . . .

'Then why won't Conrad talk about him?' asked Ronan, puzzled. 'All he would say was, he wasn't the right person to ask.'

'Ah well, they fell out. Though maybe falling out isn't the right way of putting it . . . It was when Ingram married your mother. I didn't hear of any quarrel, exactly, but Conrad always seemed to be on his own just then. Such a change it was. And then one day Ingram comes up to Conrad. I was just nearby, mending a net: not that Ingram ever took any notice of the likes of me. Conrad was sitting on a wall looking out to sea, and Ingram, he sits down beside him and says, "Well, little one, I haven't seen you for a long time." Conrad just muttered something, I couldn't hear what, and Ingram—I can remember it as if it was yesterday—Ingram says, "Now I'm married—and I'm going to be a father, did you know that? And you're sitting here all alone. You mustn't mind, you know. After all, I'm going to be King and everyone knows you're only my dog." Only he said it so charming you couldn't take offence. Leastways they fell to chatting and arranged to go hunting together next day.' Abruptly he stopped.

'Well?' demanded Ronan. 'Was that when my father was killed? Tell me—I want to know.'

Morgan sighed. 'So sad,' he murmured. 'Yes, that was the last I ever saw of him. It seems they fell foul of a she-bear in the hills.'

'And that was the scandal!' cried Derwin, suddenly remembering.

'What was?' asked Ronan.

Morgan looked embarrassed. 'Oh, there was talk. You know how people are. *I* didn't believe a word of it.'

'Talk about *what*?'

'Oh well—it was all nonsense—nothing really—not to be repeated . . .'

'If it was all nothing you'd better tell me. Otherwise I'll believe—I don't know what I'll believe!'

'Well—that is—some people said . . .' Morgan gulped

miserably, the words drying up in his mouth. He looked sideways at Ronan.

'Some people,' finished Derwin, 'said that there wasn't a bear at all.'

There was a long silence, broken by the rustling of leaves underfoot.

'You mean,' said Ronan carefully, 'that Conrad murdered my father?'

'No, of course not.' Morgan sounded really shocked. 'It was just talk.'

'Well, from what you say I shouldn't be surprised if he did,' remarked Ronan dispassionately. 'I don't think I should have liked my father. I'm glad I never met him.'

'Ronan! You don't mean that!'

'Who knows what I mean? Why should I care anyway?' Ronan quickened his pace and walked on, kicking the plants as he went.

CHAPTER 14

NEXT MORNING Conrad woke Ronan as usual, but Ronan only turned over and burrowed deeper in the blankets. Conrad put it down to the weather, cold and foggy. It was after dawn, but still dark and quiet, sounds deadened by the mist. Bushes seemed to shift and change. Once he stopped, momentarily convinced that a sudden movement had betrayed a watching figure. He heard nothing. Of course there was no one there. They had seen no one since they left the coast. Perhaps they should be keeping a watch . . . But then he slept little anyway.

The fog persisted all day, adding to the queerness of the strange land where now they tried to find their way. They had left the hills and were crossing a great flat valley. Small, still pools and streams of silent rust-red water wound among the trees. Thick, feathery grasses gave way suddenly and plunged their feet into sticky black ooze. Skeins of mist wove between the trunks of birch and alder, clung among spiders' webs, drifted over the dull rich gleam of haunted toadstool rings. When for a moment the path seemed to straighten out, the great bulk of a vast ash reared up to block the way, its bunches of keys hanging in the murk like weird creatures peering down from the branches. The tops of the tallest trees disappeared into the fog. The moisture floated like a cloud, condensing into silver droplets on the thorns of brambles and briars, soaking the grass and the bracken.

The travellers were soon drenched, cold, muddy and cross. Conrad had the problem of beating a way in the direction he knew they should go, but which the forest seemed to be trying to prevent. His eyes, deceived by the fog, kept playing tricks. Several times he turned, convinced someone was watching, hiding in the mist. But there was no one there. The others, following in his footsteps, had some warning of treacherous ground, but had to put up with branches that sprang back in their faces.

Ronan, bringing up the rear, scratched and stung by a succession of brambles, dropped further and further behind.

He was thirsty. He decided to stop for a drink. The others were out of earshot, but he could catch them up when he wanted: four men and a dragon left an obvious enough trail through the bog.

It was very quiet. The thick leaf-mould cushioned his footsteps. The still water of the pool mirrored the silvery trees so that as he cupped his hands to drink he seemed to be lowering them into the sky.

He drank, then watched as the ripples settled and the reflections took shape once more. Looking at him from the water was a face, pale, with shining eyes, green or grey, and long flowing hair. He gasped, and leant forward, stretching out a hand. The reflection shattered, and a laugh rang out, jerking him round. The girl stood just behind him, mocking.

He sprang to his feet, crying, 'Who are you?' For answer she only laughed and backed away. He followed, saying, 'Wait. Don't go.' Her dress had a watery sheen, and changed colour as she moved; her hair, too, caught the light, seeming now ashen fair, now dark. Still she smiled, and moved away, and seemed to call him nearer. He followed faster, and she dodged away behind a tree. He lost sight of her, and stopped, bewildered. Then something stung him on the cheek. He whipped round, and saw her standing under a pine tree. Laughing, she ran off, pelting him with pine cones as she went. One caught him just over the eye; blinking away the tears, he hurtled after her. He was quicker on the straight, but she twisted and jigged like a hare. Then he made a lucky guess, side-stepping round a tree, and she ran into his arms. It was like holding a wild bird, light, slender, firm. Only for a moment: eel-like, she slipped from his grasp and was gone.

Still he followed, and still she ran, until he tripped and fell headlong. When he looked up she had vanished.

In her place was a circle of dark-clad warriors, their bright spears like the spokes of a wheel of which he was the hub.

111

'Bind him,' said one.

They dragged him to his feet, and took his knife, and tied his hands behind his back. As they marched him off among a wall of spears he caught sight of the girl, silently watching him go. He twisted to catch a last glimpse of her. She had led him into a trap. The betrayal hurt more than the fact that he was now a prisoner.

The men led him unerringly along a dry path that twisted tortuously through the wet land. Several times they left the path and splashed along streams. The trail would not be easy to follow. Soon they had left the trees behind them and now walked through a marsh where tall reeds rustled over their heads. All Ronan's questions, demands, protests, went unanswered. Eventually he fell silent.

And then, emerging from a sea of reeds, he saw it: a town floating on its own reflection in a silver lake. It was surrounded by wooden walls, reached by a narrow bridge. The huts were built on stilts, huddled together. There were some small boats tied up and motionless in the still water. Beyond, connected to the shore and to the town by more bridges, squatted another, smaller island—a single building, black, domed and silent. Silent as was the town where, if people lived, they hid as he passed.

It was towards this building that Ronan was led. The bridge, slippery with weed rocked beneath his feet, disturbing bubbles that rose and burst with the scent of things rotting under the water.

His guards left as others came to take their place; hardly a word was spoken. He was hurried through doors, down passages, and at last into a great hall. There was a quiet hum of activity; there seemed to be many entrances, and people constantly coming and going. In the middle, silent, a man sat reading.

'The prisoner as instructed, Sire.'

The man looked up and stared at Ronan. He had light, colourless hair and an anonymous face; his only definite feature was a pointed nose. His eyes gave nothing away. His voice, when at last he spoke, was neutral.

112

'You don't look like an Axeman.'

'Of course I'm not!' cried Ronan indignantly.

'Then what are you?' Silence. 'You might as well tell me. I know almost all about you. We have been watching you for days. There are five of you, and a beast. You carry a bird with you. Who are you and what are you doing in my land?'

'We're only passing through. We mean no harm.'

'You are going to the territory of the Axemen. No one goes there except their friends.'

'They're no friends of ours!' Ronan's voice was getting louder while the man's continued quiet, barely more than a whisper.

'You are addressing the King,' said a guard. 'Show respect!'

'And I am a Prince,' snapped Ronan. 'Show me respect!'

The King raised an eyebrow. 'If,' he murmured, glancing down at his book, 'if you are not friends of the Axemen, what do you want in their land?'

Ronan was silent. 'I can't tell you,' he said at last. 'But we are only looking for our own.'

'And I—I am only protecting my own. You are a stranger, and strangers are not to be trusted. Lock him up until he decides to talk,' he added to the guard. 'You are continuing the watch on his companions? Of course. We may need to dispose of them.' Calmly he resumed his reading.

Ronan was led away down windowless passages. The wooden floors, built over water, shifted beneath his feet.

He was taken to a small room, also without windows. His wrists and ankles were chained, and linked to a chain in the wall. The door was locked and bolted, and he was left alone in the dark.

Time passed. Ronan kept his eyes shut to avoid staring into the shuffling gloom. There was nothing firm on which to focus. On the fringe of hearing he could sense the lap of water, and the scrabbling rats somewhere beneath him. Trying to get at him . . . He shifted suddenly, to make sure they knew he was still alive. The scrabbling stopped as the floor jerked, then, as the room stopped swaying, the stealthy scratchings began again. His thoughts were confused, and all unwelcome: no one point on which to rest . . .

113

At last there was the sound of approaching footsteps, and the glow of a torch at the door. A key grated in the lock. The door swung open, and the girl stood on the threshold.

'Have you come to gloat?' he asked, blinking against the sudden glare.

She looked at him, considering. 'Aren't you going to be nice?'

'Nice!'

'I thought you might be,' she said. 'I came to bring you some food. I didn't mean this to happen. You should have told my father what he wanted to know. Then he would have set you free.'

'So he's your father, is he? And why should I trust him any more than you?'

'Don't be angry. Do you want some food?'

'I don't know how you expect me to eat, chained up like this.'

'Oh. Does it hurt?'

'Yes.'

'Wait—I'll get the key.' She ran quickly out of the room, leaving the door open behind her. Anxiously, Ronan waited for her return, peering into the darkness. Eventually she came, laughing and jangling a bunch of keys. 'I tricked the guard,' she said gleefully. 'I kissed him on the end of his nose and sneaked the keys from behind his back.'

'Another trick?' said Ronan.

The girl looked puzzled. 'But you wanted me to undo the chains,' she pointed out.

'Oh, get on with it.'

It seemed to take an eternity until she found the right keys and released his wrists. Sighing with relief, he rubbed his cramped limbs.

The door was still open.

'You realize,' he said, 'I could take you hostage and make them let me go. You even brought a knife with the food.'

'But you won't,' she said tranquilly.

Baffled, he stared at her. She was either bird-witted or very cunning.

'Have some food,' she urged. 'I chose it myself.'

114

When he started to eat he found he was hungry. 'What's your name?' he asked.

'Mirim. And yours?'

'Ronan.'

'May I have an apple?'

'Please do.'

She selected an apple and, leaning back against the wall, bit into it. Ronan, studying her profile, began to feel increasingly unreal. She was both bewitching and bewildering, and none of it made any sense. Her accent was strange, with a sort of lilt to it. Still, at least he could understand her—they spoke the common language of the peoples who traded around the Northern Sea.

She in turn considered him, from the corner of her eye. Strangers were a rarity; a palely interesting youth who claimed to be a prince was an undreamt-of phenomenon. Although he was rather young. 'How old are you?' she asked.

'Sixteen. And you?'

'Oh—much older,' she answered, vaguely and untruthfully. 'Why won't you say where you're going?' she went on, swallowing a mouthful of apple.

Ronan stiffened. Perhaps she was setting another trap for him. 'I can't.'

'Is it a secret?'

'Yes.'

'You can tell me. I know lots of secrets.'

He stared at her in alarm. Now he was sure it was a trap.

'You'll have to tell him in the end,' she said. 'He always gets his own way. Always . . .'

She shivered and stood up. 'I have to go now.'

'Leave me the torch.'

'I'll leave it in the passage. You might want to set fire to us.'

She locked the door behind her and fixed the torch outside. A dull gleam of light filtered into the room.

'Good-night!' she called, and laughed.

Mirim was standing behind her father's chair when Ronan was

led in next day. This time he was kept waiting. As before there was a deferential scurrying in and out of the various doors as messages were brought and orders sent. Silent in the centre of the room, the King crouched over his books, oblivious, apparently, until betrayed by a furtive sideways gleam. Ronan caught Mirim's eye. She smiled at him encouragingly. He looked away, stared at the ceiling where a fly droned in quiet circles.

Eventually the King raised one finger. Ronan was led over. The King carried on writing. Ronan looked at the top of his head. There was a bald patch.

'So,' said the King, 'I hear your name is Ronan and you have reached the great age of sixteen years. Have you anything more to tell me now?'

Ronan shot an accusing look at Mirim and closed his lips tightly.

The fly settled on the table and started to wash its legs. The King spared it a small part of his attention and squashed it. 'Still nothing to say?' he murmured, flicking the corpse to the floor.

Ronan remained resolutely silent. For the first time the King looked up, cold uncoloured eyes, pointed nose, straggling eyebrows.

'I'll never tell you anything,' Ronan burst out.

'Please, Ronan,' said Mirim. 'We only want to know where you're going.'

The King ignored the interruption. 'I understand my foolish daughter has given you food and light. So much the worse for you. We shall have to use more direct methods. Garvin, you may have him. Make sure he can still speak when you have finished, otherwise you may please yourself.'

A big, pasty-faced man stepped forward, rubbing his plump hands. 'You are too good, Sire,' he crooned.

Ronan was hustled out.

'Father!' cried Mirim, dismayed. 'You promised you wouldn't hurt him.'

'*I* shan't. He may get hurt. In fact, I'm sure he will. But that's his fault.'

'But—but I trusted you . . . Father, you tricked me!'

116

'Be quiet, Mirim. And stop behaving like a child.' His voice had a sudden edge, and his eyes were full of contempt.

Mirim seemed to hear him from a distance. This wasn't happening. She felt as if someone was hurt, but she hardly knew who. Or perhaps the hurt wasn't much. Or perhaps it didn't matter. Her head was full of clouds.

Slowly she left the room. She paused, with a kind of horrified fascination, at the end of the corridor leading to the cells, then wandered on and out into the foggy air.

She crossed the bridge and followed a twisting path through the marsh. The sun, gathering strength, was unwinding strands of mist from between the reeds. Soon she drifted into the forest, weaving her way between the pools where silver birches trailed long fingers towards their reflections.

A robin, puffing up his throat, poured out his song of defiance. He seemed so sure of things.

Mirim no longer felt sure of anything. She had trusted her father in this, and he had deceived her. How many other lies had he told? It felt like one of the great houses of cards she used to build. Shake one card, and the whole would come crashing about her ears. Half-remembered incidents came back to her, other times when she had questioned things, and he had said, 'Trust me.' He was her father and he was the King. So she had to trust him. But what if he had betrayed her confidence all along? She felt as if she had been seeing him through a distorting mirror, but now the image was true. He was like a great spider sitting in a sticky web of deceit and illusion.

Either he was wise, and kindly, and honest—or, if he were not honest, perhaps he was neither kind nor wise.

And then, her mother's warning . . .

Mirim sat down on a grassy bank and watched the stream slip by. Clouds of midges danced over the water. The sun on the ripples dazzled her eyes.

Things remembered pulled her, some one way, some the other. Treacherous ground. What if her own memory was deceiving her? Perhaps she hadn't seen things straight at the time. Pulling the veil from her eyes still did not make her any more sure what was right.

Bubbles broke at the surface. Fish, vole, or only gas? There was no knowing.

With an effort she conjured up her father's face. So familiar, but so elusive.

More easily she pictured Ronan. Young, slim, with gentle eyes, skin flushed by the sun except where a white scar showed on his forehead. She had betrayed him, led him into a trap of her father's devising.

She felt so confused, so much alone. There was no one to tell her what was the right thing to do.

Her mind ran round and round like a rat in a trap. Her father, Ronan, circles of deceit . . . And even now while she hesitated Ronan was being tortured. That had to be wrong—and she was responsible.

That at least she could put right.

Mirim rose slowly to her feet. Once she made the first move there would be no way back. The house of cards would tumble down.

She gritted her teeth. It was all up to her now.

The day had clouded over. A thin, sharp wind blew through the trees, and the branches shivered. It began to rain, shattering the reflections.

A puny youngster, thought Garvin, ostentatiously checking over his instruments of torture. He would offer little resistance. Which was just as well. The scene with the King had been carefully rehearsed; privately Garvin was under orders not to damage—irreparably—a valuable hostage. Simple terror would be enough to make the boy talk.

Garvin grinned hideously. He was fully aware that he owed his position to his unfortunate appearance: an accident as a child had lost him one eye and horribly scarred a face that had originally had little to recommend it. He was appallingly ugly and his gentlest smile could make even the stout-hearted quail. He knew it, and exploited it to the full. Flicking a whip with a crack like thunder he leered revoltingly and advanced on Ronan.

As it happened Ronan was not paying much attention. His refusal to answer questions was instinctive. And since it had not been a considered decision, he didn't consider changing it: he didn't think about it at all. His mind was wholly taken up with a boiling rage. Mirim had lured him into a trap; then she had pretended friendship and betrayed his confidence. What he would like to do to her . . .

Once her decision was made, Mirim's mind seemed to clear. Rescuing Ronan was a simple problem to be tackled in logical order, like the games of chess she played by the hour with her cousin, often infuriating him by winning. It was just a matter of luring knights in one direction, castles in another, walling up the queen so the pawn could sneak away to safety.

Only she was so short of time . . . Rapidly she slipped through the trees, silent as smoke.

She found the watchers not far from home. They were hidden in the treetops, encircling the strangers. Fulke was in charge. Good. He had always had a soft spot for her. Mirim climbed the ash in which Fulke perched and slithered silently to his side. He pressed his finger to his lips as he saw her coming, but the warning was unnecessary. She peered down on the strangers. They had obviously lost the trail. They snuffled the ground like dogs, arguing, oblivious of the watching eyes. The red monster seemed to be sleeping.

Mirim put her mouth to Fulke's ear. 'Message from Saber. Army invading from north. You are to go straight away. Meet Saber in Arandale.'

Fulke nodded, put his hand to his mouth and gave a wren's alarm call three times—pause—then thrice again. He melted away and only the stirring of branches in the trees around, as if shaken by a sudden breeze, showed that his men had joined him.

So far, so very simple, thought Mirim, as she too slipped away, leaving the strangers to their fruitless scrabblings. Once safely away, she began to run.

'Saber!' she shouted, as she hurtled over the bridge. 'Saber!'

The captain came running out of the guard-house. 'What is it?'

'Hurry! We're being attacked! You must hurry!'

'Slow down a moment and explain.'

'Fulke sent a messenger—I met him—he gave me the message—went back to Fulke . . .'

'Well, what was the message?' demanded Saber, by now as agitated as Mirim pretended to be.

'An army,' gasped Mirim. 'From the north. The strangers turned northwards and met a whole army of their people— Fulke was following and saw—they're forming up to attack down the river—Fulke is going to try and hold them back at the ford—he said—reinforcements quickly!' Pausing to catch her breath, she sank to the ground, adding only, 'I'll tell Father— go!'

Saber barked a volley of orders. Men scurried from the guard-house, buckling on weapons and armour as they ran. Moments later they had swarmed across the bridge and left the town silent, brooding in the afternoon sun.

Mirim began to laugh. She was enjoying herself amazingly. Still, there was no time to waste.

Then she met her cousin, hurrying to find the source of the commotion. 'Where has Saber gone?' he demanded.

'Oh, he said the troops were lazy and needed exercise. He's taken them on a long march.'

'A foolish thing to do when there are strangers about.'

'Oh, but you're here to protect me, aren't you?' She smiled sweetly.

Irritated, he bit back a retort.

The next step was to steal some keys. The key-room was empty and Mirim had found what she wanted and slipped out again even before she'd had time to think of a lie to account for her presence if caught.

She weighed the keys in her hand, hesitating. But there was no other way. She took a torch from the wall. Swiftly she slipped down the passage, past her father's chamber, towards the part where no one ever went any more . . .

There at last was the door. It looked just the same. Except for the dust. She took a last look round. No one there.

The door was stiff from disuse. The key turned only after a struggle, and the hinges shrieked. Mirim dived through, the door clanged shut. She leaned back against it, her heart

120

thudding, listening for footsteps, a shouted challenge.

There was only silence.

The dust rose in soft eddies beneath her feet. Cobwebs clung to her face. Her breath came fast, but muffled, the sound falling dead in the felted air. Creatures stirred in crevices, patches of blackness with many legs gliding from dimness to obscurity.

Almost she turned and ran. At the end of the passage waited an enemy she had ignored for many years. She felt an immense reluctance to confront it. Finally she sat down on the floor. The dust of seven years settled about her.

Seven years since last she walked down that passage. Then, too, it had been without her father's knowledge, against his command. Then, in the room at the end lay her mother: ill, they said; dying, she read in their eyes. Mirim clutched a handful of bluebells picked in the morning dew, now limp and pathetic.

She had pushed open the door of the room and stood there, blinking. The face in the bed turned towards her, the eyes clouded and uncertain.

'Mother, it's me.'

'Mirim . . .'

'I brought you these. You always liked them.'

Her mother peered vaguely at the wilting flowers, and a smile wandered across her lips. 'How kind,' she said. 'Mirim . . . you're the only one who cares.' A tear trickled down her puckered cheek. 'Listen—' She beckoned her daughter nearer and clutched her hand, hurting her. 'You must never trust them,' she whispered urgently. '*Never*, do you understand? I thought I was watching them, but they caught me sleeping . . . sweet voices, and poison in the cup.'

She lapsed into silence for a while as her eyes turned inward on some untold path.

At last she roused herself. 'Mirim—I meant to teach you before. You must learn to protect yourself. They have the strength—you must be cunning. Here is the key to my cabinet. There you will find drugs, powders—secrets that only I know.' Her eyes glinted with a malicious guile. 'It's not too late . . . you'll find some tricks there to ruin them. It's all written down in the book. Belladonna, aconite, foxglove, narcissus, they're all there. You shall revenge me. Then I shall rest in peace.' She smiled at last, triumphant. Her gaze wandered and she sagged back, her hand losing its convulsive grip. When she spoke again it made no sense: shattered remnants of thoughts fluttering in some half-forgotten breeze. She no longer recognized her daughter.

They buried her three days later. She had died of a fever, they said. Mirim tried to believe it. But her mother's last words still lurked in a dark corner of her memory.

The chill seeped into her bones. She had never been so cold, so alone. After the desperate spurt of activity her resolution had ebbed away. But if ever she were to escape she had to go down that passage. And action would at least postpone thought.

At last she stood, and slowly walked on. She had to rescue Ronan: for the moment that would have to suffice.

There were no ghosts there, only dust. Thick dust lay over everything, blurring outlines, clouding images. There were no answers here, and the questions had been buried long ago. Mirim crossed to the window and stared out. Voices, everyday sounds, came indistinctly across the water.

There was no one to guide her, and how could she decide? There was so little difference between what was right and what was wrong. One could be alive one moment, dead the next; there was only a hair's breadth of difference. Or perhaps life and death, doing and not doing, were the same; mirror-images.

Almost she could understand: but it was all so confusing. And everywhere the dust.

The cabinet still stood in a corner. Mirim unlocked it, took out the book, turned the pages. 'To make men sleep, tincture of poppies,' she read. She found the bottle, closed and locked the cabinet, left the room, walked back down the passage.

She had a vague feeling of having failed to come to any conclusion, of having dodged the issue. She dismissed it.

The tables were set ready for supper: trenchers, cups, salt, jugs of wine. The hall was empty. She divided the contents of the bottle between the jugs. She had no idea of the proper dose, would have to trust to luck. Finally she filled a cup with drugged wine and carried it from the hall.

Ronan ached. His whole body ached abominably. Oh, but he was tired . . . He settled into the least painful position and closed his eyes.

Mirim shook him. 'Wake up!'

'Go away.'

'Ronan, come on, wake up.'

'Shan't.'

'You must. I'm rescuing you.'

'Don't want to be rescued.' Ronan turned his back on her, wincing as his muscles groaned.

She shook him again.

'Ouch!' He pushed her off.

'You've got to come now. Please! I've gone to a lot of trouble . . .'

'You!' Ronan sat up and glared at her. She was crouching beside him, torch in hand, tears running down her face unheeded.

He looked at her sceptically. 'What new trick is this?' he enquired.

'You must believe me. It's not a trick, honestly. I duped the soldiers, and doped your guards, and left drugged wine for everyone else to drink . . .'

'And no tricks?' asked Ronan.

She missed the irony. 'No. I promise. Please get up and come.'

'I shall probably regret this,' he said; but he let her pull him to his feet.

CHAPTER 15

CONRAD SAT staring at the ground. They had lost the trail. For hours they had been clutching at the slightest clue: a snapped twig, some scuffed leaves. Now, as darkness fell on the second day, he had finally to admit that he had no idea where in all this vast weltering maze Ronan might be. There was only one decision left: whether to spend the rest of his days in a vain search through this miasma, or whether to turn back to their quest. True, he had never wanted to bring Ronan; still, he had accepted responsibility for him, and now must stand by it. He had to do his duty, but how long did duty demand that he spend on a hopeless search? But how could he go looking for the kingdom, if he had lost the heir? Although they were all depending on him to find Ilyriand, and if Ronan was dead . . . He was too tired, too confused to decide. Still he sat and stared at the ground, fuming at the inaction yet refusing to stir in pursuit of more illusions.

A slug oozed past his foot, then paused, feeling the ground. If it turns to the left we go on, thought Conrad. Then he closed his eyes with a muttered oath. As well let the dragon decide, he swore to himself, angrier than ever at his own ineptitude.

Suddenly Emma exploded into frenzied braying. Furious, Conrad whipped round. 'Can't you keep that blasted goose quiet!' he yelled; and Ronan, his arm round a girl's shoulders, stepped into the clearing.

Conrad stared, the rage boiling up inside him. Then, as Emma, wings outstretched, clamoured across her path, the girl tripped and fell headlong on to Prothero. The dragon shot up with a startled squawk, caught Derwin off balance and sent him flying into the mud. Conrad burst out laughing, steadied Ronan with one hand, and, smiling in overwhelming relief, held out the other to help the girl to her feet.

124

For Mirim, its accidental recipient, that glowing smile was the most disturbing feature of a bewildering day. She stared at Conrad, tall, black and silver in the moonlight.

'Listen!' cried Derwin, whose sharp ears had caught a sound. They froze, and Conrad too heard the rustle of many hurrying footsteps.

'Friends?' he whispered.

Ronan shook his head.

'Get going. Quickly,' ordered Conrad. 'But *quietly*. Derwin, you'll lead. Go east. I'll head them off and catch you up later. Now go!'

He seized his bow and vanished into the darkness. Mirim gazed after him. She knew him: she had met him in dreams. Even his abrupt disappearance failed to disconcert her. For the moment his existence was enough; she hugged it to herself, a tangible, caressing warmth. The forest sparkled in the starlight, and the wind sang.

Conrad circled round the enemy. They were dangerously close. Several men, perhaps ten or twenty. He began to call out commands and questions in as many different voices as he could contrive, then he crashed off through the undergrowth, scuffing up dead leaves, splashing through water, telling himself to make less noise.

Falling silent a moment, he heard the pursuit veer towards him. They were almost on him. Faster now he went, away from the clearing. No doubt his pursuers knew the forest better, but by following unhesitatingly each path that opened he managed to keep them at a distance, even to draw a little further ahead.

On he went, ducking and twisting through the trees, half running, half walking. Each time he stopped the following footsteps were there. He struggled through a thicket of alder, tripped and fell full length into a shallow pond, lurched up spluttering, ran on.

The hectic chase went on until, panting and dizzy, he saw a great tree with branches beginning low to the ground, almost like a staircase. Without pausing he went up it. Clinging to the trunk against which his heart pounded painfully, he looked down.

His pursuers walked straight beneath him: ten archers, and two men, more richly dressed, wearing swords. Conrad watched them out of sight. Suddenly it struck him he was enjoying himself. Smiling, he slipped down the tree and set off once more, then paused to see if they were following. The forest was wrapped in a dense listening silence. Deliberately he sought a dry twig and stepped on it. It snapped; and instantly there came the small stealthy sounds of the pursuit. He ran, twisting and dodging, always feeling, as if tied to his heels, the insistent following feet.

Then the path petered out. The forest was dense about him. He blundered in the almost dark, arms outstretched. Thorn trees hemmed him in. Desperately he flailed around, and, scratched and bleeding, burst through a clinging morass of brambles on to a straight, clean, moonlit path. He ran down it full tilt, sensing the hunt close behind him, his back tingling where an arrow might at any moment strike. A stream crossed the path; he splashed through it and across a muddy bank.

Struggling to catch his breath, he staggered on, chest heaving and the blood thundering in his ears. A tree root caught his ankle and he slithered to the ground.

As his breathing calmed he realized that the hunt had stopped. Puzzled, he started back down the path.

He saw them by the stream. One of the swordsmen was kneeling, staring at the single line of footprints in the mud. Already the men were beginning to turn away. Conrad took up his bow. They had realized that they had been tricked, and there was only one way to make them continue to follow him: he would have to make them angry. The kneeling man wore a hat stuck through with a feather. Deliberately Conrad took aim at the hat and, grinning, loosed his arrow. Time stretched. He watched as with an awful paralysing slowness, horrifyingly, inevitably, the man began to rise straight into the path of the arrow. It took him full in the throat. His arms flung out; he arched back, and fell.

The hunt changed then; it was no longer any kind of game.

126

There followed an endless time of running. Conrad was soon completely lost, and tacked at random through the trees, concerned only to keep out of reach of his pursuers. Several times they nearly caught him, but always he managed to slip away, by doubling back, by hiding, by shooting arrows to keep them at bay while he dragged air painfully back into his shuddering lungs. Eventually his arrows and his strength were spent. His pursuers too were exhausted, and the chase took on a nightmarish quality where hunters and hunted dragged themselves forward on leaden feet.

The terrain was changing: for some time they had been moving uphill. The marsh was left behind. Here the forest was more open, beech trees, gnarled and twisted, clenched between mossy boulders half-concealed by sprouting bracken. The light was growing. Conrad crested the hill, met the dawning sun; and stopped. It was the end.

Before him, on either side, stretched out a ravine, sheer, rocky, tumbling down to a river far below.

Conrad turned, to see the hunters step out from the trees, daggers raised, implacable. He read his death in their eyes.

The dawn was chill, colourless, empty. A thrush whistled briefly, then faltered and fell silent. Conrad reached for his knife: he could at least die fighting, a proper death even if unseen and unsung. Then he hesitated, watching his enemies, now close upon him. They seemed men much like himself. They looked tired. He had not the slightest inclination to kill them.

Suddenly he sickened of the whole business, and turned away. He stepped off into the void and dropped like a stone.

The sky between the trees was intensely, overwhelmingly black, scratched by the silver arc of the moon and stabbed by the throbbing glare of the stars. Mirim shivered, flinging her arms wide, scraping her skin against sharp pine needles.

Someone fell over, noisily. 'Stop!' came an urgent whisper from the dark. 'Ronan can't walk any further.'

'Ssh!' hissed Derwin.

They crouched in the silence, listening. Shafts of moonlight fell between the trees. Shadows shifted, stilled, wavered again. The wind.

'Just when we could do with some fog it's finally lifted,' muttered Derwin. 'Prothero, can you manage to carry Ronan?'

'I'll need extra rations to keep my strength up.'

'As much as you like, when we're out of here.'

'Load him on.'

Mirim touched Derwin on the shoulder. 'Your leader . . .'

'Conrad?'

'Conrad,' she repeated. 'He said to head east.'

'Yes.'

'That's the land of the Axemen.'

'Close?'

'Three—four hours.'

'Good. That's where we're going.'

'Are you friends of the Axemen?'

'No. They've got something we want.'

'There's a river. It marks the boundary between their land and mine. There's only one bridge.'

'Can't we swim across the river?'

'No—there are cliffs, and rapids.'

'Is the bridge guarded?'

'Yes. The Axemen have a guard-house on the far side.'

Derwin was silent for a moment. 'Can you direct us?' he asked.

'This way.'

The cavalcade moved on, Mirim now in the lead, Ronan, lying among the baggage on Prothero's back, swaying into sleep.

It was the still dark just before dawn. Cracks of light at the windows of the hut showed where the Axemen still watched. A dog whined. It was the middle of the night and he had not been fed. The moon cast deep shadows into the ravine. It was cold. He stood up. The short line that tethered him to the bridge dragged at his neck. He crouched down again. His eyes fixed on the building, where cracks of light showed at the windows, he whined again. The whines overflowed into a yelp, then he put his head back and howled. The door opened, a figure appeared, yelling, picked up a stone and threw it at him. He had no room to dodge: the stone caught him on the leg.

Whimpering, the dog slumped down, licking the new injury and the other sore patches on his legs, twisting about in a fruitless attempt to reach the area at the back of his neck which always itched.

The door opened again, and instantly on his feet, the dog barked furiously. But there was only something thrown out into the night, then the door slammed shut once more. The lights went out.

Gradually the dog quietened, and as his barking died away he became aware of another sound—low, almost imperceptible—from the other direction. Stiff with suspicion, his hackles rising, he stared into the blackness, growling softly at the back of his throat.

It was a strange, gentle sound, peaceful, unperturbed. It spoke to him of birds singing on sunlit spring mornings. The dog sank back on his haunches, puzzled. Uncertain what to do, he fell to licking his side.

The sound was growing steadily more definite, closer. With it was a smell. A good smell.

Without taking the flute from his lips or wavering in its play, Derwin walked along the bridge, moving so sweetly as hardly to seem to move at all. Calmly, he slid to the ground near the dog. The music still wound, trance-like, hypnotic. With the steady slowness of a snail gliding he stretched his free hand out along the ground, palm upwards, bearing a lump of meat.

The dog's tail began to sway. He snuffled at the meat, jerked it away and gulped it down. His nose returned, sniffing lengthily at Derwin's hand, then he licked it, his tongue warm.

Quietly Derwin reached into his pocket, took out more meat and offered it piece by piece to the hungry animal. By the time the food was finished, the dog was completely relaxed, sitting close to wash himself. Unerringly Derwin's fingers found the itchy place on the dog's neck and rubbed it. The dog lowered his chin into the man's lap and looked up at him, searching his eyes.

Derwin caressed the shaggy back, angry as he felt the sores, the bony ribs. He whispered reassuringly as he took out his knife and cut the dog's tether. Then at last he stood, put away his flute, walked past the fort. The dog trotted at his heels.

The others, following quietly in single file, found them some distance up the track, sitting side by side. The dog, introduced to them, accepted them with a certain reserve. Emma greeted him with equal suspicion.

'I shall call him Kerrin,' Derwin announced. 'When it's light, Ferdy, you'll have to see what you can do for these sores.'

'Are you meaning to keep him?' asked Ferdy. 'Conrad won't like it. A girl and a dog in one night.'

'Oh, I don't know,' answered Derwin. 'We already have a goose and a dragon—why not a little more livestock? Come on, let's see if we can find a place where Conrad can track us but the Axemen can't!'

For a while they followed the Axemen's road, a track hacked through the forest, marked by churned mud and by dead and dying trees. Towards dawn they came to a stream. They turned down it, splashed along for a while, then hid in a small hollow among a group of thorn trees. They waited all day in vain. They kept watch, but saw no one, neither Conrad nor the Axemen.

They passed the time in sleeping, in hearing Ronan's story, in sorting out of their packs some spare clothes for Mirim— Morgan had noticed that in her flimsy dress she was shivering with cold—and in wondering if at any moment savage warriors would come howling out of the trees to slaughter them all.

As darkness fell they shared a cold meal, not daring to light a fire. Suddenly Kerrin growled, his hackles rising.

Conrad slithered down into the hollow. He was covered in mud and blood, his clothes torn and filthy. He slumped down and wearily closed his eyes.

Ferdy, clucking, went to fetch his bag of medicines. The others clustered round. 'What happened?' asked Derwin.

'I went for a swim,' Conrad answered sourly.

'There, I said he'd turn up,' Prothero remarked to Morgan. 'There are some things you can never really say goodbye to. Plagues and pestilences, for instance.'

'Never would have thought it,' marvelled Morgan. 'Still, he'll probably die of his wounds.'

But once the mud was washed off, most of the injuries

appeared superficial. A long cut down the side of his face, another on his arm, were the only ones still bleeding. Ferdy dressed the wounds with flower-gentle and insisted on lighting a small fire so that he could make a drink of ground ivy. Conrad sipped thankfully at the hot, pungent liquid and lay back, his eyes half closed.

'How did you find us?' asked Derwin, bringing some food.

'A dragon's trail isn't difficult to follow. As about a hundred very unfriendly-looking warriors with axes also discovered. It's all right,' he added. 'They were scared off by the prints from Prothero's flat feet. If they'd known the only thing about him as big as his feet is his conceit it would have been a different story.'

'Do you think they'll come back?' asked Ferdy nervously.

'Probably. But Prothero will fight them off, won't you?'

Conrad pushed away the food. He was too tired to eat. He felt sick. All day, since he had woken, sodden and aching, on the muddy bank where the river had thrown him, he had carried at the back of his mind the feeling of falling and through it the image of the man in the hat toppling backwards, arms outstretched, an arrow in his throat. I didn't mean to kill him, he kept repeating; but every step he had taken through the forest seemed to have led inevitably to that moment when he loosed the arrow, and the man stood up. If only he could sleep . . . But the images were stronger when he closed his eyes. 'Where did that dog come from?' he asked abruptly.

It was the chance Ronan had been waiting for. Eagerly he recounted the events of the previous night, explaining how cunningly Mirim had duped her people, sending them this way and that so that she could rescue him. 'So you see,' he ended, 'I owe my life to Mirim. We all do. She guided us to the bridge, and if it hadn't been for her I'd never have got out of that dungeon alive.'

'And how,' enquired Conrad, 'did you get into it in the first place?'

There was a silence, broken by Mirim. 'I tricked him. I led him into a trap.'

Conrad gave her one short, contemptuous stare, then turned away. He was furiously angry. 'So,' he said carefully to Ronan, 'first she tricked you, then she betrayed her father—'

'She changed sides,' said Ronan defensively.

'And when will she change them again? Send her back before she does any more damage—or give her to the Axemen, they'll know what to do with her.'

'No! She's with us now!'

'You little idiot! We all owe our lives to her, do we, to that traitor? You fool, it was she who put us all in danger! A man died because of her cunning little schemes!'

'You'll pay for that!' cried Ronan, choking with rage. He sprang up and drew his dagger.

'I could kill you with both hands behind my back,' whispered Conrad, white-faced, motionless.

'Get up!' shrieked Ronan. 'Defend yourself!'

'Stop it!' begged Derwin, moving between them.

'Don't interfere,' snapped Ronan; and to Conrad, 'I command you on your allegiance. Defend yourself!'

Conrad rose, and stated flatly, '*I* command this expedition. The girl goes back to her people. Put that knife away. *Do as you're told!*'

'Are you challenging my right to rule? Who's being disloyal now? Is it true then? Is it true you murdered my father?'

'Oh, sit on their heads, somebody,' growled Prothero. But the others stood back. The quarrel had gone too far not to be settled. Only Mirim intervened, clutching Ronan's arm. 'Please, no! He'll kill you!' The Prince's only answer was to shake her off.

Conrad stared at him, tight-lipped, then drew out his knife. With a cry of triumph Ronan leapt forward and stabbed viciously, but the other slipped easily to one side. Ronan whirled round. Warily the two men circled each other, long shadows flickering in the firelight. Several times Ronan lunged; each time Conrad evaded the blow. An evil smile glittered on his face, and he still held his knife ready. But he was more tired and hurt than he knew, and as he dodged yet again he stumbled. Ronan struck. The knife plunged into Conrad's shoulder. He staggered and fell, and Ronan went after him, clutching his knife now dark with blood. They rolled over, first one then the other on top. But

Conrad was bleeding from his shoulder and from his earlier wounds: blood ran into his eyes so he could barely see. His strength was ebbing away. Ronan felt it, and waited his chance. Suddenly Conrad went limp. Ronan whipped back his knife to strike, then realized his opponent was unconscious. Cursing with rage and frustration, he hurled his dagger away. It stuck, quivering, in a tree.

CHAPTER 16

NEXT MORNING Conrad slept late. By then it was impossible to finish the quarrel, but, unresolved, it lay heavy between them.

'You realize,' said Derwin, 'that we're half-way home? We've found the land of the Axemen. Mirim doesn't know the way to the fortress, but as it lies on the west coast we only have to walk westwards until we meet the sea and then we're bound—'

'You've not told her where we're going?' interrupted Conrad.

'Well, no, but . . .'

'She must not know.'

'But, Conrad, you can't really think she's a spy. After all, she did get Ronan out of trouble.'

'After getting him in it—and proving how little value she places on faith and loyalty. I'll not trust her an inch.'

'There's no need to trust me,' said Mirim, in a small tight voice. 'I don't want to know where you're going.' She stared at him defiantly: and Conrad found he stood alone in a circle of hostile faces.

Over a month had passed since they left Fallond. It was early May, but the weather felt more like winter. They kept watch by night, not daring to light fires for warmth. By day they walked cautiously, fearing ambush.

Conrad's position as leader made it easy to blame him when things went wrong, for sore feet, empty stomachs, foul weather. He made no attempt to mend the situation, becoming ever more silent, bitter and brooding as they turned increasingly against him.

Ronan thought constantly of the people at home, relying on him. His mother, sitting by Emerick's bed, counting the hours. They must *hurry*. But everything seemed to be going wrong. Time was slipping away, they had no means of returning to

Fallond, and they didn't even know where they were.

Conrad had an ally in Mirim, little though he knew it or could have believed it. Her overtures of friendship were rudely repulsed. The colder and harder he seemed, the more attractive she found him. She imagined herself soothing his hurts, affording him a refuge from the cruelty of others. She had lived long enough in dreams to slip easily into this dream walking.

They came one evening to the sea, grey, spume-tossed and desolate. They camped by the shore as the sun went down and night came cold and bleak. Huddled in his blanket, Conrad considered which way to turn next, mapping out their journey in his mind. The coast on which they had been wrecked ran from east to west. This shore, running north and south, was the one they had originally been seeking, the one on which the fortress of the Axemen stood. If they turned northwards, and they did not find the fortress, at least they would soon know that they were heading in the wrong direction. But they had no way of knowing how far south the Axemen's country stretched: if they went south they could walk for weeks and still not know whether the fortress lay in front or behind.

'We'll go north,' he stated as they breakfasted.

'South,' said the others in chorus.

'You go north if you like,' cried Ronan belligerently. 'We're going south.'

'I think we should go north,' said Mirim unexpectedly.

'What do you know about it?' asked Conrad suspiciously.

She coloured. 'Nothing. Only I think we should all stick together.'

His suspicions deepened. But they went north.

Soon the coast became lower, flatter, spongy underfoot. Water squelched in over their boots, biting insects pursued them in clouds, fog blotted out the view.

Then one night a wind got up, blowing the fog away and soaking them with a driving rain. In the morning the view was clear. Before them stretched marshes, dreary with the long babbling melancholy of curlews. Beyond, the coast dwindled away as the sea curved round, cutting off their path.

'Well done!' said Ronan bitterly. 'So that's what we've got

from following our great leader. Three whole days of walking for nothing. Now we've got to go all the way back!'

Without a word Conrad turned and headed south through the recriminations of his fellow-travellers, his face bleak and cold as the hail that began to lash their faces.

'Don't mind me,' said Prothero. 'I always enjoy a little stroll.' He turned his lumbering bulk and headed back the way they had come, the piled-up baggage swaying as he went.

Mirim was the only one to enjoy the journey. She felt as if she had dropped out of the world, leaving behind her the doubts and uncertainties of her previous life. She was revelling in a glorious freedom. There was no one to tell her how to behave, no one to make her dress demurely and sit up straight. She could wear boy's clothes, laugh and joke with the men.

At night, wrapped up against the cold, she would watch the stars through the treetops and listen to her sleeping companions—Morgan snored, and Prothero rumbled—and to the scufflings of the creatures with which she shared this new world, mice scurrying, hedgehogs, heavy-footed, snuffling as if with a permanent cold.

It was all so different; and if at times she missed soft beds and warm baths, she soon grew to love fresh air, the smell of the earth and the shock of cold stream water on her shivering skin.

She missed her friends sometimes too, the girls with whom she used to gossip, but she felt now she had grown beyond them. The Fallonders now were her friends and all her family.

They would—when Conrad was away hunting—have told her their destination, but she refused to listen. She didn't want to know where they were going. She preferred to believe the journey would last for ever.

At sunset one evening they camped in the lee of some stunted pines which clung defiantly to the rocky cliff. For once it was dry: a starry moonlit night. An owl hooted overhead, a sudden clamour above the distant roar of the sea. Conrad too went off hunting, and the others, after eating, settled down pleasurably to abuse him.

'And another thing—' Ronan was saying.

'I think you're all being very unfair,' interrupted Mirim. 'You can't blame him for the weather.'

'But if he hadn't made us trail all that way north we wouldn't still be sitting here in the cold.'

'Well, he provided you with that meat you've been eating,' said Mirim, changing tack.

'It was tough,' said Ronan, as if that answered everything. 'I'm going to light a fire. I'm cold.' There was plenty of dead wood around and they soon had it going, not a discreet little cooking fire, prudently hidden and carefully guarded, but a great hot roaring blaze.

Prothero turned round to toast his back. 'Funny sort of leader who doesn't know where he's going,' he rumbled.

'That's right,' said Ferdy. 'He's forever looking down his nose at us, and for why, I'd like to know?'

'Well, I think he's unhappy—and—and he has problems,' said Mirim.

'What problems has he got that we haven't?' demanded Ronan.

'Very true, in this sad world,' agreed Morgan, shaking his head. 'Still, it's like your sweet nature to defend him, Mirim. It makes it all the more distressing that he should be so cruel to you.'

'He's not cruel—well, that is . . .' She paused a moment. 'He's lonely,' she went on cautiously. 'You're all so unfriendly to him.'

'And whose fault is that?' enquired Ronan.

'Sad,' said Morgan. 'Poor Conrad, for all he's a king's son I've never known him happy. Always carrying the burdens of the world on his shoulders. I remember my mother used to say happiness is a matter of choice, not of circumstance. There's a lot of truth in it, a truth I've always lived by. Make the best of things,' he ended earnestly.

The others looked at him with expressions nicely blended of awe and blank astonishment.

'But,' faltered Derwin, 'I've known you be just a little tiny bit pessimistic at times.'

'Never,' asserted Morgan. 'You mustn't confuse pessimism with realism. If I didn't look at things on the bright side, why, in this vale of sorrows I don't know as I'd have the strength to carry on ... What are you all laughing at?'

'Never mind,' said Mirim, taking pity on him. 'Would you like me to sing for you?'

'That would be nice,' he said. 'I like to hear you sing.'

So Mirim sang, a nonsensical song, but sweet. Derwin joined in with his flute.

Conrad, returning from the hunt, paused and looked down at the little circle. The fire, cracking in the chilly air, threw a warm light on their faces. The girl's voice and the flute blended in a soft and gentle music. The shadows of the twisted pines by contrast seemed all the darker.

'It's to be hoped,' he said savagely, breaking into the circle of firelight, 'that there are no Axemen about. One could hear you five miles off.'

The music ended abruptly.

'If it's a choice between bringing our enemies down on us and freezing to death, I'd rather die warm,' snapped Ronan.

Conrad made no reply, but, throwing down his catch—one thin and pathetic rabbit—kicked out the fire and huddled under his blanket.

Silently the others lay down, passing eventually into an uneasy sleep.

The coastline was becoming more rugged, slashed with rocky inlets. Not daring to go too far inland lest they miss the fortress, they plodded from one headland to the next and the next. And it rained: a chill, penetrating endless rain. They began to think of little but hot baths and dry clothes.

Derwin, to keep his spirits up, started to sing. Conrad whipped round angrily. 'Quiet, man!' he snapped. 'Can't you get it into your head this is hostile territory?'

Ronan snorted. 'We've seen no Axemen. I don't think I believe in them any more. If they exist at all, I swear they don't live here.'

'You're wrong,' said Conrad. 'Look about you. There's a

blight on this land. I can feel it, even if you can't.'

Ronan started to argue, and then, as they turned a corner, the angry words died on their lips.

Reared up, pale against the sea, silent with menace, it stood: a cairn built up of skulls. More than twice a man's height, and the base as broad. Skulls arranged in ordered rows, save where with the slip of time the bones of one had crumbled into another. Empty eyes gaped, tier upon tier. Here and there some creeping plant had found a hold and grew through hollow sockets.

The old fireside tale came abruptly to life. This was the land where their ancestors had died, defenceless, on a summer afternoon.

The wind shivered, spattering them with a few hard specks of snow.

From then on they went more carefully beneath looming crags where enemies might lurk waiting, with axes, and death in their eyes. Yet still they saw no one, though the cliff-tops now bore a path, old or little-used, but discernible, and sometimes they saw rocks crudely carved or hacked with strange devices.

As darkness fell they huddled into the indifferent shelter of an overhanging cliff, settling to a meal which, as they dared not light a fire, was cold, stale and comfortless. Conrad left them to it and, looking for a good place to mount guard, trudged to the top of the ridge.

A sullen blot on the pallid sea, the fortress lay not half a mile away, straddling the next headland. It was surrounded on three sides by the sea and on the fourth by a high wall, massive, malevolent, pierced with windows like empty eyes. In the dim evening its outlines were blurred, insubstantial, like some obscene fungus melting into decay. Beneath shifting showers of snow and sea-birds it squatted, silent, brooding.

So far they had travelled to find this fortress and the key to Ilyriand. Now he saw it, Conrad realized that their quest was as vain as it was foolish. That they should come so far to the stronghold of their enemies, there to scrabble on the ground for a key lost half a thousand years ago, was mere absurdity.

Night deepened, blank over a starless sea. Snow fell in a ghostly glimmer, muffling the distant whisper of the sea, settling

139

like a shroud on the dead stones.

Conrad let the dry dust of his hopes spill through his fingers. There was no returning, no point in going on. As well walk into the sea. Better. A clean washing into oblivion . . .

High overhead a rent appeared in the clouds. The snow had ceased, and a mounting wind scoured the sky. Stars flickered, and the moon shone, a few days past the full. In its glow the fortress re-appeared, now a thing of black shadow and shifting silver light.

Without any conscious decision, Conrad set off towards it, his footsteps crunching in the snow.

Though he went cautiously he was stiff with cold. The ground was stony and the moonlight deceptive. Several times he slipped, but there was no shouted challenge. Nothing but the endless calling of the sea.

The fortress loomed larger. He stared up at the gate, black and forbidding. Still he saw no one. Then again he stumbled and almost fell. The obstacle rolled over by his feet; teeth grinned at him from the snow. A skull. The rest of the body lay nearby. Looking around he realized that in the shadows among the rocks were other shapes: bodies, the bones stripped of their flesh but still clad in tattered shreds of clothes. There were weapons too: axes and knives. Another skeleton lay right in his path, its skull cloven by an axe which lay still in the wound between the two halves of the vacantly smiling jaws.

All was silent, and in the fortress there was no light save that of the moon.

The gate was open; he walked in. In the courtyard there were more bodies, things smashed, the marks of fire. He wandered on, bones crunching beneath his boots. The shattered remains of timber doors creaked in the wind. Through a great hall he went, along dark passages, up stone steps. Everywhere the dead lay as they had fallen. He mounted a spiral staircase, his steps echoing in the silence. Suddenly he caught a movement, and a scrabbling noise. Bones shifted; a rat burst out and scurried away.

He came out at last on top of a tower, and took great lungfuls of the chilly air. The pale moon swam high. The wind whipped his hair, bones lay around his feet, and a salt spray stung his eyes.

So far and futile a journey; there was nothing here but old stone and dry bones.

Mirim stirred, then lay still, cocooned in the warmth of her blanket and of some sweet, fast-fading dream. She heard voices arguing in whispers, and caught only snatches of the talk. Then she heard the others moving off, their footsteps muffled and subdued.

Silence fell. She lay sleepily, savouring the moment. The morning seemed full of promise, like waking on a summer's day. She sat up, pushing the hair from her eyes. The weather had changed in the night, the unseasonable snow melted away. It was a grey morning, misty and still. Droplets of moisture clung to the grass; the hillside faded, then came back into view as skeins of cloud drifted in from the sea.

She bathed her face in the dew, gasping at its chill. It was odd that they should have left her on her own, but she felt no resentment, glad to be alone to discover whatever it was that the morning offered. She wandered off down the slope to a spot where the cliff dipped and shelved more gently. In a few minutes she found herself on the beach.

The Fallonders had lived all their lives by the sea and paid little attention to its beauties or its terrors. But for Mirim it was a new and magical world.

The tide was out. Waves murmured over a stretch of clean-washed sand. A flight of birds skimmed low, wingtips kissing the water. Gulls, feet planted in shallow pools, drowsed fluffed up with their heads on their chests. Air and water merged in the texture of a feather. Along a shoal of stones Mirim found tiny shells, round, long, oval, or twisted into turrets, delicate with translucent colours, silver, grey, blushed with the shades of dawn. Billowing like clouds of down, strands of mist drifted in from the sea. Sometimes a watery sun glimmered through, reflected on the sand.

Wandering on, Mirim came to a place where the cliff slumped down on to the beach in a huddle of gleaming rocks. Amongst

141

them were little pools. Her eye caught by a sudden movement, Mirim crouched down and looked into an enchanted world. At first the pool seemed empty except for the fringing weeds, but as she remained still, strange creatures began to appear. A fish, long and thin with spots on its side, wound round a stone, found a hole and trickled into it. Then its face re-appeared, peering from the hole with a sort of absent-minded curiosity. There were many-coloured snails gliding over the rocks; and a crab. She had seen a picture of a crab in a book at home, and recognized it with delight—its huge front claws, its eyes on stalks, and the fringe of plantlets that grew on its back. Then, amazingly, it began to walk quite steadily sideways. Pincers gesticulating as if beating time, it sidled majestically across the pool and melted into a shadowy corner. Nearby was a miniature forest made up of little tubes, each with a feathery crown. Disturbed by some movement, the feathers vanished. A creature with five arms had wrapped itself around a snail; as the tip of an arm lifted, Mirim caught a glimpse of countless minute tentacles, each blindly groping. Walking up the side of the pool was a thing like a dark purple pincushion, its numberless prickles all arguing with themselves which way to go. Then, with a thrill, Mirim realized that the water was full of tiny, almost invisible dragons. Their bodies had no colour and she could see right through them, could even see their hearts beating. She wondered if Prothero knew his relations lurked here in this secret world. Busy and important, they scurried about, then suddenly one was seized by a flower. There was a brief struggle as the petals groped and clutched, then the dragon escaped. Intrigued, Mirim felt in her pocket and found some crumbs. She dropped one down to the flower. It missed, and rolled away. Cautiously she put her hand into the water and steered another crumb towards the flower: instantly the petals curved round, grasping the food, engulfing it.

Mirim drifted on from pool to pool, pausing each time to gaze on different small dramas. With their curtains of weed they reminded her of the plays she had seen sometimes enacted in her father's hall. More and more she felt as if these things were happening for her alone: this day was hers.

Abruptly she realized the tide was rising. Laughing, she retreated, the water lapping at her heels. Then for a while she stayed to watch the waves, the sea always different, always the same, so peaceful its roar, so comforting its vast unending emptiness.

At last she turned away and wandered up the beach. She felt no need of food or drink: she was light as air, she floated. She came to a path which led her by easy stages up the cliff, winding to and fro between boulders bright with lichen and tussocks of grey grass. The path led her almost beneath the walls of a fortress, ruinous and irrelevant, and brought her to the wreckage of a tree, stunted in its growth, but very old, and only recently fallen, its wounds still fresh.

Jumping lightly up she began to scramble over: then she felt something under her hand—a hard, metal object, almost buried in the fabric of the tree. The wood flaked to powder under her probing fingers, and the object fell into her hand. It was cylindrical, ornately carved, and gold: as the sun pierced through the mist it flashed and shone.

It was dark by the time Mirim returned. Kerrin greeted her enthusiastically, jumping up to lick her face. The others sat around glum and silent.

'Oh, there you are,' said Ronan, without evident interest. 'Where have you been?'

'By the sea,' said Mirim vaguely. 'I found this.'

In two strides Conrad was on her. 'I'll take that,' he said roughly, snatching it from her hand; then, as he saw Ronan at his shoulder, relinquishing it reluctantly.

Ronan took it to the light of the fire, the others closing around him, peering eagerly.

Mirim, excluded, watched but made no comment. She found herself some food and settled down at a distance to eat, her back against a rock and her eyes on the quiet gleam of the sea.

CHAPTER 17

'IT MUST be the key,' said Ronan definitely. 'Look, there's writing on it. I can't make it out . . . Must be in the old language.'

'Let me look,' asked Ferdy. He pored over the inscription, but could make out only one word: 'Ilyriand'.

As he spoke a hush fell. They stared at the key. The land of their forefathers rose as by magic out of old stories.

Ronan put out his hand for the key and Ferdy, a little unwillingly, passed it over.

'Keep it safe,' said Conrad. 'Don't show it to anyone. Don't tell Mirim what it is.'

Ronan, stowing it carefully away, for once did not argue: he had no wish to show it to anyone. Anyone at all.

'Well,' smiled Derwin. 'That's two problems solved. We have the key, and we don't need to bother about the Axemen. Someone has disposed of them for us. Their territory must nowadays be all north-east of here—we've walked through it, and out of it, without even seeing them.'

'That's as may be,' said Morgan. 'But I don't think I much want to meet the somebody who did the disposing.'

'It's curious,' remarked Conrad thoughtfully. 'I saw no other weapons among the dead, only axes and knives, all of the same design. It's as if they ran mad and slaughtered each other.'

'What a nice comforting thought,' said Prothero brightly. 'A whole new enemy that disposes of its foes by sending them mad. I wonder when we'll bump into them?'

'Look out for them,' suggested Conrad. 'You'll have a lot in common.'

From the fortress they set off south-east. At last they were back on the map, in which they now had almost boundless confidence. If the fortress existed, and the key existed, then so must Ilyriand: it seemed only a walk away.

Their route led them up onto a high, undulating moorland, dotted with rocks and occasional groves of trees. Their confidence did not last long. There was little cover. They felt like mice on a landscape hung over by the watchful eyes of hawks and owls. Conrad as usual led the way, pretending an assurance he did not feel. He began to fancy, each time he approached the crest of a rise, that he would come suddenly face to face with some dark featureless foe.

Though they saw no one, there were frequent signs of human presence. There were great stones grouped into circles, or lines, and sometimes huge boulders reared up on end. Often the trees were hung with chimes, discs of bone that rang softly, almost below hearing, muffled by the wind that stirred them.

'This place gives me the shivers,' complained Ferdy, as they hurried through one such chiming grove.

'I wonder if we'll meet *my* ancestors,' said Prothero thoughtfully.

Morgan itched. The others lay breathing peacefully, but for Morgan sleep was far away. The truth was, he needed a bath. He hadn't had one since he couldn't remember when, and he was beginning not to relish his own company. If, he thought, turning over for the hundredth time, he were to bathe, wash his clothes and hang them in a tree, they might be dry by morning. With a stifled groan he stood up and put on his boots. Prothero, 'on guard' with half an eye open, watched him go without comment.

His blanket rolled under his arm, Morgan set off the way they had come. He had glimpsed in passing a pool set rather oddly on top of a small hill, surrounded by a narrow belt of trees and offering reasonable privacy.

The pool lay still, serene, unclouded, a mirror to the moon and stars. Birch trees stood about it, chimes tinkling softly in the slender branches. A barely discernible ripple told where the water seeped from the rock beneath. For a moment Morgan hesitated, suddenly uneasy as if there were watching eyes hidden among the trees. There was a rustling sound as some small creature scrabbled among the dry leaves; then the listening silence returned.

Morgan took off his clothes and dropped them in the water. Then he gritted his teeth and waded in. It was bitingly cold. As the water mounted to his knees his courage almost failed him; then he flung himself full length, flailing up the ooze of ages undisturbed. Rapidly he rubbed himself down, then retreated to the bank. The night air stung his skin. A high wind had risen; clouds blotted out the stars and it was very dark. Morgan groped for his clothes and rubbed them together in the water. At least no one could see him. If there was anyone watching . . . Finally he huddled into his blanket, pulled on his boots and, clutching his sodden clothes at arm's length, squelched back to camp, taking with him a slight aroma of mud.

Behind him, the water of the pool gleamed no longer; sullied, it stank. The branches of the trees about shook in the angry wind. The chimes clattered.

Next day, Conrad's feeling of being watched deepened until it became almost tangible, like a presence snuffling at his heels. He found himself continually glancing around, searching the horizon. There was nothing to be seen, but still he could not shake off the feeling that somewhere, just out of sight, there was *something*.

When he noticed that Kerrin was also uneasy, trotting along with ears pricked, head turning from side to side, Conrad's suspicions sharpened. He dropped to the rear, convinced that it was from behind that the threat came. Then he felt it from in front. Soon it was so strong that he could smell the menace, feel it furring on his tongue. Sometimes he heard a panting right in his ear, but as he swung round it vanished. He tried to hurry the others, but their feet seemed weighed down as if something were clutching at their heels, pulling them down into ground that looked firm and felt like glue.

Wearily they trudged uphill, their eyes on the ground. More and more slowly they went. Then Conrad raised his head.

At the crest of the rise stood three figures, dark against the

146

sullen sky. The first had the head of a wolf, the second the head of a stag, the third the head of an owl.

Kerrin barked sharply, once, then slumped on his belly, whining.

The Wolf raised his hand. 'Halt!' The command rang out, urgent, but silent: it spoke only in their minds.

For a moment they stood staring, then Derwin snatched out his knife. The Stag turned and looked at him from eyes that were no eyes but only darkness visible.

The dagger spun from his hand and fell to the ground. Gasping, Derwin reached towards it, but his hand would not move. His arm remained stretched out, paralysed.

Ronan, first to recover, asked, 'Who are you? What do you want?'

'Silence!' The soundless voice spoke again, seething with menace. There was no disobeying.

The Wolf pointed at Morgan. The others felt set aside, of no account. Pictures formed in their minds: a quiet pool, surrounded by trees, sacred, haunted by gods. Morgan, splashing in the holy water, defiling, desecrating. His life was forfeit.

Wordlessly he walked forward. The others watched him go, no thought of protest in their minds. Punishment followed transgression as night after day.

The soundless voice spoke again, of an endless empty falling forgetting . . .

When Ronan woke the sun was low in the sky. There was no sign of Morgan or his captors. The others still lay sleeping.

'Come on, wake up!' cried Ronan, shaking them. 'We must go after him.'

'No,' muttered Conrad, his eyes black.

'What do you mean?'

Conrad could hear Ronan shouting, but could see only the still pool, the chiming trees, the flash of silver knives, blood flowing in a red tide, a warm salty gushing, choking at the back of his throat.

'No,' he whispered again.

'But they're going to kill him!'

147

Shaking his head, trying to banish the dream, Conrad blinked and swallowed. 'We can't save him. There's no way. He broke their laws. He has to die.'

Ronan stared at him, his face contorted with rage. 'You're scared!' he hissed. 'Any excuse will serve a coward!'

Conrad swallowed again. He still felt the blood would gush from his mouth when he spoke. 'You felt their power,' he said slowly. 'We can't fight them. The only chance would be to kill them as they slept. You want to do that?'

'Yes,' said Ronan.

'No,' said Derwin. 'There must be some other way—I don't know what, but we'll think of something.'

'We can't just leave him,' said Mirim uncertainly.

'Of course we can't,' agreed Ferdy, sounding more definite than he felt. 'I mean, all he did was *wash*. I don't see why . . . Anyway, poor old Morgan, he didn't want to come in the first place.'

'Off you go, then,' said Prothero. 'I'll stay here and look after the baggage. I saw enough of the ways of the wizards in Fallond, I'm not tangling with any nasty foreign ones.'

'Very well,' said Conrad heavily. 'But, Derwin, do think of something, for pity's sake.'

They set off straight away, leaving Prothero in charge of the baggage and of Emma, tethered and calling protestingly as they disappeared. They hurried on by starlight until, in the darkest part of the night, they could walk no more. Derwin racked his brains for some device or stratagem, but could think of nothing. 'Something will turn up,' he decided, and went to sleep.

Derwin yawned and rolled over. It was still dark but he could hear some curious muffled noises. He sat up. Nearby Conrad was kneeling, bow in hand. Out of the fog-darkened dawn came an eerie high-pitched cry.

'What is it?' whispered Derwin.

'Some sort of animal, I think,' answered Conrad. 'But no kind I ever heard before.'

They waited. Slowly the darkness lifted, and they saw coming towards them out of the mist a strange creature, grey, long-legged, long-necked, with a long head and pointed ears. Conrad pulled back the string of his bow.

'No!' Derwin whispered urgently. He stood, cautiously he advanced. The animal watched him approach, curious, but poised ready for instant flight.

Derwin inched nearer, heedless of the wet grass on his bare feet, then stopped. The animal snorted and threw up its head, drops of moisture spraying from the long dark hair that fringed the arch of its neck. It took a couple of steps forward, almost dancing on its long legs, then paused, swishing its tail, sniffling through wide nostrils. Derwin slowly held up his hand and touched the animal's neck, wet but warm.

Crooning encouragement, Derwin sidled closer, running his hand over the firm wide shoulders, laughing as the creature snuffled at his face and blew hot breath on his cheek. Carefully he stooped, picked up a handful of leaves and grass and held it out. Arching its neck, the animal inspected the offering, then graciously accepted it. Its lips, brushing Derwin's hand, were amazingly soft for so large and powerful a creature. Holding his breath, Derwin stretched up his hand to the mane of hair, steadying himself, then vaulted on to the animal's broad back. The animal twisted round its long neck and looked at Derwin enquiringly.

'Oh you beauty,' whispered Derwin. He wriggled forward and held on tight with his knees. The animal began to move, at an awkward, jarring pace that threatened to throw Derwin to the ground and shook every bone in his body. Then the animal lengthened its stride, running faster, but smoothly. Derwin felt the wind on his face, streaming through his hair, and an enormous sense of power between his legs as the drumming hooves beat on the ground. There were similar creatures all round him now. A great black one seemed to call a challenge; still faster they went, the black and his grey, galloping shoulder to shoulder, the world whirling by in a noise like thunder.

Conrad watched incredulously as Derwin vanished into the mist on the back of the wild beast.

'I do believe that was a horse,' said Ferdy, appearing at his elbow. 'I've read about them. It's said that men in the south often ride them. Fascinating.'

'As if I didn't have problems enough!' exclaimed Conrad, kicking violently at a rock and taking a sour satisfaction in hurting his foot.

But Derwin returned a few minutes later, still mounted on the grey horse, accompanied by several others, and looking decidedly smug. 'Do you know,' he said, 'I'm beginning to get an idea . . .'

Morgan walked, mindless, barely aware of setting one foot in front of the other. Before the blank gaze of his captors he knew he had sinned and must die. On he trudged, carrying his guilt, seeking only to be free of it.

Sometimes, like a fly flailing in a web, his mind would try to clear, fighting the cloying numbness for a memory of light and air. Then a masked face would turn towards him and darkness fall again.

His captors spoke not at all, or only with their minds, and the journey wound on in a silence broken only by the sound of the wind and the far-off calling of a kite.

At night Morgan was commanded to sleep, and he slept, dreamless almost, though somewhere deep inside the fly still fluttered in the web.

In the chill hour before dawn, he woke. Nearby he could make out the shapes of the Wolf and the Stag huddled in their cloaks, sleeping. The Owl sat staring at the sky.

Morgan shook his head, trying to clear it. The pressure was less now. If only they would let him alone for a minute, so he could remember . . . The wind rose and sighed. A faint echo woke in his brain: the sea. He tried to concentrate, to conjure up blue waves in this black desert. But the waves slipped away and he drowned in sleep.

Another day passed, or it might have been several. There was no knowing. Then it was night again.

Morgan opened his eyes, abruptly conscious and aware. Something had woken him. His captors were also awake, sitting up and listening. Then he heard it again, a plaintive beckoning music, calling, calling, then dying away. It seemed to come from among some rocks not far distant, deep shadowed by the moon.

And then, on the other side, lights shining, dancing and soaring, circling, winking out, spinning high into the sky.

The Wolf spoke silently to his companions, who rose and stepped soft-footed into the darkness, one towards the lights, the other drawn by the music. Morgan watched as the Wolf gazed first one way, then the other, all his attention absorbed.

Very quietly Morgan rose to his knees and, wincing at the pounding of his heart, began softly to crawl away, not daring to look, his body shuddering in anticipation of a blow from behind.

Suddenly it came: the Wolf crashed down on him and he fell on his face, all the breath blown from his body.

'Well, get up man.' The voice was familiar. Morgan, feeling the weight pulled off him, blinked upwards. Conrad was standing over him. By his side lay the Wolf: his head had fallen off. No, his mask had fallen off.

'Quick,' said Conrad, pulling Morgan to his feet. He led the way to where they had left the horses. Derwin's voice met them, calling cheerfully, 'All's well. They are both sleeping peacefully.'

'Then let's go.'

Morgan found himself thrown up behind Ronan on the back of one of the great beasts. He clutched frantically at Ronan's waist as they lurched forward. Ronan glanced round, his eyes gleaming with excitement. 'Are you scared?'

'What—is—this animal?' gasped Morgan. 'It's awful! I was better off where I was. Oh—I feel sick!'

The horses trotted on through the hours of darkness, then, as the sun rose, broke into a canter. Their hooves seemed hardly to touch the ground which previously the travellers had crossed with so much effort. Over the undulating ground they went, running smooth as a ship before the wind.

By mid-morning they were back at the hillside where Prothero was waiting for them. 'Oh, you're back are you?' said the dragon, and Emma honked a rapturous welcome.

They stopped to eat, and Morgan recovered enough to ask the question that had been puzzling him. 'What *were* those lights?'

Ronan grinned. 'Glow-worms! Mirim's idea—and when that owl came over to see what it was I sneaked up behind and

151

knocked him out. And on the other side Derwin was playing his flute and when the other man went over Ferdy jumped him. Good, wasn't it? It was Derwin's idea, mostly—' he added conscientiously, '—after we found the horses and realized they'd carry us fast enough to escape from those spooks.'

'Time to move on,' said Conrad.

Ronan looked at him. 'Of course,' he said to Morgan, 'some people would have left you to it. It's good to know who your friends are.'

CHAPTER 18

FOR THREE days they swept along. The horses moved swiftly, covering the distances as if the map were rolling away beneath their feet. Even Prothero managed a sort of lumbering trot. The Fallonders' spirits began to rise: they had the key, they knew where they were, and they were making up for lost time. For a while their quest had seemed hopeless; now they felt they had a fighting chance. If only they could keep up this pace. They had covered more than half the distance in a little less than two months; but they still had the return journey to make, and no ship. In five months the fleet would set sail from Fallond. It would be a hollow victory if the travellers found Ilyriand, but too late.

Then the country began to change: moorland gave way to the dark tree-clad slopes of a range of mountains. They soon realized that horses were not built for mountain-climbing. A stumble, when Ferdy was thrown and knocked cold, settled the matter. They parted from the horses with regret, at losing friends, and at having to travel on foot. Derwin's grey followed them for a while, whickering anxiously as they toiled up a steep slope pocked with mossy boulders and thickly strewn with pine needles. Then he whinnied one last time, and disappeared back into the shadow of the trees.

The forest was a secret, twilight place, alive with creatures of light and shade, glimpsed briefly and silently vanishing. High up, unseen, the tree canopy rang with the piping calls of countless birds. And it was warmer, away from the wind. Small, pale flowers lay on the ground like quiet stars.

They made camp close to a clear bubbling stream where kingfishers flashed and dippers ran beneath the water. Conrad went hunting to replenish their stores, and the others settled down, enjoying the peace.

153

Prothero's stomach rumbled. The dragon's appetite had been growing lately as there was less to satisfy it. Sometimes he would turn to look at himself, worried: he felt he was being stretched out, long and thin. 'Do you think I'm growing?' he asked Derwin.

'Hungry, are you?' Derwin yawned. 'Never mind, Conrad should be back soon.'

After supper, Ferdy got out the map and stared at it in the firelight. 'Are we going fast enough?' he said. 'It's still an awfully long way—'

'Quiet!' snapped Conrad. 'Not in front of her.'

'Why not?' demanded Ronan. 'We're miles away from her home now. You can't still believe she's been sent as a spy. She's with us now. *I* trust her.'

Mirim looked up hopefully. Conrad refused to meet her eyes. 'But I don't. Once a traitor, always a traitor.'

'I foresee treachery,' said Prothero. 'But not from Mirim.'

Conrad snorted in derision. 'What do *you* know about it?'

Prothero stared at him from great yellow eyes. 'That is for me to know and you to find out.'

'Oh do stop arguing,' Mirim broke in. 'I don't want to know where we're going. I'm going to wash. You can talk all you like while I'm gone.'

She picked her way through the gathering twilight towards the stream. After washing she slumped down on the bank, head in hands. By her feet was a small sage plant. She put out a hand to stroke its downy leaves and a wave of scent brought back a picture from years before—her mother in the herb garden planting out a bush of sage, carefully settling the roots, then sitting back on her heels, brushing the earth from her hands with a grunt of satisfaction. 'Wait until summer, child. Bees love sage.' And in June the bees had flocked to it till the whole bush hummed and each purple flower was tipped with black and gold.

'What's the matter?'

Mirim looked up through a film of tears to see Ronan crouching before her, solicitous. She couldn't bear him, so hot and so close.

'Nothing,' she choked out, and ran off.

Morgan, a little later, came across her, the tears pouring down her face as she stared into the stream.

'That's right, little Mirim. Have a good cry.' His knee joints cracked as he lowered himself down beside her.

She sniffed and wiped her face on her arm. 'I wish I hadn't come.'

'I didn't want to come either,' sighed Morgan.

'I don't know what I'm doing here. I don't belong. Nobody wants me.'

'Nobody likes me either,' sympathized Morgan.

'I wish I was dead!'

'Ah well, that's a wish as will likely soon be granted.'

Mirim stared at him. 'Are you trying to cheer me up?'

'That's right, little one. Put a brave face on it.'

Mirim, despite herself, began to laugh.

The next day's travelling was hard, continuously uphill, following a narrow winding path between mossy boulders. Ronan was wrapped up in his own thoughts, or he might have noticed the tracks.

By mid-afternoon they were exhausted. Coming to a point where the slope levelled out, Prothero took control. 'This is the first place for two days where all of me can lie down flat.' He subsided with a heavy sigh. 'Could someone please remove the baggage?'

'All right,' said Conrad. 'We'll rest here the night.' Bow in hand, he disappeared.

He returned just before sunset, heavy-laden.

'Good hunting?' asked Derwin.

'Mmm.' Conrad threw down the bloody pile, then stretched. 'Keep close to the fire tonight,' he said abruptly.

'Why?' demanded Ronan. But Conrad had walked off to wash in the stream and made no reply.

Ferdy busied himself over the cooking pot. He had found some tubers which did not seem to be poisonous. With luck they would taste better cooked. He added some herbs, and stirred. A succulent smell wafted round the clearing.

Conrad returned, and started skinning and gutting his catch.
Darkness fell.

Suddenly Conrad was on his feet. Almost in the same movement he snatched a rabbit from the pile and a brand from the fire, and ran off.

'Whatever—' began Derwin. Kerrin stood, hackles raised, growling, erupting into a bark. Then he charged off after Conrad.

The others stared mystified.

Then they heard two sounds, not far off: the howling of wolves, and a girl's terrified scream.

Mirim.

For a moment that seemed forever, Ronan was frozen to the spot, paralysed with horror. Then he too began to run, stumbling in the dark. Thorns tore at his skin, a branch crashed against his head, roots clutched at his heels. He fell, staggered to his feet, confused. Which way?

There was the sound of wolves yapping and snarling as they tore their prey to pieces. He fell again, scrambled to his knees, saw the shadow leaping on him, screamed . . .

'Quiet, boy!' Conrad was standing over him, torch in hand, Mirim's body thrown over his shoulder. Ronan felt Kerrin nuzzling at him and clutched at his rough coat. 'Back to the fire!' ordered Conrad.

Moments later they met Derwin and Ferdy, each carrying a torch in one hand and a knife in the other.

'What's happening?' called Derwin. 'Is Mirim all right?'

'Fainted, I think, but sound enough,' said Conrad. 'Now can we get back to the fire? The wolves will have finished that rabbit by now.'

Back at the camp, Conrad and Derwin built up a roaring fire. They all sat close to it. Grey shapes circled silently, vague walking shadows between the trees. Kerrin hunched, growling softly between his teeth. Emma kept quiet. Ferdy patched up Ronan, who was bleeding from several long scratches on his legs and arms and a deep gash on his cheek. 'And what use you thought you'd be fighting wolves with your bare hands I'd like to know,' said Ferdy severely as he slapped on a poultice of nailwort. Ronan winced.

Mirim, recovered from her fainting fit, crawled to Conrad's side. Greatly daring, she took his hand. 'Thank you,' she said.

Conrad glanced down at her hand, then at her face. 'Next time do as you're told.'

Derwin made a catapult and took pot shots at the prowling wolves.

'I suppose we are going in the right direction?' said Ferdy, staring doubtfully at the map. 'There should be forest all the way there.'

They had reached the crest of the range. And on the far side the forest vanished. Below them the eastern slopes stretched out dry and brown down into hazy emptiness that shimmered under a burning sun. The only plants were dry tussocks of grass and thorny twigs sparsely decorated with a few, reluctant green leaves.

A hot wind hissed, stirring the dust.

Conrad took a cursory glance over Ferdy's shoulder at the map. 'Trees can die,' he said drily, 'but I don't think mountains move. We go that way.' He pointed south-east, across the plain.

'Oh well,' said Derwin brightly. 'At least the sun's shining.'

'Yes,' said Morgan. 'Get sunburnt I shouldn't wonder.'

'That's right,' agreed Prothero, scratching. 'Every silver lining has its cloud.'

Perhaps it was the sun in their eyes, or the unaccustomed heat that made them sleepy and inattentive: either way, they were taken totally by surprise when a cloud of dust suddenly resolved into a band of horsemen, rapidly approaching. There was nowhere to hide, nothing to do but stand and wait.

The horsemen trotted towards them, their pace unchanging. There were fifty or sixty of them, wearing white robes, their heads bound with scarves that fluttered behind them as they rode. Their horses too were white, bearing harnesses hung with tiny mirrors that sparkled and dazzled in the sun.

Nearer still they came. Conrad's hand went to his bow.

They passed within a few feet, without a glance, until the last turned on them a bored, incurious stare. His eyes flickered

157

briefly as they rested on the dragon, then he looked away.

The dust settled slowly. Derwin let out his breath in a long sigh. 'They didn't seem very interested in us, did they?'

'Or we were lucky,' said Conrad. 'Perhaps they had more pressing business. We'll keep a better guard, in case they come back.'

'You do fuss,' Ronan joined in. 'Obviously the people here are friendly.'

By the time evening fell they had seen no more of the horsemen, but they were close to a small town of white, flat-topped houses, flushed pink by the setting sun.

Derwin was all for going into the town. A change of diet—and of company—would be extremely welcome.

'No,' said Conrad flatly. 'We'll rest here for a while, then move on around midnight, then rest again during the hottest part of the day. I didn't like the look of those horsemen and we'll need to keep our wits about us if we're going to get across this plain without being caught. And since you're so keen for some extra activity, you can keep watch. Wake us at midnight.'

Derwin would have argued, but the others, tired out, had dropped where they stood and had obviously no intention of going anywhere. He shrugged and yielded with apparent good grace.

It was a marvellous night, the velvet blackness of the sky illuminated by great sweeps of stars. Lightning flickered silently on the rims of the hills.

Derwin sat watching. The others breathed steadily—and more or less noisily—as they slept; but he felt vibrantly awake. From somewhere the other side of the town, emerging from the endless zizzing of insects, he could hear a drum beating, rising, falling, sometimes stopping for a moment but always starting again. At last he stood up, groping for his boots, and slipped away. Kerrin woke instantly, and trotted at his heels.

Derwin followed the sound of the drum through the empty streets. He saw no one. The houses were hidden behind high walls, gates closed against curious eyes. The sound became more distinct: the drum was accompanied by some stringed instruments, and by a low-pitched horn. Eventually he found the musicians, in the grounds of a ruined house. They took no notice of him and continued to play. He sat down on the remains of a wall to listen. The music was strange at first, but he began after a while to recognize recurring patterns. The rhythm was complex, the beat set by the drummer's left hand countered—attacked, almost—by the more intricate poundings of his right. The plucking of the stringed instrument created yet a third rhythm, and through it all the horn wound snake-like, linking the sounds or breaking them apart.

Almost without thinking, Derwin took the flute from his pocket and at first diffidently, then with more assurance, joined in. The music of the others moved over to let him in; a theme he introduced was taken up by the horn, embellished by the drum, then thrown back to him. Like children playing with a ball, the music was tossed back and forth, each player juggling with it for a while, each instrument celebrating its virtuosity, before flicking it to the next. At last the drummer stumbled, and the music came to a crashing halt. They all laughed. The horn-player picked up a jug, took a drink, and passed it to Derwin. The liquid was luke-warm, bitter and invigorating. As the jug went from hand to hand, Derwin felt a sudden surge of homesickness. There had been too little music on this journey. A faint, sad tune came to his mind, a song of Fallond's pine-clad mountains, clear waterfalls, the soft, cold beauty of snow, a haunting evocation in this hot and arid land. For a while the flute whispered its melancholy song alone; then one by one the others joined in, transposing, transmuting the theme with elements of their own; separate strands spinning into a single thread, while stars fell from the sky above the flicker of summer lightning.

For hours they played, their lack of a common verbal language no barrier to a warm, intoxicating comradeship. The dog curled up sociably by his feet, Derwin felt thoroughly at ease; what was alien in his surroundings was all exciting. The drummer, the natural leader of the group, had extraordinarily mobile eyebrows which conveyed a world of meaning. The horn-player had a long, melancholy countenance and drooping moustache, his general air of despondency belied by twinkling eyes. The best of friends, thought Derwin hazily. It was with immense reluctance, and some unsteadiness, that as dawn approached he said farewell to them and wandered back to camp, Kerrin as always tagging at his heels.

Conrad had woken, later than he had intended, to find Derwin gone. By then the wind had obliterated his footsteps. Conrad knew well enough where the truant had gone, but was not about to go chasing after him in the dark. In fact he was tempted not even to wait for him. He roused the others and bullied them into moving further into the shelter of some rocks, then sat staring in the direction of the town, alternating between thinking he would never see Derwin again, and deciding what best to call him when he did. The disloyal, treacherous, disobedient reprobate—he deserved all he got. Probably be boiled in oil, or fed to the fishes . . .

Hours later they heard sounds of someone making unsteady progress towards them, then a noise as of a body falling.

'Get off,' said a voice. 'Stop licking me. Kerrin, let me up! Stop it!'

A few moments later Derwin ambled up.

'Where—have—you—been?' asked Conrad.

'Visiting friends,' said Derwin amiably. 'Nice chaps.' He took out his flute, blew a short trill, then stuck it behind his ear.

'I ordered you to stay here *on guard*!' said Conrad, gritting his teeth.

'Oh well,' said Derwin vaguely, and hiccuped. 'Where's my flute? I had it a moment ago.' He blinked around owlishly.

'What if they had taken you prisoner and made you tell them where we were?'

'But they didn't. Where *is* my flute?' He dropped on to hands and knees and groped in the dust.

'You deserve to be whipped,' ground out Conrad.

Derwin, ignoring him, sat up. 'Incredible music they have. I haven't enjoyed myself so much in years.'

'You went off,' yelled Conrad. 'Against my orders, and left us sleeping. I trusted you to keep watch, and you went off leaving us to be slaughtered in our sleep!'

'What a lot of fuss about nothing,' complained Derwin. 'You sound like a mother duck.' He went back to groping in the sand for his flute, mumbling, 'Quack, quack! Quack, quack!'

He stopped abruptly when Conrad, throwing caution to the winds, hurled the whole of their remaining water in his face.

'What did you do that for?' Derwin enquired, sitting up, very dignified. Kerrin, growling, flew at Conrad and bit him on the leg.

CHAPTER 19

THEY WENT down towards the town, eager and curious, except for Conrad, who was tight-lipped and angry—angry that he had been disobeyed, still more because he had been proved wrong. Unable to give vent to his fury, he smarted and glared unforgivingly about.

The town was at the meeting of three roads and a river and already, early in the morning of another hot day, brimmed with activity. There was so much noise, of men and of animals, that at first they could make little sense of the scene. They were constantly buffeted by the crowds, and their attention pulled this way and that by shouts and clangs and flashes of colour.

Trees grew along the main street; in their shade sheets were laid out, and on them goods arranged. Strange vegetables and curious fruits in small neat piles; stacks of round yellow cheeses, stinking; heaps of mysterious gold and orange titbits, enticingly scented; cooking pots; the long hooded robes which seemed to be the local dress; leather shoes and harnesses; knives with handles intricately worked and glinting in the sun. A man yoked to a pair of urns poured cups of some pale frothy liquid. Another juggled with shiny skittles, and another played a pipe. Several small boys gathered round the travellers, pulling at their clothes, shouting at them, holding out their hands. Receiving nothing, they continued to follow, shouting what sounded like abuse. In the general din the Fallonders hardly noticed. Everywhere animals bleated and bellowed and whined, while people called, gesticulated, offered, begged, haggled. It was all very tempting, but they had nothing to barter.

Eventually they stopped by a well, hoping to get at least a drink of water without payment. Then Derwin, who held Emma firmly clasped under one arm, was accosted by a man in a brown robe. The man held out some pieces of copper and pointed at the

162

goose. Derwin shook his head. The man groped in his robe and produced more copper, holding it out with one hand and pulling at the goose with the other. Emma pecked the man, Derwin clutched her to his chest and turned away. The man went off, yelling angrily.

'Why turn down a good offer?' enquired Ferdy maliciously.

Derwin, looking worried, called Kerrin to his side.

'Look at that!' cried Mirim, pointing to a boy who, with many flourishes, was thrusting flaming torches into his mouth.

Prothero snorted. 'That's nothing! I could do better than that when I was still in the egg.' He threw back his head and belched out a great gout of blue flame.

The effect on the bystanders was astonishing. As one, they threw themselves on their faces and covered their heads with their arms. Prothero, his flame dwindling, stared at them incredulously. 'Well!' he exclaimed. 'At last a really appreciative audience.'

'You should not be doing this,' said a voice severely. Derwin turned and saw a thin, bearded man and behind him, smiling and bobbing, his friend the drummer.

'I am Cassian,' said the bearded man. 'I am cousin of him. I am poet. I am speaking well your language. Is good?' His eyes swept over the group and fell on Conrad. 'To you, Esteemed Leader, I am bidding—welcome!' With an elaborate flourish he bowed to the ground before Conrad.

Conrad looked wonderingly at Cassian. The foreigner wore a white, embroidered robe, its hood thrown back to reveal luxuriant black curls, glossy cheeks, and melting brown eyes. Awkwardly Conrad nodded back.

'Most respected travellers,' Cassian went on, with eloquent waves of his arms. 'Not only—' he bowed to Derwin, '—a most accomplished musician, but also a great dragon beast of magic powers!'

'What do you mean, magic powers?' demanded Prothero, suspecting sarcasm.

'The sacred blue flame, O Magnificent One! None may be looking on it save they of blood royal!'

'Sounds like a lot of rot to me,' said Ronan.

163

'No, you saw them all fall flat on their faces,' said Derwin. 'Must be something in it.'

Cassian, meanwhile, had been conferring in his own language with a young man in blue. He turned to the dragon, and asked, 'O Wise One, this man is humbly asking that you are telling his fortune?'

'Whatever next!' exclaimed Ronan, disgusted.

'Hush!' said Conrad, who was staring at Cassian, fascinated.

'Please, O Magical One, are you deigning to do this small thing?'

'All right,' said Prothero unexpectedly. He addressed the man in blue. 'You will be neither rich nor poor. You will marry three wives and bury two. The third will bury you.'

Cassian rapidly translated. The man asked a question, and Cassian turned back to the dragon. 'The man says, will he be having sons?'

'Four,' answered Prothero instantly. 'They will be strong, and valiant, and respect their father. The fourth will be a dreamer: but he will go far.'

The man turned away with a nod of satisfaction. Cassian caught his sleeve, there was a short argument. Finally the man shrugged and passed over some silver.

'What was that about?' asked Mirim.

'He is paying for the wisdom of so magnificent a seer. Else he would not be valuing it highly. I am looking after the money for you,' he added.

'But that's cheating!' Ronan cried, shocked. 'You mean that man is paying for whatever rubbish Prothero cares to spout at him?'

'Hush, hush! You are needing food, isn't it?' asked Cassian, gesturing at their travel-worn appearance.

A young woman had pressed forward and murmured in Cassian's ear. Money changed hands. Cassian turned to the dragon who was sitting looking rather puzzled. 'She is a widow, and is having two suitors. She is saying, which shall she marry?'

Prothero looked hard at the woman. She lowered her head and hid her face in her sleeve. 'Do not marry the young man,' he said. 'He has blood on his hands. As for the old man . . . ' He paused. 'As for the old man, marry him only if you want blood on yours.'

Cassian, taken aback, hesitated, then translated. There was a gasp from the crowd and the widow hurried away.

'What on earth did you say that for?' demanded Morgan. 'That poor woman . . . '

But Prothero only shook his head, still with the same curious expression, and turned to listen to the next. For now the crowd, greatly impressed, clamoured for the dragon's prophecies, pressing their money into Cassian's ready hand, while he, with considerable skill, kept them in order, and translated, and shouted, 'Hear ye! A seer who speaks only the truth! Come hear his words if you be not afraid!'

'We've got to stop him,' said Ronan. 'He's taken leave of his senses.'

'He never had any,' remarked Conrad drily. 'At least he's being useful for once.'

'That's just the sort of cowardly expedience I'd expect from you,' sneered Ronan. 'He's cheating—' He stopped in alarm, hearing Prothero's latest pronouncement, to a grey-haired old man of obvious wealth and stature.

'You are the seventh son of a seventh son,' said Prothero. 'You have seven sons, thirteen wives and too many daughters. You will have all you ask for and die happy.'

'Whatever did he say a thing like that for?' gasped Ferdy. 'At least he might keep to things that can't be checked. There's going to be trouble . . . '

But there was no trouble, rather, as the translation finished, a congratulatory acknowledgement from the old man.

'Did you translate what he said?' Ferdy demanded of Cassian.

'Of course. This is a true magician.'

Startled, the Fallonders stared at each other.

'Roll up! Roll up! This way for the Prophet! Hear your fortune from the Dragon of the Sacred Flame!' Cassian was calling as he sized up the crowd and manœuvred the wealthiest to the front of the queue.

'I don't think I believe this,' said Ronan faintly.

'Seeing's believing,' yawned Derwin. Settling himself in a

patch of shade he closed his eyes. It had been a long night. His head hurt.

At last Prothero called a halt. 'No more,' he said. 'Seeing the future is hard work.' And as the supplicants clustered round he shouted, 'Be off with you!' and spouted out an enormous gust of blue flame, watching in satisfaction as the whole crowd threw themselves on their faces. Moments later the square was deserted, except for the travellers, and Cassian.

Cassian was busy counting the money. 'Not a fortune,' he murmured, 'but good. Properly managed . . . '

Prothero regarded him with a cynical eye. 'Hoy, you! Stop muttering that gobbledegook you talk round here. I want food. I assume I have earned some dinner?'

'Anything, O Wise One. Any delicacy that money is buying. What is your heart's desire?'

'Hmmm. Well, my stomach's desire might be for tender young virgin fried with best herbs and spices . . . '

'Er, anything, O Masterful one,' said Cassian hesitantly.

'. . . on the other hand I might settle for venison. With onions, they're good for my flame.'

Cassian took them to an inn where, he assured them, they would get the best food in town. The inn was furnished with long tables and benches, and lit by guttering torches. It lacked a fourth wall, so Prothero was able to stretch out in the road and keep an eye on the cooking, which proceeded with much sizzling and appetizing aromas in a dingy alcove at the back.

Derwin's companions of the previous night arrived and strains of music soon began to mingle with the sounds of cooking. Cassian poured out wine for them all; 'A very good year,' he assured them. Used only to the thin ale of the north, the Fallonders drank deeply. Only Derwin treated the wine with some caution, though this was soon dispelled by the intoxicating music and the tantalizing smells.

At last the meal arrived—less a meal, more a feast. The table groaned with an array of dishes each bearing a different food. There were bowls of brightly coloured rice; pancakes; several different kinds of fritters; small chunks of meat black on the outside and pink inside, so highly spiced that they made the eyes water; sauces, some cool, some agonizingly hot; little balls whose bland exterior concealed an explosion of different tastes within. Cassian waxed lyrical, explaining the contents and preparation of each delicacy. His guests ate hungrily and appreciatively—all except Morgan, who declared it would give him a stomach-ache and refused to eat anything but a rather rubbery pancake, after which he lapsed into a gloom punctuated only by an occasional belch.

For Prothero there was a vast platter of venison fried not only with onions, but also, as Cassian explained, with garlic and ginger, paprika and scallions, coriander and cumin. He wolfed down every last scrap, celebrated with an enormous belch of blue flame which caused more pandemonium than ever in the confined space, then closed his eyes and appeared to sleep.

The plates and dishes were cleared away. The music resumed. More jugs of wine appeared. Shadows danced on the walls.

Conrad had been sitting silent for a while, drinking but not attending to the conversation. Now he spoke suddenly. 'Cassian.'

'Yes?'

'You speak many languages, don't you?'

'All the languages in the world,' said Cassian modestly.

'Show him the key,' Conrad told Ronan. Ronan hesitated. 'We need to know what that inscription says,' Conrad insisted.

Reluctantly Ronan fumbled at his neck, took out the key, passed it over. Cassian took it, eager for a chance to show off his learning. Then his face fell. 'It is very ancient runic script,' he said finally.

'We know that,' said Conrad impatiently. 'What does it say?'

'Alas, it is passing my skill to read such a tongue. There are few now who can do so. But—' He brightened visibly. 'I can be taking you where one can be reading it for you. I can be taking you—' He paused for dramatic effect. '—To the City!'

'What's the City?' asked Conrad.

Cassian closed his eyes in horror. 'Not knowing of the City!' he lamented. 'Such barbarians . . . Azastan, greatest city of this great land of Ashmael. The city of towers and minarets and waterfalls that sparkle in the sun . . . The city of dreams where all things are possible and the impossible is undreamt of . . . '

'There would be someone there who could translate this inscription?' Conrad interrupted.

'Yes,' said Cassian simply.

'Then we will go.'

'But we don't even know where it is,' objected Ronan.

'It is lying some four, maybe five days' march away.'

'But which way?' persisted Ronan.

'Which direction is it you are going?'

'South-east.'

'Then it is on your way!' exclaimed Cassian in triumph. 'And truly it is worth any journey just to be seeing the marvels of Azastan. I was born there,' he added. 'Now I am coming to be your guide, isn't it?' He looked at Conrad and smiled, teeth flashing, the torchlight kindling a blue sheen in his glossy black hair.

'Then that settles it,' said Conrad.

Ronan hesitated, wanting to argue but unable to think of any valid objections. He looked uncertainly at Cassian, then round at his companions. Derwin, who had been playing with the other musicians, had just returned and was telling a joke. Everyone laughed.

Cassian took a long drink, then set his cup down determinedly. 'I am telling you one of my Poems,' he announced. 'Now—to translate . . . '

He closed his eyes and recited:

'When upon the bridge of hours

I am sitting to count the seeds of time . . . What are you thinking?' he asked, opening his eyes.

'Very nice,' said Derwin. 'How does it go on?'

'Ah. Yes. That is, at present it is going no further.'

'Oh. Well—what does it mean?'

'I am not knowing,' confessed Cassian, spreading out his hands and giving an apologetic smile. 'I thought it is sounding well, isn't it?'

'Oh, it does, it does,' Derwin assured him. 'Um—"When upon . . . "?'

'When upon the bridge of hours

I am sitting to count the seeds of time,' Cassian repeated, satisfied. Then, catching sight of a man who had just come in carrying a wide flat bowl, he started to his feet and hurried across the room. He returned carrying the bowl and wearing a triumphant smile. 'Behold! Grasshoppers!'

The bowl was indeed full of grasshoppers, some six inches long, piled on top of each other and feebly stirring. Derwin contemplated them doubtfully.

'You are indeed fortunate,' Cassian went on. 'There is only two, maybe three nights in a year you can be eating grass-hoppers.'

'Eat them?' Derwin's tone lacked enthusiasm.

'Wait until you are tasting them fried!' He darted off clutching the bowl and issuing commands.

Fried, the grasshoppers were delicious.

'Why are there two moons?' asked Mirim.

'You're drunk,' said Ferdy severely. 'Have a grasshopper.'

Mirim rose to her feet and set off rather unsteadily towards the door.

'Where are you going?' called Ronan.

She turned, swaying as she tried to bring him into focus. 'I am going,' she answered with immense dignity, 'to be sick.'

Moist-eyed, Cassian wove an arm round Conrad's shoulders. 'Ah, Connie,' he sighed, breathing into his new friend's face an odour pungent with wine and garlic. Conrad flinched, but Cassian was too involved to notice. 'Ah my friend, I am very much touched—*here*!' He clutched at his heart, then dramatically dashed away a tear. 'I am thanking for your trust. I will take you to the city. You will not regret it. My life upon it!'

'That's a dangerous thing to say,' remarked Prothero.

'Ah,' said Cassian. 'Lord Dragon, you are now telling our fortunes, isn't it?'

'No,' said Prothero.

'Oh come on,' sneered Conrad. 'Surely you can make something up for us?'

Prothero looked at him. 'All right. Don't go to the city.'

'That's not much of a prophecy,' Conrad yawned. 'The trouble with you is, you're getting too big for your paws.' He laughed. The more he thought about it, the funnier his remark became. His wit was amazing. He laughed some more.

Everyone laughed. Cassian fell off the bench. His giggles subsiding into hiccups, he sat on the floor and began dreamily to recite: 'When upon the bridge of time—No, is not right.'

'When upon the bridge of hours?' suggested Ferdy.

'No,' said Derwin. 'When upon the count of hours
I sit and bridge the time of seeds . . . '

Everyone laughed.

'When upon the bridge . . . '

'When upon . . . '

The room began to float.

'This is the road to Azastan?' asked Conrad.

'Oh yes,' smiled Cassian.

'We are travelling north,' Conrad pointed out.

'The road is bending,' explained Cassian.

Conrad stared ahead. The dusty track led straight on over the plain until it vanished into the haze. 'Why?' he asked baldly.

'Alas, I cannot tell,' lamented Cassian. 'The makers of roads may have many reasons we are not knowing.'

The sun was sinking to their left as they continued to walk along a road that had deviated hardly at all since morning.

'The city lies to the north,' said Conrad flatly.

Cassian looked up at him apologetically. 'Perhaps,' he admitted. 'A little.'

'A little! This road leads due north.'

'You are most wise, Esteemed Leader. But truly you must be going to the city. Wait until you are seeing such wonders! Then you are being thankful to your most humble guide.' He spread his hands wide, his teeth flashing in the most conciliatory of smiles, beads of perspiration trickling around the swell of his throat.

'I hope you're right,' said Conrad.

It was difficult to be angry with Cassian. He was so anxious to please, and had besides so much charm, so much mute, sad appeal in those doe-like eyes. In the days that followed they all, one way or another, fell under his spell.

His use of their language improved rapidly. He had a quick ear and was soon dropping his native idiosyncrasies in favour of the Fallonders' turns of speech. In return he taught Ferdy, also quick to learn, some of his own language, and much about his land. They would walk along gravely conversing in Ashmaeli, while for Ferdy, plants and animals he had only read of in dusty scripts came to life and grew.

Morgan disliked intensely the foreignness of the place; but Cassian had a remedy for aching bones that worked wonders.

Prothero too demanded a remedy, for sore skin. His back seemed always itching in the heat. Cassian procured a jar of the most marvellously soothing aromatic oil.

It was a pleasant journey, even if in the wrong direction. Cassian brought them around sunset each day to a village or town where he found them lodgings out of the cold night air, and ordered their meals, and introduced them to cousins, and the friends of cousins who bade them welcome to Ashmael. When their money ran short Cassian organized another fortune-telling session, and Prothero revelled in a respect he had never met before. When Mirim finally rebelled against her borrowed clothes, Cassian brought her the dress of an Ashmaeli maid: a gorgeous filmy tunic of some soft, floating fabric, leggings to match, and silver shoes.

By the time they had been travelling north for four days, only Ronan still regarded Cassian with a tinge of suspicion—and Emma, who pecked him whenever she could.

Conrad stood and looked where Cassian pointed, along the twists and turns of the road snaking down out of the brown hills, down to where, on the banks of a green river, lay the city.

Surrounding it were great walls made from the trunks of huge trees, clad in bronze. Within the walls, soaring above them, were towers, spires and minarets; twisted, pointed, spiralling to the sky. The sun glared, dazzled, exploded against pinnacles of beaten gold. Vast gates stood open and through them passed a stream of people; some on white horses with harnesses sparkling, some carrying litters curtained with silks, some driving laden wagons, all brightly dressed, vivid as butterflies. On the river floated ships with painted sails. All hurrying to the city.

'Azastan,' breathed Cassian. 'Come quickly. The gates close at sunset.'

'No,' said Conrad, still staring at the city, feeling miserably conscious of his dull clothes, travel-stained and old. He wished himself back in the cold mountains of Fallond. 'We must find somewhere to hide.'

'What?'

'Why?'

'We'll find somewhere off the road,' said Conrad, 'where we can't be seen. Ferdy, you copy the inscription from the key. Tomorrow morning Cassian and I will take the copy to the city. The rest of you will remain in hiding.'

'I told you not to go,' Prothero reminded him.

'It's a bit late to change our minds now,' Derwin pointed out.

'The coward's got cold feet again,' jeered Ronan. 'I don't know why we don't have Emma as our leader. At least she'd be more consistent.'

'No, is an excellent plan, Esteemed Leader,' Cassian broke in. 'Tonight we camp under the stars, tomorrow you and I go together to prepare a welcome for our friends.' He beamed on them all.

Next morning, just before leaving, Conrad called Derwin aside and gave him some whispered instructions.

Derwin raised his eyebrows, but made no comment, watching as Conrad followed Cassian down into Azastan.

CHAPTER 20

THE DOOR opened. Conrad turned and saw her.

A small, slight figure, wreathed in translucent silks. Her black hair was coiled onto her head and entwined with jewels. A gold chain wound round her waist and hips, bracelets circled her wrists. At her side, weaving around her legs, was a sinuous spotted cat. Her eyes, ringed with some black substance, were huge, their expression amused, detached.

'You are the man from the north?' Her voice was low, vibrant. She spoke his language carefully.

'I am Conrad, son of Emerick, Fallond's King.' He couldn't take his eyes off her.

She smiled. The sun rose. 'Then welcome, Prince.'

'And you?'

She stooped to caress the great cat's long neck. 'I think it may have escaped your notice that these others—' she gestured delicately '—are lying with their faces to the ground. I am Almira, Queen of Ashmael.'

'I beg your pardon, Lady. Would you have me do likewise?'

'Oh no.' She smiled again. 'For you too are of royal blood, are you not?'

Cassian had brought him to the library of the royal palace— the fount of all learning, all wisdom, he said. A huge hall lined from floor to ceiling with shelves full of books bound in leather and gold. The room was thronged with men consulting books, writing at marble tables, sitting together quietly debating. Conrad remembered the library at Fallond, a small dusty room where scripts piled higgledy-piggledy as they might. Cassian had left him to stare while, he said, he consulted the librarian.

All work in the library had stopped when the Queen entered. She and Conrad, and the softly purring cat, might have been alone in the room.

173

'They tell me you have an inscription you wish translated.'

Wordlessly he handed it to her. Her fingers, briefly touching his, were cool and soft. She reminded him of Alina, but younger. She could not have been more than twenty. So young, and yet with so much power.

Almira studied the paper for a few moments, then looked up. 'From what was this copied?'

'From a wall—the castle in Fallond.' The prepared lie came automatically to his lips and was instantly regretted. To deceive such a woman . . .

She looked back at the paper, then smiled at him. 'We shall need to study this further. This is a language few now can read. Come and see me later. In the mean time you will like to refresh yourself. Go with my servants, they do not speak your tongue but they will look after you.' She called out an order, turned and was gone, leaving a wave of perfume coiling in the air.

A man with a long grey beard, wearing a white robe and golden slippers, beckoned Conrad from the room, and down a long corridor. On either side were carved wooden doors, and archways leading into other passages. 'Where are you taking me?' asked Conrad, but the man with the grey beard only grinned, and shrugged. Walking half sideways, half backwards, he beckoned Conrad further on.

At last the man flung open a door and ushered Conrad into a large chamber, its low ceiling supported by ornate pillars, studded with blue and gold. One wall opened onto a courtyard where fountains played; in the middle of the room was a sunken area which two men were already filling from great jugs of hot water. There were mirrors everywhere, and Conrad winced, catching sight of his reflection, dusty, ill-shaven, his clothes torn and travel-stained. Greybeard, nodding and smiling, gestured towards the bath.

Slowly Conrad removed his clothes, folding them and laying them on a stool. As he stepped down into the bath he saw one of the servants pick up the clothes, and carry them out at arm's length. Sinking into the warm, soft, sweet-scented water, he abruptly decided not to care.

The bath was large enough to swim a few strokes either way,

and deep enough to sink completely and lie on the bottom. Which he did, surfacing to find Greybeard peering anxiously down at him. He laughed, relaxing in the warmth. This was luxury such as he had never known or dreamt of, and after months of hard travel and weeks of bickering and argument it was unexpected and overwhelming. If these people had meant him harm, he reasoned, they could have killed him many times by now. Letting down his last defences, he floated in the warm water, thinking of Almira.

At last he stood up, relaxed enough to let one of the servants scrub his back. As he walked up the steps of the bath the other servant poured a jug of clean water over him, and then enveloped him in a vast, soft towel, before leading him to a couch.

Conrad lounged back and watched, amused, as the servants shaved and manicured him, and cut his hair. A sense of unreality was stealing over him, intensified by the silence. As they could not speak his language, they did not speak at all, except with gestures, and soft touches at his shoulders.

When his toilet was complete they brought him clothes: trousers and tunic of some light, soft material, silver in colour. They felt like a caress against his skin. For his feet, sandals: silver again, and wonderfully comfortable. Then from a box of jewels, Greybeard selected rings which he slipped on to Conrad's fingers and a pendant which sparkled and shone against his naked throat.

Conrad stood and looked in a mirror. He liked what he saw.

Almira leaned against a balcony, gazing down on the lights of the city. Dusk was falling and the gates were closed against the desert. Within the walls, so many people, all crowding and jostling, all needing to be fed.

She heard a crying and shouting and turned, the curtains billowing around her. A troop of soldiers were hustling along another captive, a screaming woman. People shouted abuse. They had no idea. They thought one had only to wave one's hand to bring wagons laden with food. Yet where was it to come from? Only along a narrow strip by the river was the land fertile. The rest was desert, useless dust. And still they bred. She had tried every way she could think of to stop them, but still they would breed. Most of the infants died, of course, but still too many survived, ill-fed, sickly, unprofitable; a running sore on Azastan's fair face.

And now the edict: every family with more than two children must give the surplus to the River God. Any person voluntarily sacrificing all offspring to be rewarded with gold. Yet they could not see the justice of it. They would not understand that a little resolution now would ensure prosperity later. It was fortunate that she knew she was right. Only to her was it given to see the end of things: if they suffered a little now, it was for the greater good. When the Empire was supreme once more, then she would be vindicated. She would live forever as the saviour of Ashmael.

Almira sighed, looking from the city out to the barren hills, flushed red by the setting sun. They had not always been lifeless. She had read the old histories. Time was that an endless forest stretched where now there was sand, in the old days before Ashmael's greatness. They had cleared the forest to grow crops and gradually their numbers had increased. More people needed more food, but more people meant more power. Those had been the golden days, days of building, of conquest, of the dawn of the city. They had found metal ores in the hills, they had built roads, they had cleared more fields for crops and used the timber to fuel the furnaces which blazed day and night, turning out iron for their weapons, silver, gold and bronze to clad all Azastan in a flame of glory.

Absent-mindedly Almira caressed the tracery around the window. How had it happened? The records of that time spoke of no sudden disasters, no catastrophes, but the land had crumbled away between their fingers. The city still remained, but all else was gone, the wealth of land and empire which once had nourished it. The rains began to fail, the sun burned brighter, the fields had turned to dust. And now Azastan stood on the brink of the desert, fighting back the invading sand.

By the Sacred Flame it should be so no longer! Just in time came the barbarian from the north with a message that spoke of Ilyriand. The secret land, hidden behind the mountains, a fabled land that lacked nothing. Only show her where it lay and she would rebuild Azastan in Ilyriand, twice as beautiful, three times as magnificent.

The barbarian had lied. A single reading of the inscription had been enough to tell that. He knew more than he had said: well, he would reveal it.

It was now full dark. She moved away from the balcony, threw herself down on the bed. The cheetah unwound itself from the rug and leapt up to lie beside her. It pressed close, hot breath fanning her cheek, yellow eyes gazing into black.

Night had fallen when Greybeard returned to lead Conrad once more, along endless passages and into an empty room. Bowing and gesturing, he left. Conrad looked round the room. It was furnished with low tables and with chairs that were like voluptuous beds. The walls were lined with silken tapestries, finely woven with hunting scenes. Riders waving spears followed big spotted cats with jewelled collars, urging them on, watching while the cats fell on their prey and tore it to pieces. The tapestries were beautifully worked, vivid, meticulously detailed. Conrad wondered who had made them. He found it difficult to imagine a woman bending over a tray of silks, selecting the best red to depict the blood running down an animal's throat. He turned from them in some distaste and walked to the window.

Beneath him, in the dark, a fountain murmured and splashed. Waves of scent from some unseen flowers rose on the night air. From the streets beyond the palace walls came faint echoes of music. Conrad looked towards the hills, lit by the shimmer of lightning. At least his companions were safely hidden.

He paused, wondering why he had thought of that. Was he not safe in the city? He had been made more than welcome, treated with the respect due to a prince . . . Still, his instincts were to keep secret the whereabouts of his companions, and of the key. No doubt it was simply the long habit of mistrust—and yet he was glad he had told Derwin to move higher up the hills. Not even Cassian knew where they were now.

A sudden flare of noise disturbed his reverie. People were coming, someone shouting. The door flew open. Almira stood

177

on the threshold, her eyes glittering, her cheeks flushed with anger. She turned, waved a command. Her followers vanished. Smiling, she walked into the room.

'I am sorry,' she said. 'Affairs of state . . . you know how it is . . . ' A wave of perfume engulfed him.

'Some wine,' she said, and poured it with her own hands. It was thick, warm and potent. Still, he was thirsty.

'I have a map to show you,' she said, opening a drawer. 'Come, sit beside me.'

Gingerly he sat on the edge of the sofa, then forgot his unease as he looked at the map, eagerly comparing it with his image of the map he had been following for so long.

'Show me where Fallond lies,' she invited.

'Oh—far to the north. It is not shown on this map. We have been travelling for many weeks.'

'And where are you going—Ilyriand?'

He looked at her. 'You know of Ilyriand?'

'I have heard of it. And it is mentioned in the inscription. It lies somewhere in these mountains, I believe?' She ran a long finger down the map.

'Have you deciphered the inscription?' he asked, continuing to ignore her question.

She smiled. 'Later,' she said. 'Some more wine?' Preoccupied, he allowed his cup to be replenished. 'We have a story,' she went on, 'that the people of Ilyriand left and travelled to the north. Now you are returning?'

To gain time he drank from his cup and watched as again she refilled it. Such fine slender hands she had. The nails were painted red.

'You know,' she said, 'we shall be neighbours, when you are King of Ilyriand.'

'But I am not to be King!' he exclaimed.

She looked at him, puzzled. 'You are the King's son?'

'The King's younger son,' Conrad explained bitterly. 'His elder son died six months before his own son was born. The boy travels with me.'

Almira stared at him, frowning. 'I find it difficult to understand that a man of your quality should be the mere

178

follower of an old man and a boy.'

The air seemed thick. Trying to steady himself, Conrad turned away and took a deep draught of wine. It tasted odd.

'The inscription,' she said. 'Or rather, the copy—is not very clear. I will need to see the original. It is with your companions no doubt. Tell me where they are, and I will send to fetch it.'

'I—' He paused. His head felt strange.

'I can help you.' She smiled into his eyes. 'I can help you to claim your kingdom,' she said. 'To take what is rightfully yours.'

The world was turning. She was right, and she was beautiful. She recognized his true worth. All his faith and loyalty had earned him nothing but mistrust and resentment. He had no friends, they hated him, he owed them nothing. He would take what should be his and share it with his queen.

It was very hot in the room. Or very cold. One or the other. He blinked, and flames flickered in his eyes. His mouth was dry. He took a sip of wine. The goblet seemed curiously heavy, marvellously smooth, hard and curved. Slowly, with infinite caution, he set it down again. The table seemed a long way off, and shifting slightly. How long his arm was. He stared down at his hand, far off, watching the fingers wriggle. How very strange they were. He felt a smile spread slowly across his face and heard himself laughing.

There was a voice somewhere in the distance. It made no sense. Then her hand touched his arm, tingling like a thousand spiders dancing on stilts. His head rose reluctantly.

'Conrad!' The voice again, insistent. 'Where are your companions?'

Smiling vaguely, he told her.

Conrad woke to darkness. He was lying, chained by the ankles, on a cold damp stone floor in what he supposed was a dungeon. It stank.

His head hurt and he felt sick.

Between horror and incredulity he pieced together what had happened.

He had betrayed his friends. Betrayed his trust. Abandoned the stand of selfless loyalty behind which he had sheltered so long.

It had all been a sham. He had protected himself against the mistrust of others by a conviction of his own virtue and contempt for their inferiority. Now it had all turned round. They had been right to distrust him, right to despise him. And if he was not what he thought himself, then what was he?

He had been drugged and hadn't known what he was doing. No, he had been drugged and had known exactly what he was doing. He had wanted what was not his, and had willingly put at risk the lives of his companions. Perhaps they were already dead. He only hoped his own death would not be much delayed. He had no use for his life now, no wish to continue living with the self he had just discovered.

It all began with Ingram, and the bear. There *had* been a bear. His enemies had said there was no such thing and accused him of murdering his brother. Indignantly he had denied it, taking refuge in his slandered virtue. The bear was real, and it had killed Ingram. But the truth was a little more complicated than that.

They were always together; he, Ingram and Alina. Inseparable. Until it was decided that Alina and Ingram were to wed. Abruptly Conrad was on his own.

It was hot that morning they went hunting. Ingram laughed at him. 'I'm going to be a father, you know that?' As ever he strode in front. He saw the bear cub first, pounced, bundled it into his cloak.

'Look! A present for my bride! I shall teach it to dance.'

He stood exultant, laughing at the struggling bundle.

Behind him, a dark shape.

Motionless, speechless, Conrad watched.

The she-bear charged with astonishing speed. Ingram was down, fighting, the bear on top of him. He fought to the end.

Still Conrad stood immobile. The bear shook the body one last time, dropped it and glared around. The cub, extricating itself from the cloak, nuzzled against its mother's legs. She sniffed it. The two trotted away.

He had tried to carry the body back, but he was far from the castle. In the end, exhausted, he abandoned it and returned to Fallond covered in his brother's blood.

The wolves found the body first.

And the talk began.

How long had that time been? Between seeing the bear snuffling through the bushes and the moment it charged? Long enough, maybe, to have shouted a warning. Had he been paralysed with fear? Or was it jealousy that froze the words on his lips? And then the child, a smelly squalling runt, laying claim to it all—Fallond, Alina's love.

Last night he had wanted to get his own back.

He slept, and woke to find Cassian looking sadly down at him.

'Is not fitting you should be lying in the mud, Esteemed Leader,' he said remorsefully. 'I am much distressed.'

'Why did you bring us here?' enquired Conrad.

Cassian's expression lightened. 'It is beautiful, isn't it? My lovely city. You have been very lucky, Esteemed Leader, it is not given to many to see the palace as you have seen it—and to meet the Queen, praise her name! Is she not the most exquisite and amazing of women?'

'Indeed,' said Conrad drily. 'Cassian, I trusted you. You said you would guide us. And you brought us here to betray us.'

Cassian looked affronted. 'Of course. I am Spy. Is my profession. I am very good Spy.'

'Your—profession—stinks,' said Conrad.

Cassian sighed deeply. 'I have offended you,' he lamented. 'Was not my intention. You are all very dear to my heart. Even the goose,' he added reflectively. 'I am very sad to betray my friends. But alas, what else is there for me? One must live. In my soul I am Poet. But people will not pay for poetry. Treachery has good market value. Nobody is wanting Art.'

Conrad frowned. 'Am I expected to feel sorry for you?' he demanded.

'Please,' said Cassian. 'Then I know you have forgiven me. I wish you nothing but good.'

'Oh well . . . ' Conrad felt too little at ease with himself to pursue the matter. He looked up at Cassian's anxious face and smiled reluctantly.

'No ill feeling? Friends, yes? Good! I must go. Farewell,

Esteemed Leader. I have been proud to guide you.'

With a last beaming smile Cassian went out. The noise of clanging bolts drowned his departing footsteps.

They came for Conrad at dusk. Two silent guards pulled him to his feet and once more along those endless winding passages.

At last they entered a room, a long low hall full of people, light, music, voices. At the centre of a long table on a raised platform sat Almira, toying with some titbits on a golden plate. She looked up at Conrad, considering. He stared back impassively.

'On what was the inscription written?' she enquired at last.

There was no reply.

'Where are your companions?'

Conrad's heart leapt in incredulous relief. So she hadn't found them. He turned his back on her, trying to hide his joy.

'Teach him some manners,' said Almira quietly.

A big man all in red stepped forward and hit Conrad neatly in the gut. As he doubled up, the man lashed out with the back of his ringed hand. Conrad's head was jerked back, blood spurting from a wound on his cheek. Again and again the big man hit him. He welcomed the pain like a brother.

'The inscription,' repeated Almira. 'Where did you find it?'

Again no response.

With an exclamation of impatience the Queen rose, came rapidly towards him, and slapped him repeatedly around the head and face. Still he stared back at her, his eyes blurred but blank and unyielding.

She shrugged, and turned away. 'Kill him,' she said.

CHAPTER 21

RONAN WATCHED as Conrad and Cassian disappeared past the palace gates. He had borrowed Cassian's spare robe which he wore with the hood up, and thus disguised had attracted no attention at all. It had been quite fun following them, though he was not quite sure why he had allowed Mirim to chivy him into doing so. Conrad would be furious if he found out. Not that that mattered.

He settled down in a doorway to wait. He had a good view of the palace gates and of the continuous trickle of people coming and going, some importantly, with servants about them—one even carried on a litter on the shoulders of four men, with horns sounding and dogs barking—but most more humbly. No one was refused admittance, though some did not stay long, and left looking downcast. But of Conrad there was no sign.

As minutes, then hours, passed, Ronan's excitement ebbed away. He began to feel both thirsty and bored. No one took any notice of him—not surprisingly, as the city seemed about equally divided between those who were exceedingly busy, and those, like Ronan, who had nothing better to do than sit in patches of shade and watch the day slide by. Most of the activity was centred on the river, where boats were being loaded and unloaded, and boxes and barrels carried along the quay towards a side entrance to the palace. The water shimmered temptingly in the sun. Ronan, hot in his borrowed robes, thrust away the longing to plunge into its cool depths, and sat resolutely on. Almost he fell asleep, among the dust, and the hazy heat, and the muffled cries of the porters, the distant wailing of a baby . . .

A growing sense of unease dispelled his drowsiness. Too much time had gone by. Something must have gone wrong. For the first time he began to take seriously Prothero's forebodings of catastrophe. He panicked. All very well for Mirim to beg him to follow Conrad, but what was he supposed to do now? The sun was low, the day nearly over. It was all up to him. He had not the slightest idea what to do. He felt horribly alone, out of his element, like a jellyfish left stranded on the beach. Conrad would have known what to do, he thought. The shadows lengthened. Work had ceased on the quay, and the sounds of the city took on an evening quiet. Still he sat in a desperate indecision.

Kerrin pricked up his ears, then trotted away into the darkness. With the dog at his heels, Ronan stepped into the firelight, grim-faced and stiff. He ignored their questions, saying, 'Pack up quickly. We'll spend the night near the gates. Something is wrong. We can't go into the city tonight—the gates are closed, I only just got out in time—but we'll go in first thing tomorrow.'

'But what's happened?' asked Derwin again.

Ronan looked at him, a hunted expression in his eyes. 'I don't know. They went into the palace and didn't come out again. There's something . . . Come on, hurry up.'

'Never any peace,' grumbled Prothero. 'Well, you can't say I didn't tell you so.'

They camped behind some rocks close to the city gates. Ronan would allow no fire; he could produce no reasons, but they accepted his authority, and settled down, some to sleep.

Derwin lay with his eyes fixed on the stars, thinking round in circles. Sleep was far away. At last he gave up the pretence, and threw back his blanket. Mirim, tossing and turning, was obviously not sleeping either. She hadn't said a word all evening. Derwin hesitated, but decided to leave her to herself. He could see Ronan at a little distance silhouetted against the sky, huddled in a characteristic posture, elbows on knees and chin cupped in hands. Stepping softly, Derwin went over and dropped down beside him. 'Well, Prince?' he asked.

Ronan looked up quickly. His eyes were very bright. 'Well what?' he said.

'What are you going to do?'

Ronan half smiled. 'I haven't the least idea,' he admitted ruefully. 'Oh, Derwin, I'm frightened.'

Taken aback, Derwin could think of nothing to say. He was still trying to marshal some words of comfort when there was a sudden clamour from the city. The great gates crashed open, and out thundered a troop of horsemen. Galloping hard, they vanished down the road. When the dust had settled, the moment had passed. 'Don't worry,' said Ronan, looking determined. 'I'll think of something.'

The night passed slowly, with one more interruption, as the horsemen, more slowly this time, returned to the city and the gates clanged shut behind them.

They waited next morning until the crowds were thick at the gates, then entered the city by ones and twos so as not to attract attention. Prothero was difficult to disguise, but Derwin loaded him with baggage and led him in through the dust sent up by a herd of goats.

They were in the city unchallenged. They began to feel quite hopeful—until they turned a corner, and the palace came into view. Vast and implacable, it squatted by the riverside, the dazzle from its white marble walls hurting the eyes. Its crystal towers shattered the sun's rays, hurling them back in defiance. The huge doors gaped where the guards stood, spears in hand.

Another whole day of staring at the palace and of anxious consultation produced only the most basic plan. Mirim and Morgan, with Emma and baggage, were to wait by the bridge. At dusk the others would go into the palace and look for Conrad. 'You'll have to look after Mirim,' said Ronan to Morgan. 'And, here—look after the key. Don't let anyone else have it—throw it into the river if you must.'

'You'll have to look after Morgan,' murmured Derwin to Mirim. 'Otherwise he'll probably throw himself into the river.'

Night was falling. Mirim crouched by the bridge, feeling very conspicuous. There were few people around now. Morgan sat by her, white-faced. The minutes crawled by. Then Mirim's attention was caught by a patch of shadow that seemed to be shifting, sneaking towards them. She stiffened, touched Morgan's arm.

The thing moved into the moonlight. It was the travesty of a man, legless, contorted, pulling itself along on its hands. The face had no nose, only half a mouth, one eye that glittered askew. Determinedly the cripple shuffled towards them, stopped so near they could smell him, held out a hand.

Mirim felt feverishly in her pockets, found one of Prothero's coins, held it out to the clutching fingers.

The cripple stuffed the coin in his mouth and scuttled off crablike, mumbling weird triumphant cries. A woman ran out, snatched the coin, more people appeared and clustered around shouting.

Mirim watched in horror. She was shaking all over.

Other figures came out of the dark, pressed round her with outstretched hands, fetid breath, hollow eyes.

Desperately Mirim shook her head, pulled out her empty pockets. They clutched at her clothes, shouting, shoving. The stench caught her throat and she retched.

They went in the end, when they found she had nothing more to give.

Morgan came out of the shadows, tried awkwardly to comfort her.

'That poor man—did you see? Oh those poor people—And they were so horrible . . . ' she was crying incoherently.

'Never mind, little one. There, there . . . What a nasty experience for you . . . '

'But can't we do something to help them?'

'You mustn't upset yourself so.'

'But there must be something we can do!'

'I'm afraid they're not the only ones, my dear. If we knew all the suffering there was in the world we wouldn't get up in the morning.'

'That poor man . . . His face, did you see his face?'

'There, there, little one,' said Morgan uselessly. 'There, there.'

The sun sank fire-red, sending a wash as of blood across the river and staining the marble walls of the palace.

'Well, here goes,' said Ferdy nervously. 'Do you really think this will work?'

'Have you got any better ideas?' demanded Ronan.

'Run away?' suggested Ferdy hopefully.

Ronan deigned no reply, but marched, head high, towards the palace gates.

The guards thrust forward their spears, shouting a challenge. Prothero took a deep breath and blew out a long quivering blue flame. Wailing and dropping their spears, the guards fell flat on their faces.

'I still don't think it'll work,' remarked Ferdy, stepping over them.

They flitted down the long, echoing passages. Archways on either side gave glimpses of tree-lined courtyards, or led to yet more silent corridors. When they came to a door they peered in; most of the rooms seemed to be empty. They saw few people, and many of those they met paid them no attention. Whenever anyone did accost them, a puff of blue flame sent the challenger diving rapidly for the floor. But there was no sign of Conrad.

At last Ronan called a halt. 'I don't think this is going to work . . . ' he began.

'What did I say?' murmured Ferdy.

'. . . sooner or later the guards will pick themselves up and come looking for us. We could wander for hours without finding Conrad.'

'Then we'd better ask someone,' said Derwin. 'Here . . . ' He beckoned Ferdy back to the last room they had looked into, a larder stacked with sacks and jars. 'We'd better have you looking more impressive,' he added, emptying a bag of flour over Ferdy's head.

Ferdy choked a protest, but was told only to close his eyes and mouth while Derwin rummaged along the shelves. When he had finished, Ferdy looked not so much impressive as horrendous, his face chalk-white, with vivid red scars on his cheeks, while his hair and eyebrows were green. Ferdy spluttered a good deal, but was kindly advised not to worry as it was all edible.

'Here,' said Derwin, holding a vast white tablecloth. 'You'd better put this on.'

Carefully he wound it round, covering Ferdy's tattered clothes.

'Mmm. That looks very awe-inspiring.'

'But I can't walk,' wailed Ferdy.

'Then glide. That'll look even more impressive.'

'There's someone coming,' called Ronan.

'Right,' said Derwin. 'Now's your chance. Command the fellow to tell you where Conrad is.'

Swallowing hard, Ferdy shuffled out into the passage and held up his hand in what he hoped was a grand gesture. 'Hold!' he cried. 'I conjure you . . . '

But the man had taken one look, dropped the bowl he was carrying, and fled.

'I think that impressed him,' said Derwin.

'This is quite tasty,' remarked Prothero, poking in the ruins of the dropped food.

'Come on,' called Ronan. 'He must have been taking that food to someone. This way.'

Kerrin, who had been making sure the man was really gone, returned, took a quick sniff at the food, then trotted after them, panting eagerly.

They went down another passage and through a curtained archway. As a door opened they were suddenly aware of the hum of many voices. Slipping back behind the curtain they watched a servant pass carrying some empty dishes. Ronan gestured to the others to remain, then crept out to investigate. The door had been left ajar, and peering in, he saw that their search was at an end.

In a moment he rejoined the others and told them what he had seen. 'Ferdy, Prothero, you're going to have to be very impressive.' He gave them a crooked smile. 'We'll just have to hope it works.'

The next few minutes were rather confused. There was a gong in the corridor; Derwin hit it. They hurled open the double doors and burst into the dining hall. Prothero belched blue fire. Kerrin barked. Ferdy flung his arms into the air, was for a moment tongue-tied, then screeched a wild ululating chant. Derwin and Ronan released Conrad. Of the Ashmaelis only the Queen did not throw herself to the floor; she tried to rally her people, but was drowned out by Ferdy and by bellows from Prothero and Kerrin's frenzied barking.

Then they were off and running, Conrad bundled on Prothero's back.

And they realized they didn't know the way out.

'Why do they have to live in a rabbit-warren?' panted Derwin.

On they fled, hurtling down one identical passage after another, dreading always to hear the pounding of feet behind them. They lost all sense of direction and were trusting only to blind chance.

In the end blind chance led them to an archway which opened on to a terrace lit with stars. They tore down it, seeing freedom at the end, but their cries of triumph were cut short. The terrace ended abruptly; abruptly, they fell into the river.

'Here! Over here!' Mirim was calling. She and Morgan helped them out of the water. Conrad was on his feet now, though dizzy and confused.

They ran through the streets of the empty city. All was quiet under the moonlight. Here and there they saw people huddled on the ground, mere bundles of rags; but the beggars made no move. Only sometimes their eyes gleamed as the travellers passed.

Then Ronan, in the lead, turned a corner, checked, and gestured to the others to stop. Derwin joined him at the corner. Before them reared the east gates, massive, unclimbable. Guards stood on the wall, black against the dark sky.

'Come on, Prothero,' whispered Derwin. 'Do your stuff!'

'Not again!' sighed the dragon. 'My fires are getting rather low, you know. And all that cold water wasn't good for them either.'

'Come on!'

Still grumbling, Prothero cleared his throat, then stomped forward and bellowed. The blue flame flared, the guards vanished, Derwin ran to the wheel that opened the gates and spun it round. The gates slipped silently apart. They were out of the city.

'We've made it!' exclaimed Ferdy. 'They can't stop us now.'

'I wouldn't be too sure of that,' said Morgan.

'For once,' said Derwin, 'I'm inclined to agree with you.'

But although they looked often behind them as they went,

189

dawn came with no sign of pursuit. As the sun rose higher they began to relax, and slow their pace; but Ronan remembered the fast horses and hunting dogs he had seen in the city. He said nothing, except to urge them on, but at mid-morning they had to rest.

By now they were travelling through barren, rocky hills. Azastan was out of sight, and even Morgan began to think that their adversaries had thought the chase not worth while.

They stopped in the shade of some rocks. Conrad slumped down and closed his eyes.

'Are you all right?' asked Ronan.

Conrad was silent for a while, remembering. 'How did you find me?' he asked eventually.

Ronan told him, unable to keep the pride from his voice as he explained how he had followed them into the city, watched all day outside the palace, organized the others, led the daring rescue against all the odds . . . Conrad listened in total silence, his face slightly averted, staring at the rocks.

'I should never have trusted Cassian,' said Ronan judiciously. 'Still, all's well that ends well!'

Conrad, with an effort, turned to look into the Prince's eager face. Ronan, he realized, had forgotten all his previous rancour in the joy of the rescue. There was nothing now in his eyes but triumph and affection.

Still Conrad said nothing. He looked round, saw that, with the exception of Derwin, who had walked back down the track, the others were all asleep. Strange, he reflected, that all the time he had been trying to win Ronan's admiration with his pose of right-thinking and heroic leader, he had inspired nothing but resentment. The roles had been reversed: he had needed to be rescued, and Ronan, triumphant, had ceased to look on him as a rival. He had Ronan's affection, now that he deserved nothing but contempt.

And he could not even ease his guilt with a confession, for that in itself would be a betrayal: a betrayal of the innocent pride in Ronan's eyes.

He could think of nothing whatever to say.

Suddenly Kerrin shot barking up the track, Derwin panting

after him. 'Quick!' he called. 'Wake up! They're coming!'

'What is it?' groaned Ferdy, muzzy with sleep.

Derwin stood up, gasping for breath. 'They're coming after us from the city—with horses—dogs . . . '

'How far off?' asked Ronan.

'Not far—and moving fast. The dogs will have our scent.'

'Then we'd better move quickly. Lead on!'

Snatching up his pack, Derwin hurried up the path, Kerrin at his heels. The others began to follow wearily behind.

Conrad caught Ronan's arm. 'Keep the others going,' he said. 'I'll stay here—hold off the pursuit as long as I can.'

'I'm not leaving you,' cried Ronan indignantly.

'You have a duty to escape if you can.'

'I don't care. I won't leave you behind.'

Conrad hesitated. 'Will you not do as I tell you?' he appealed.

'No!' There was a stubborn set to Ronan's narrow jaw and his grey eyes shone with an heroic fervour.

The others had disappeared round a bend. There was a silence around the two figures.

A beetle was walking down a rock. Fixing his eyes on it, Conrad began to speak, his voice arid as the hills. 'It was not Cassian who betrayed you. It was I. I wanted to be King in Ilyriand, and Almira my Queen.' His lips twisted. 'I was a fool as well as a traitor. You should have left me to my fate.'

For one long moment Ronan stood, as the light died in his eyes. Then, without a word, he turned and ran after the others.

Conrad was left alone to find death. It would be an easy sacrifice. The difficult thing would have been to go on living.

There was, for a time, a silence between the life that had gone and the death that approached. The sun burned. High above a great bird, eagle or vulture, arced slowly through the blue air.

Limping a little, Conrad walked back down the track. After a while he came to the top of a ridge, and saw them. They were now near the edge of the plain, would soon be climbing into the hills. There were perhaps a hundred riders, or a hundred and fifty—it was difficult to tell with the glaring sun and the swirling dust. Dogs ran before them, their low baying echoing faintly in the still air. He had still a little while to wait.

191

He retraced his steps once more, to take up his stand in a narrow, rocky gully where the horses would have to pick their way no more than two or three abreast. If he was lucky he might hold them for a little while. He had as many arrows as he was likely to need. He could only hope Derwin would have time to think of some stratagem to conceal his companions and put the dogs off the scent. The pursuers might even be content with his death alone, though he doubted it.

Time passed. The sounds of the chase came closer, the rhythmic barking, the clatter of stones under the horses' hooves. Then they were in the gully. Almira led, hair and robe streaming loose, then the other riders jostling, the sun glaring on spears and shields.

For one disastrous moment Conrad hesitated. She saw him, hurled her spear. It took him in the side and he sprawled headlong.

The dogs were almost on him. In a moment he would be torn to pieces. With all the strength he could find, he struggled to his knees and bent an arrow to his bow. He could see her lips curved in a savage smile. Through a red mist he aimed, and shot.

The arrow glinted, falling in the sunlight. It took her full in the throat. Her arms flung out; she arched back, and fell. Her horse reared, snorting. Shouts rang out. Shouts of joy?

Conrad watched through a daze as the horsemen halted, calling off the dogs. Then one of the soldiers walked towards him, carrying the blood-stained arrow. He bent and handed it to Conrad, gazing at the wound in his side. He made a sign, then turned and walked away. The soldiers remounted and trotted off, dragging the body behind them in the dust.

Conrad clutched the red-stained arrow and felt his own blood run out into the sand.

They could hardly believe their luck. Before them yawned a great ravine, and over it a ramshackle bridge of rope and planks. They hurried across.

'Burn it,' ordered Ronan. 'Prothero, set fire to it!'

'Stop,' cried Derwin. 'Where's Conrad?'

'He's not coming,' snapped Ronan. 'Prothero, get on with it.'

'You left him? On his own?'

'He betrayed us. He deserves to die. Anyway he must be dead by now and if we don't get this bridge down we'll all be killed.'

For a brief moment Derwin stared at his Prince, then he ran back across the bridge. Ferdy hesitated, then shrugged and followed. 'Stay here!' screamed Ronan, his face contorted. Mirim ran past him, back down the track.

Conrad still lay where he had fallen. He was unconscious, but breathing faintly. Ferdy pursed his lips and looked grave when he saw the gaping wound, but he anointed it with a salve of dragonwort and dittany and bandaged it tightly. Of the pursuit there was no sign.

'Is he dead?' asked Ronan when they returned to the bridge, carrying their sagging burden.

'Not yet,' answered Ferdy briefly.

'He should be,' said Ronan bitterly.

'Why? What made you call him a traitor?' asked Derwin.

'He confessed it. He told me to leave him to die because he had betrayed us.'

'And you believed him?'

Ronan stared at him, silent, doubting.

He seized his moment as soon as Conrad recovered consciousness, opening his eyes on a harsh blue sky he had not expected to see again.

'What did happen in Azastan?' Ronan demanded.

Conrad blinked, trying to bring him into focus. 'The Queen asked me where you were and I told her. She offered to help me become King in Ilyriand.'

Gasps of astonishment.

'You see!' cried Ronan.

Prothero snorted in derision. 'So why are you all so shocked? What else should he do? The way you'd all been carrying on at him at every turn you can hardly blame him for wanting to change sides.'

Derwin gave a crack of laughter. 'You know, Prothero's right. Ronan's been abusing him ever since Mirim joined us, and the rest of us have been egging him on. We're an ungrateful and

193

insubordinate crew, you know. I can't blame him for wanting to ditch us.'

'And I'm sure he's not telling the whole truth anyway,' cut in Mirim. 'I expect that so-called Queen used all sorts of magic and sorcery and—and things, and it wasn't his fault at all!'

'Indeed,' lamented Morgan. 'The best of us may fall when faced with temptation.'

Ronan stared round at them disbelievingly. 'You're all taking his side against me! How can you? Where is your loyalty?'

'Loyalty has to be deserved,' said Derwin soberly.

Ronan flinched, incredulous. 'Don't you understand? *He betrayed us!*'

'Perhaps he did once. But what of the rest of the time? What of all we've been through together?'

'But . . . ' Ronan paused, marshalling his arguments. The world seemed to be dropping away under his feet. 'But this was the time that mattered. Don't you see, he's been with us so far because he wanted to get to Ilyriand? And he wants it for himself. He said so. How can I tell that, if once we get there, he won't betray us again?'

'You can't,' answered Conrad, breaking into the argument that had been raging over his head. He wished this wasn't happening, but it was. 'You'll have to decide whether you can trust me. I no longer know whether I can trust myself. But—'He paused, panting for breath and wincing as the pain bit into his side. 'But I'm not wholly bad, even if I'm not as virtuous as I thought I was. If you need me, you'll have to make do with me as I am. Being a ruler, after all, has little to do with absolutes.'

'I don't need you to teach me how to rule!'

'It's a wise prince that learns from his subjects,' remarked Morgan sententiously.

'And you should all of you treat me with more respect!' commanded Ronan, falling back on an old grievance.

'Balderdash,' said Prothero. '*Sire*.'

'You know what I think?' Derwin cut in before the explosion.

'What do you think?' demanded Ronan.

'I think this is a rotten time for a discussion on ethics. I'm hungry.'

194

'That's right,' said Conrad wearily. 'Let me rest first. You can cut my head off afterwards.'

Ronan felt his anger seep away into a vast and sickening disappointment. He tried to stoke up his wrath once more, opened his mouth to speak, then closed it and walked off.

'A lot of fuss about nothing,' muttered Prothero. 'Though it proves something—even heroes can be useless incumbrances!' Conrad's description of him still rankled.

Conrad looked at him, his face relaxing into the shadow of a smile. 'And useless incumbrances can be very heroic?'

The dragon looked at him in astonishment. 'Well, well. Next thing you'll be saying you're grateful.'

'I should be. Later, maybe.'

Next morning Conrad was feverish, rambling in a delirium which persisted for many days. The wound on his side refused to heal and he grew steadily weaker. They fashioned a litter for him on Prothero's back and continued their journey, for the barren hills provided little shelter and no food. They travelled only in the early morning and the late afternoon, and rested in what shade they could find when the heat became too much to bear.

On the ninth day they came down out of the hills. Another barren, scrubby plain stretched before them, but through it, fringed with green, wound a narrow river. They camped on its banks. Ronan and Derwin took bows and went hunting, but they saw few animals and those they missed. At dusk they returned empty-handed. They would need better luck on the morrow.

CHAPTER 22

IN THE middle of the night Morgan woke. For a while he lay watching the stars march overhead, while his stomach gnawed and rumbled. For himself he didn't mind, but it was a pity these young things should be doomed to a slow death by starvation. A nasty end, or so he'd heard.

Then he had an idea, one which at first seemed so unthinkable that he tried to dismiss it, only it kept creeping back, and becoming gradually more persuasive. He would go and look for some food. He might even find some, in a village or somewhere. If the worst came to the worst—which it probably would—and he died without finding any, well at least he would be one less mouth to share the others' rations. His decision made, he put on his boots, heaved himself to his feet, and plodded off.

He had not gone far when he became aware he was not alone in the night: various scufflings and snufflings seemed to follow his track. Once there was a shrill scream which made the hairs at the back of his neck stand up and sent chill shivers down his spine. But no slavering, ravenous beast appeared out of the dark and, reflecting that being eaten was probably no more unpleasant than dying of starvation and was at least less wasteful, he carried on.

He followed the course of the river, reasoning that if there were a settlement anywhere, it would be near water. The moon and the stars shed light enough for him to pick out his path, so that he only occasionally stubbed his toes and fell over quite rarely.

By dawn he had travelled several miles and was feeling hungrier than ever. Some chattering finches taking their morning drink at the river's edge were too small to bother with, even if he had been able to catch them; but a plump duck, dabbling tail up in the early sunshine, was another matter. As if guessing his thoughts, the duck took off in alarm, wings cracking—and abruptly fell from the sky at his feet.

Morgan gazed unbelievingly at the bird. There must be a catch, he thought, and then he saw the boys. They were eight or ten years old, and quite naked. One carried some sticks, the other a sling. For a moment they stared at him round-eyed; then they turned and ran. Pausing only to pick up the duck, Morgan hurried after.

Fortunately the village was not far away. Puffing and blowing and feeling his age, Morgan limped up the track, to find what appeared to be the entire population of the village already standing waiting for him. None of them was wearing any clothes, though some carried tall spears. Morgan stopped, deterred as much by so vast an area of unabashed nudity as by the sudden thought that these could well be cannibals. Then, swallowing slightly and averting his eyes, he walked up to them and dropped the duck.

The villagers stared at it, and at him. Somewhere a cock crowed. The silence continued. Morgan cleared his throat, said, 'How do you do?' and held out his hand to the nearest of the villagers. A low muttering ran round the group, then silence fell again. Morgan let his hand drop.

A gift, he thought, a token of friendship. Desperately he felt in his pockets, but found nothing suitable. A dirty handkerchief seemed unlikely to appeal. Then he remembered his knife, took it from his belt and held it out handle foremost.

There was a shrill chorus of shouts and cries; they all seemed very excited. Pushing through from the back of the crowd came a tall, broad man whose muscles rippled like the sea. Gravely he took the knife, offering his own in exchange. Morgan accepted it, and a great sigh went up. The crowd formed themselves into a circle, and Morgan found himself in the middle of an arena, alone with the large warrior, and with a knife in his hand. 'No,' he cried. 'You don't understand. I don't want to fight. I just wanted something to eat.'

The villagers took no notice, embarking on their own war cries. One would shout a phrase, the others howl back a response. Their champion pranced up and down and circled

197

around, stamping his feet. Suddenly, in a flashing lunge, he dived at Morgan who, with a moan of despair, promptly dropped the knife and fell to the ground, rolling himself in a ball and hoping that the end would come quickly.

The roaring chorus faltered and stopped. The warrior plucked uncertainly at Morgan's back, trying to disentangle a limb, without success: as he pushed, Morgan rolled this way and that, but remained as uncooperative as a woodlouse.

Eventually he became aware that the noise had died down, and felt himself being rolled firmly, if approximately, into a sitting position. Cautiously he opened an eye and peeped through his fingers. Squatting in front of him was an elderly, bearded man, wearing, he was relieved to note, a long white robe. The old man was evidently a person of importance: the crowd stood in a respectful hush.

Leaning forward, the old man began to draw in the dust. He drew a figure holding a spear, and pointed to the warrior. Then he drew a second figure lying flat, its head severed, and pointed to Morgan, who swallowed sickly. Grunting and shaking his head, the old man rubbed out the drawing and, for greater effect, stood up and jumped on it. Squatting down again, he smoothed the dust and set to work again. This time he drew two figures side by side, pointing first to himself, then to Morgan, and smiling energetically.

Very gingerly Morgan began to unwind, and tried to assemble his features into a reciprocal smile. The resultant grimace, though not endearing, was effective: the old man beamed, leaned forward and rubbed Morgan's nose with his own.

With roars of approval, the crowd rushed forward, jostling each other in their eagerness to share in the greeting. Morgan found himself clasped to an endless succession of bare and sweaty chests, his nose ruthlessly rubbed until it began to feel quite flat.

At last the greetings were over, and the villagers stood waiting for him to make the next move. He fingered his nose ruefully: it really was sore. Pulling himself together and remembering what he had come for, he in turn began to draw in the dust.

First he drew a figure, and pointed to himself. Then he

pointed to his mouth, made chewing motions, and rubbed his stomach. The old man watched intently. Morgan began to warm to his task. This wasn't his sort of thing, but really it was quite fun. He pointed in the direction from which he had come, drew five more figures in the dust, and made the same mime of eating. He thought of trying to draw a dragon, a goose and a dog, decided it was beyond his powers, and added three more man-like figures.

The villagers clustered round, peering at the drawings and talking eagerly. Then the old man turned to Morgan, repeatedly touching his clothes and pointing to the figures in the dust. Eventually Morgan realized he was asking if his companions also wore clothes; smiling at the simplicity of these people, he gestured from his clothes to the drawings and smiled reassuringly. The old man pointed to his mouth, then to the figures, then to the clothes. Morgan smiled again, more doubtfully: but it was the cue for action. Many of the villagers disappeared at top speed.

First to return was an enormously fat woman who slammed a bowl of beans down before Morgan and grinned triumphantly. Kneeling down she made a grab at his boots and pulled vigorously. A short struggle ensued, at the end of which she panted away victorious, and settled down to the arduous task of inserting her own vast calves into the recently vacated footwear.

The appearance of Morgan's socks, slightly holed and redolent of much walking in hot weather, caused a momentary panic, but the villagers rose to the occasion, one even being curious enough to exchange them—by force—for a loaf of some sort.

Rapidly the pile of food grew. A youth with a sack of flour managed to relieve Morgan of his tunic with amazing ease; but it took the concerted efforts of several villagers to peel off his breeches, and a squabble ensued as to who would have the honour of wearing them.

Eventually the bartering was completed and Morgan, mother-naked, tried to shrink into the sand. Grinning, the villagers hauled him to his feet, loaded the bundles of food onto their heads, and set off in the direction he had indicated. The lucky winners of articles of clothing thrust out their chests and walked proudly, while the fat woman, her feet wedged half-way into the boots, staggered in the rear. Morgan, dizzy at the extent of his sacrifice, his tender feet wincing at the hot earth, shuffled along with his eyes closed.

Kerrin barked furiously.

'Someone coming.'

'Morgan?'

'No—that is—not unless . . . ' Derwin's voice died away, his gaze fixed on the approaching band. He hushed the dog and waited. Conrad was asleep, tossing restlessly. In the shadow of the cliff Prothero sprawled, apparently in more peaceful slumber.

The group of people filed into the gully, put down their bundles, and waited, smiling amiably. Derwin smiled back absently, his attention taken by a hand which had appeared from amongst the bare knees and was now groping forward. It located and seized a blanket, then vanished back among the legs clutching its prize. There was a short commotion, then out stepped Morgan, decently wrapped.

'I meant it for the best,' he sighed. 'But I never do anything right.'

Ferdy greeted the villagers, haltingly, in Cassian's language. The old man replied, with some hesitation: it was clearly not his native tongue either. A conversation ensued, then Ferdy turned to his companions: 'They've brought food to exchange for our clothes—all of them. I've told them we need clothes to protect us from the sun. They say we can starve if we like.'

'Offer to share,' said Derwin. 'There must be things in our baggage we can do without now.'

Ferdy spoke again with the old man, then turned back. 'They say they outnumber us and what we don't give them they can take.'

At that moment Prothero reared up growling and let out a spurt of flame. The villagers turned, seeing the dragon for the first time, and panicked.

The dragon roared, the villagers screamed, Kerrin barked, the old man plucked at Ferdy's sleeve.

Ferdy turned to Derwin and shouted through the din, 'They agree to share.'

When things had quietened down they sorted through their baggage. There seemed no point now in keeping clothes designed for a Fallond winter. As the villagers seemed to regard clothes as decorative rather than functional, they raised no objection, and accepted the furs and woollens with low cries of wonder and admiration. They accepted also various articles which in Fallond had been thought essential and which on the journey had proved totally useless. Conversely, tucked into nooks and crannies, were a few items which they had thought had been left behind, and which they had regretted ever since. Prothero gazed at the mounting pile of irrelevant clutter which he had been humping around over the miles, and closed his eyes, too moved to speak.

As the sorting and bargaining came to an end the old man came over to Ferdy who was crouched anxiously by Conrad's side. The old man stooped over him and peered into his eyes, then sniffed at the medicine Ferdy had prepared and shook his head. Beckoning, he led Ferdy out of the gully and began to search the bare hillside. Eventually he found a dry twig which looked to Ferdy's eyes much like any other twig. Gesturing excitedly, the old man began to dig.

Slowly, for the earth was hard and unyielding, he uncovered a large tuber. Grunting with effort, he hacked around it with a stone, and at last prised it loose. This, he explained, was the only thing which would break the sick man's fever.

Back in the camp he pounded up some of the root in a bowl, mixed it with water, and muttered charms over it. Then he poured a little over Conrad's forehead, stomach and feet, and very carefully trickled a few drops between the parched lips.

'Are you sure he knows what he's doing?' asked Mirim.

'No—but neither do I,' answered Ferdy. 'My remedies haven't done any good at all.'

The old man, satisfied, looked up. 'You come to the village,' he said. 'I look after you. I Nabukar. Chief. We friends. Yes?'

They spent several days in the village, and found there peace of a kind, despite their urgency to be off on the last lap of their quest. Conrad's fever broke and he began to mend, though slowly. He was very quiet, spoke hardly at all, but sat and watched the slow trickling of each day's uneventful passing.

Dawn was the liveliest time. Flocks of birds flew over, honking or chattering, and the shrieks and laughs of the women filing down to fetch water rang on the still fresh air. The men left to forage for what food they could find. Then, as the sun rose, life slowed. The sky was empty except for the eternally droning flies. The women settled to the monotonous pounding of roots into flour. The children, round-bellied and insect-legged, scratched in the sand.

Derwin, naturally, found plenty to do, suggesting improvements to the design of the huts, producing a more efficiently-shaped pestle to grind the flour, learning to play the local musical instruments and teaching the village musicians to make flutes like his own. Ferdy too was busy, at first looking after Conrad, later accompanying the men as they hunted for food, learning their language, the names of their plants, which could be eaten and which were good for medicine. Morgan got on well with the women of the village, invoking screams of delighted laughter as he solemnly showed them how to sew Fallond-fashion. Mirim found there a stark beauty, and peace. She spent much of her time watching the small prowlings and quiet wars of the bizarre insects which seemed to own the land. Ronan fell into a dream, staring south and east into a desert blank and empty as his grey eyes. Ilyriand lay that way, beyond the desert. Only Prothero grumbled: he said the heat made his skin itch. No one took any more notice of him than usual.

Late one afternoon Mirim was, as often, wandering around outside the village, peering into holes and under rocks. She found an exuberance of small creatures—small as compared to a dog, for instance, but for what they claimed to be absurdly large, and very odd, invested with the qualities of dream, or nightmare. There were caterpillars more than a foot long, and striped in bands of blue, green, yellow, red, black, blue, green, yellow, red, black all down their fat and undulating bodies.

There were millipedes, equally huge, but shiny black, their legs flowing like a river. There were vast furry spiders with eyes swivelling on stalks and groping jaws; beetles of all shapes, sizes and hues; lizards that were rarely more than a flash of colour among the rocks. There were other, more sinister creatures that were dead leaves clinging to twigs until a fly or a cockroach wandered by: then they were sudden death, crunching, head first, scattering discarded wings.

Mirim was contemplating a horned beetle, wondering if it was poisonous, when Derwin appeared, closely followed as usual by Kerrin.

'What are you looking at?' he asked.

'This—isn't it beautiful? Like a miniature dragon.'

Derwin peered closer, then offered the beetle his finger.

'It looks very fierce,' said Mirim apprehensively.

'Mmm. I'm terrified.'

The beetle stepped on to Derwin's finger and paused, swaying its pointed horns. Derwin raised his hand and gravely considered the insect, nose to nose. Kerrin, after a desultory sniff, had settled down at his side and was washing a paw.

Abruptly the beetle opened its wing-cases and flew off, whirring. Derwin smiled and straightened up. 'Very fetching,' he said. 'I like the horns. I think there's some food ready. Are you coming?'

The sun was beginning to mellow and the shadows were lengthening. It was almost cool. The sky was filling with birds returning to their roosts and bats waking for a night's hunting.

They walked in a silence suddenly shattered by a demoniac scream. A figure hurtled down from a rock and landed in front of them in a shower of stones. 'Ambushed!' grinned Ronan. His hair was damp from swimming in the river and beads of moisture ran down his chest.

'You—you *varmint*!' cried Derwin, and lunged at him.

Ronan fled, Derwin at his heels, Mirim and Kerrin in pursuit, the dog barking wildly.

Shrieking with laughter, they hurtled into the village and collapsed on the ground. Then Mirim noticed Conrad. The setting sun lit up his hair: there were strands of silver among the black, and lines around his eyes.

'He's getting *old*,' thought Mirim, horrified. She tried to deny it, to restore the glamour that she had always seen surrounding Conrad; but it had gone, in a moment, irrevocably. Now he was only ordinary, and she was left wondering that he had ever seemed anything more. She felt a bewildering sense of loss, and acute embarrassment. She had little appetite for supper.

Darkness had fallen. It was very peaceful. Reluctantly Conrad stirred himself into activity. 'It's time we moved on. Ferdy, ask the Chief which is the best way across the desert.'

Ferdy turned to Nabukar. The Chief answered at length, with much throwing up of hands and low wailing choruses from the other villagers. 'He says there is no way across the desert.'

'But we can't stay here for ever!' cried Ronan.

'Oh I don't know. I suppose there are worse places,' said Ferdy.

'Wherever we go is bound to be worse,' Morgan stated lugubriously.

'Ask him again,' said Conrad.

On the day before they were to leave, they were woken by the sound of drums. The villagers, who in the usual way had little enough excuse for celebrations, were determined to make full use of this one. The festivities had taken a long time to prepare. The men had scoured around for some extra delicacies, including the leaves of a sinister-looking plant. Then the women had spent hours chewing the leaves, spitting the ensuing mess into a vast communal bowl, adding more or less noxious ingredients.

It was part farewell, part tribute to the clearly magical strangers, part wake, for everyone knew it was impossible to cross the desert. The travellers were going to their doom.

The feasting went on all day, as did the drinking—the liquid in the vast bowl tasted surprisingly good—and the dancing, a rhythmic shuffling which was equally intoxicating. A warm and delighted feeling of comradeship enveloped them, shot through with moments of panic when they remembered that tomorrow they had to depart.

Nabukar's second wife approached, carrying a large pot and grinning broadly.

'She says this is something special,' Ferdy translated. 'They were very lucky to find them.' He peered into the pot and recoiled. It was full of bloated white maggots, wriggling. 'Let the others taste first,' he said hastily to the woman. She looked a little disappointed but passed on.

One by one the travellers looked, blenched, and declined. At each refusal the woman looked more crestfallen, and a disapproving silence began to grow among the villagers. 'Someone's going to have to . . . ' muttered Derwin, and he forced his reluctant fingers to stretch out and catch one of the soft, clammy bodies. Wearing a fixed grin which he hoped showed intense gratification, he raised it to his lips. It squirmed. His gorge rose. He hesitated, glancing up at the woman. She was watching him expectantly. Deftly he palmed the maggot, then let it slip down his sleeve, chewing and miming extreme pleasure. 'Delicious,' he declared with a warm smile at the woman. 'Really, you should try one,' he said to Morgan, who was staring at him pop-eyed in horror.

The woman offered the pot hopefully to Morgan, who shied away, then returned to Derwin, smiling trustfully.

There was no option but to repeat the performance—not once, but many times. As a boy, Derwin had delighted in tricks of sleight of hand, and he had lost none of his old skill: but his sleeve began to get a little crowded, and he was uncomfortably aware that some of the maggots were beginning to make their escape. He could feel one scratching around in his armpit, and another making a determined bid for freedom via the back of his neck.

'Really, that is enough,' he said firmly. 'Let your people share now.'

Reluctantly, and pressing on him one last delicacy, the woman moved away, just as the topmost maggot arrived at his ear. He caught sight of Mirim, who was staring riveted as his tunic wriggled.

'Excuse me, a call of nature,' he said, and retreated, carefully.

He found, among some rocks, a dampish spot which he hoped

would be more to the maggots' taste than they had been to his. It took a long time to disentangle them from his clothing. One was caught in his breeches for ages.

On his way back a cliff moved. It was Prothero, rubbing his back against a rock.

'Do you want some help?' asked Derwin. 'Where does it itch?'

'Down . . . down a bit more . . . left a bit . . . up a bit . . . aaaah . . . '

'Are you content, now we are going?' asked Derwin presently.

'No—don't stop—ooh—no, of course I'm not content. But if we've got to commit suicide we might as well get it over with.'

'You are looking on the bright side, aren't you? You must have been taking lessons from Morgan.'

'Well, do *you* think we'll cross that desert?'

'Oh, I don't know. I suppose I have to think it'll be all right . . . It's not that I particularly want to stay here, it's not that I don't want to get to Ilyriand, it just seems like so much effort making a move.'

'Well, I can't see the point of any of it. I have a nasty feeling that if Ilyriand actually exists and if we ever get there, I shan't be allowed to stay. But we'll never get there anyway.'

Derwin looked out south-east, where they had to go. A great sweep of stars did nothing to dispel the darkness of the desert. Nearby, around the fire, was a tiny pool of light and life; beyond, all was chill, empty night.

CHAPTER 23

Two weeks later it had become clear that Nabukar was right: there was no way across the desert. It was a naked land, barren, featureless, devoid of life. As far as they walked, they seemed to make no progress, for, save that the landscape dissolved into a haze at noon and vanished altogether in the black cold of night, they saw no change. There was only dust, and stones, and the angry glare of the sun, as if they were trudging through a nightmare, chained to the spot while the world like a treadmill slipped away beneath them.

They spoke little. The desert encouraged introspection, not conversation, and they walked along each busy with his own thoughts or, as the sun rose higher, lack of them.

They had not found any water since they had set out, nor was there any sign that there might be water ahead. The land unrolled in a series of dips and scarps, brown, dusty, monotonous. Once they thought they heard birds flying over in the night, but when dawn came the sky was empty. Empty also of clouds. There were no plants to be seen, and the only signs of animal life were occasional strange tracks in the sand. Whatever it was came out only after dark, burrowing deep from the heat of the day. Kerrin, nosing among the rocks, failed to unearth even a beetle.

According to the map, to the south-east lay the mountains, and beyond them Ilyriand.

The desert seemed to stretch for ever in every direction, like some insatiable animal engulfing all it met and leaving nothing but the dry husks of life that had been.

'This all used to be forest,' said Ferdy. 'Nabukar told me. I couldn't understand why there was no desert marked on the map. But he said there was forest once, then people came to fell the trees. The wind blew the earth away. Nothing was left but sand.'

'How do we know the same thing hasn't happened to Ilyriand?' asked Derwin.

'We don't.'

At any rate it was too late to turn back now. They walked on because there was no point in walking back.

The goose seemed to suffer most, beak open, panting, or pecking at the dust in a forlorn search for green grass.

One morning they woke to find Emma gone. Derwin, missing her, was relieved. Perhaps she would have better luck. 'She might even find Ilyriand,' he said.

'How do you know I didn't eat her?' growled Prothero.

'That isn't a joking matter,' said Derwin shortly.

'No,' said Prothero. 'It isn't.'

They looked through their supplies and found there was only enough left for three more days. 'We'll halve our rations,' said Conrad. 'Make it do six.'

They trudged on.

Next day Morgan refused to move. 'Kill me,' he said. 'I can't go on. You can eat me if you like.'

Derwin stared at him, revolted. 'I'd rather not, thank you. Anyway, there's not much point—there's only enough water for five days at the most.'

'Either we all survive, or none,' declared Ronan heroically.

'Speak for yourselves,' Prothero interrupted. 'I'll eat him.'

'Prothero!'

'Well, why shouldn't I? I'm a dragon, aren't I? He's my lawful prey.'

'Oh do stop talking such nonsense, all of you,' cried Mirim. 'As if we didn't have enough problems!'

'Come on, Morgan,' said Derwin. 'I'll help you.'

They packed up and moved on. The subject was dropped: but to the knowledge that death from heat, thirst and starvation was only days away, was added the realization that a vast dragon walked beside them. Prothero had grown a good deal since they set out, and his temper was becoming ever more uncertain. Armed with massive claws and teeth, breathing fire, lashing his spiked tail, he could kill them all if he wished. And now he was hungry.

Another day gone. How many now? The desert was like a quicksand, swallowing the days. Conrad screwed the stopper back on the water bag.

Derwin caught his expression. 'How much left?'

'A mouthful apiece. No more.'

'Perhaps we'll find a stream tomorrow,' said Derwin optimistically. Conrad gave him a derisory look. 'Oh well,' muttered Derwin. 'Never say die.'

Conrad settled himself down and shivered. Once the sun set the wind got up and now it was cold. 'Wish you hadn't come?' he enquired, with a trace of irony.

'Oh no—I wouldn't have missed it for worlds. After all, we've had a marvellous time, haven't we?'

Conrad blinked, but made no reply.

'What about you—wish you'd stayed at home?' asked Derwin.

'Oh—I don't know. I don't seem very sure of anything now. I've spent a lot of time lately discovering I'm not what I thought I was, but it doesn't seem to help me to find out what I am. I don't think I know what I think about anything until it's too late. When I've lost a thing is when I know I cared for it.'

Derwin, disturbed by so much unaccustomed talkativeness, shifted uncomfortably. Kerrin whined and nuzzled his leg. Poor Kerrin, he was thirsty too, and how thin he was getting. Derwin ran his hand over the dog's head, fondled his ears. And what about Emma? Where was she?

The others were asleep now, or at least silent and unmoving, each an isolated little huddle, barely discernible from the surrounding rocks.

Conrad lay watching the stars, his mind back in Fallond, where Emerick lay—if he still lived—and Alina bent over her embroidery, and Osric told tales of far away, and snow fell from the mountains.

At last, as the sky paled towards dawn, he too fell asleep, wondering even in his dreams what it was that he sought.

Prothero woke to two very strong sensations: one of overwhelming thirst, the other of relief. Eventually he realized his back had stopped itching. He turned to look, and saw there was something lying on it. Something that looked like a folded sail, or a pile of leathery blankets. He stared at it perplexed, wondering who had put it there. Then it moved. There was something under it. He jumped in alarm. The thing unfurled: it was a pair of wings. It was his pair of wings.

He collapsed in a heap, contemplating this marvel. The wings had sprouted through a split in his skin. They were floppy, but seemed to be hardening, stirring with a life of their own.

After a while it occurred to him that if they were wings, they might fly. He wriggled his shoulders, flexed his back. Nothing happened. Then a hitherto unsuspected muscle came suddenly into play and the wings unfolded and flapped, cracking like a sail taking the wind. Somebody stopped snoring and stirred. Prothero lay still. This was his, they would have no part of it. Cautiously he got up and crept away, uphill.

The moon had set but there was enough starlight to see by, and in the cold it was easier walking than by day. Which was just as well. The great mass of uncoordinated flappiness wobbled and swayed: the dragon lurched, trying to keep his feet. The stiffening wings became ever more unwieldy and uncontrolled. Several times he fell and slithered back in a shower of sand, but each time he picked himself up and crawled on, always upwards. He knew he must go up. It was the single solid idea in a shaking, shifting world.

Perhaps, he thought hazily as he shuffled up the hill, perhaps this is the way dragons die. The trouble with being the only one of your kind is you know you're unique but don't know how. But it seems a fitting end for a dragon. Gouting fire to soar through the air and crash to earth in ruins, like a flaming brand tossed in the night. Or like a shooting star.

By now he had reached the edge of the scarp. He stopped and looked back into the darkness where his companions lay sleeping. They've never known me, he reflected. They've always regarded me as a sort of self-propelled baggage-cart-cum-tinder-box. Poor blind humans. Well, they won't learn different now.

He had recovered his breath but his heart was still pounding.

His brain seemed very clear, except at the centre a small seed of fear.

Standing on the brink he let out a great spurt of fire, a brief flicker of light in the vaster darkness. And he jumped.

And flew. Spreading in the wind his wings took him gliding, down, then surging with a new inner life, up, spiralling up towards the stars. The cold night was his, the air his element. Flaming he flew.

In the empty uncoloured chill of dawn a deer lifted its head from drinking, and died. The dragon stooped from the sky, his teeth met unerringly in the animal's neck; blood, hot and salt, spurted into his mouth. The warm life flooded into him; the deer's life was his. He lifted his head. Blood trickled down his jaws, and he knew the sweet appalling joy of killing. A dragon's power is death. He ate, drank, and killed again. And again. Blood filled his mind.

Conrad woke reluctantly that last morning. His companions were stirring, except for Morgan, breathing in rasping snores, looking as if he would pass from this sleep to his last, unaware. Ferdy looked almost as bad, his face grey and his eyes unfocused. Then Conrad realized Prothero was missing. He crawled to his feet and looked around. The dragon was nowhere in sight. A trail of prints led away. It was several hours old, the edges blurred by the wind.

Conrad sighed. He had thought the time for decisions was past. Now he had to choose whether to urge his companions on in a last faint hope of finding water, or whether to look for Prothero. The dragon might have abandoned them; or he might need help. Though what help was possible now?

For a moment Conrad hesitated. He had an overwhelming desire to do nothing at all. Confound the animal, he thought. Then, muttering thickly to Derwin with a tongue reluctant to obey him, 'Going to look for Prothero,' he set off following the footprints.

The trail was strange. Prothero seemed to have been carrying something that had brushed along the ground, and several times he had fallen over. As the sun rose higher Conrad too began to stumble and fall. The slope he was climbing began to assume the proportions of some precipitous mountainside, one that was constantly slipping from under his feet, trickling away to leave him flailing at the air. Before long he was crawling on hands and knees. The sand shimmered, shifting into visions of ice and water falling from snow-clad rocks. I died a long time ago, he thought, why am I bothering. Then, abruptly, *I don't want to die*.

In one last effort he reached the summit, and collapsed. It was after all only a little hill. The trail ended. Just like that. Conrad peered down the drop. His eyes were swollen and the sun was inside his head. There was no sign of Prothero. Confound it, he muttered, where the blazes is the pestilential dragon?

The sand danced. The sun swooped. The world dissolved. Blast you, Prothero, he thought, as his thought ended.

The wind blew. Morgan and Ferdy, both unconscious, were already half buried by the sand. Mirim and Ronan sat hand in hand for comfort. Kerrin lay with his head on Derwin's chest. There was silence, except for the wind, and sometimes Kerrin whimpered. It had all been said, or was better left unspoken.

Dreamily Ronan watched the speck in the sky. A vulture, he thought, as it began to take shape. I hope it will wait until we're dead.

Mirim followed his gaze, and shivered, but did not look away. There was nothing else to look at. Only the black shape of death, growing larger as it flew towards them.

Ronan frowned, puzzled. I'm going mad, he thought.

The shape grew, hovered over them, a shade blocking out the sun. Then with a clap of wings it landed. It was Prothero carrying an enormous eggshell.

Now I know I'm mad, thought Ronan. I'm seeing things. He looked at Mirim. She could see it too.

'Would you like some water?' asked Prothero, offering the eggshell.

Conrad woke to the sound of a goose honking.

212

He opened his eyes and saw a winged dragon chewing on a carcass.

He closed his eyes again.

'Are you awake? Would you like some more water?' said a voice. Mirim.

Conrad struggled to a sitting position and looked round. They were all there, Emma too, in a green river valley running down from the mountains to the desert.

But the dragon had wings. How very odd.

'Oh, he's alive, is he?' enquired Prothero, sauntering over. 'I must say I'm glad. After all the trouble I had finding him and bringing him here it would have been downright ungrateful of him to peg out now.'

Conrad choked down some water. 'How did I get here?'

'Flying—on dragon-back,' announced Prothero grandly. 'Now isn't that dandy?'

Conrad looked at him, blinked, gave up and went back to sleep.

CHAPTER 24

MIRIM WAS away bathing in the river. Ferdy got the map out and passed it around. It was not of much help. It showed clearly enough where they were: this was the only valley to penetrate a mountain wall that stretched unbroken north and south for mile after mile. And still the valley was not depicted as a pass, but as coming to a blind end. On the far side of the mountains was written 'Ilyriand'. In between was a blank space.

'Not much use, is it?' commented Ronan. 'It doesn't look as if they wanted anyone to find their way back.'

'But it was drawn by someone coming *from* Ilyriand,' replied Ferdy. 'It's not a map of Ilyriand, it's a map of the outside world.'

'You know,' said Derwin, 'even if we had been able to cross the desert we'd never have found this place if Prothero hadn't learnt to fly.'

Prothero smiled serenely. 'What was it the wizard said? "Take the dragon," wasn't it. Excellent man. A true visionary.'

'That's not what you said at the time,' retorted Ronan.

'Much good may it do us,' added Morgan. 'There's no way out. If Ilyriand is still there we're obviously doomed to die on the threshold.'

'Prothero,' said Derwin, having a sudden thought. 'Couldn't you fly up the valley and see where it leads? Or perhaps if you flew over the mountains you could see how to get over them? Or perhaps you could carry us over?'

'Yes—and perhaps,' answered the dragon sourly, 'I could break my wings trying to fly in a valley that's narrower than I am. And perhaps I could get frostbite trying to fly above the clouds.'

'You can't help?' asked Derwin.

'No,' said Prothero crossly, then, relenting slightly, 'I can't. I already looked.'

The sun was high now and the valley beginning to throb with heat. Mirim returned, looking damp and cool. Conrad stood up: 'There's not much point in sitting talking about it. Let's move on.'

The valley soon became very narrow indeed, turning sharply to the left and becoming a mere cleft in the massive mountainside, hardly any wider than the bed of the river that gurgled down it. The sun's heat was cut off as by a door closing, and the summer sounds of birds and insects faded away. They walked in silence as, relentlessly, the mountains closed in on them. They felt like ants crawling. Prothero stared straight ahead, his wing-tips brushing the cliffs on either side, trying not to think of being trapped here for ever.

And then, round another bend, the mountains moved in once more. The gap between them, no more than the width of a man's arms outstretched, was filled by the stream, brown, silent and sullen.

They stopped.

'It must widen out again further up,' said Derwin. Prothero made no comment.

Conrad was already taking his boots off. He stepped down into the water, wincing at the cold. Barking excitedly, Kerrin jumped in after him. They splashed off upstream, rounded another bend and vanished. Gradually the sound of splashing died away. The others waited. Someone shifted position and a stone rattled, startling the silence.

Then, faintly, they heard Kerrin barking. Then, silence once more. A silence that seemed to last for ever.

'Where are they?' burst out Ronan, unable to bear it any longer.

Nobody answered.

And then, finally, splashing sounds growing nearer. Kerrin came into view, swimming. He crawled out, shuddering, and shook himself. Ronan cursed as the shower caught him full in the face.

Still there was no sign of Conrad. No one spoke. The silence dragged on. At last Derwin began to pull off his boots. 'I'd better go and look.'

'Ssh!' hissed Mirim. Kerrin, ears pricked, whined softly. Then they could all hear the sound of someone splashing through the water.

Slowly Conrad waded down the stream and dragged himself up the bank. 'There's no way through,' he said dully. 'The stream gets narrower, then it disappears into solid rock.'

'There must be a way,' cried Ronan. 'You didn't try hard enough.'

Conrad, his head bowed, made no reply.

'You got us into this mess,' shouted Ronan, his frustration turning into anger. 'You get us out of it.'

'All right.' Conrad shook himself. 'Let's have another look at the map.'

Ferdy spread it out for them all to see. Mirim looked at it with interest: it was the first time she had seen it.

'Look,' said Derwin, 'it's marked clearly enough: "Gateway to Ilyriand".'

'If there's a gate, it's shut,' remarked Morgan glumly.

'A gate usually has a key,' said Conrad. 'Ronan, show us the key.'

Ronan pulled it out. It lay dull in his hand.

'Anyone seen a keyhole?' asked Derwin.

'If only,' sighed Ronan, 'if only we knew what the inscription means.'

'But I do!' said Mirim, startled.

'You don't!' said Derwin.

'You can't!' said Ronan.

'The only reason I went to that accursed city,' said Conrad, 'was to find out the meaning of the inscription. And *you knew all the time*?'

Mirim cowered in the face of this concerted attack. 'I didn't know you—didn't know,' she stammered. 'Is it important?'

Conrad groaned and buried his head in his hands.

'It only tells us the way to get into Ilyriand,' explained Ronan with as much patience as he could muster.

'But why do you want to know?' asked Mirim, still bewildered.

'Because that's where we're going!' shouted Ronan.

'You never told me,' she said.

There was a moment's total silence, while they thought back.

'I suppose that's true,' agreed Ronan reluctantly. 'It's all your fault,' he went on at Conrad. 'You said we weren't to discuss our journey with her.'

'I know. I'm sorry. Anyway, what does the inscription mean?'

'I don't see why I should tell you,' muttered Mirim, sulking.

'Because,' replied Ronan, getting very grand, 'Ilyriand is my ancestral kingdom, that I am going now to reclaim.'

'No, it isn't!' said Mirim.

'Yes it is!' shouted Ronan, becoming heated. 'I tell you, I am heir to the throne of Ilyriand.'

'No you're not,' Mirim contradicted. 'I am. I am descended in direct line from Dale, son of Tancred, son of Eldon, King in Ilyriand.'

The silence, compounded of bewilderment and disbelief, which greeted this announcement was broken by a laugh. Conrad was shaking with uncontrollable mirth.

'What's so funny?' demanded the aggrieved Prince.

'Can't you see? Oh Ronan, all the time you and I have been quarrelling over who should be King in Ilyriand we have been labouring to bring the rightful Queen to the threshold of her realm.'

'You don't believe that, do you?'

'I rather think I do. After all, you and I are descended only from Tancred's younger son, and we both know that makes all the difference, don't we? Mirim, tell me, how do you reckon your descent? Because we have always believed that the only survivors from the people of Ilyriand were those who travelled to Fallond, and that Tancred's only surviving son was Wendell who was born in the north.'

Mirim folded her hands in her lap and began to recite. 'I am the daughter of Vedis daughter of Arvin, son of Chalmer, son of . . .'

'Spare us the whole genealogy,' snapped Ronan.

Mirim looked at him scornfully and continued. The names rolled from her tongue like waves on the shore, monotonous, inevitable. At last they sensed she was reaching the climax.

217

'. . . Son of Theodoric, son of Dale, son of Tancred, son of Eldon. Dale was but an infant at the time of the massacre and was saved by his nurse and brought with some fifty others, sole—as we thought—survivors of the people of Ilyriand, to the lake-side where since we have dwelt.'

She ended. Silence fell. Ronan looked round at his companions, seeking a denial. None responded. Angrily he jumped to his feet and strode off. Carefully they avoided watching him go.

Ronan slumped down on a rock and glared at the mountains. The dust shimmered, mocking him with shifting illusions, danced, dissolved. There was a sour taste in his mouth. He felt sick.

A lizard poked its head out of a hole and smirked at him. Violently he hurled a stone at it and swore when he missed. The lizard vanished. The stone tumbled on down the slope, taking others with it, leaving behind a cloud of dust.

For a while Ronan gave himself up completely to his feelings: rage, chiefly, and disappointment. It was all so unfair. To have travelled so far, come through so much, to reclaim his kingdom, only just as it was within his grasp to have it snatched from him.

As he sat unmoving the small creatures of the valley began to re-emerge. The lizard came out of its hole and scuttered off, dancing on the hot stones. A beetle appeared, pushing a large pile of dung. Carefully it negotiated a stone, legs and feelers flailing. Then another beetle arrived and took hold of the dung from the other side. A struggle ensued, first one beetle then the other gaining ground, feet shuffling, shoulders straining. Then as one slipped and fell on its back the other shot forward and lost its grip. The dung escaped and rolled off downhill. Cheated of their plunder, the beetles wandered off, forlornly waving their antennae. One walked straight into the jaws of the lizard, lurking behind a rock. Briefly the lizard wore a macabre moustache of wriggling legs; then with an audible crunch the beetle vanished.

Ronan watched the drama dispassionately. He had no emotion to spare for insects.

Emotion, he reflected, was a trap. If he had learnt one thing

218

from this journey, he had learnt that. Trust was a beetle. Behind every rock was a lizard waiting to gobble it up. What was it Conrad had said? 'Kingship is not a matter of absolutes.' Not that he need take any notice of Conrad. Still, there was something in it. He would have to compromise. If he couldn't have what he wanted, he would grab what he could get.

Conrad wondered if someone should go after Ronan. Perhaps on the whole it would be better to leave him be. He felt sorry for him: Ronan was not of an age or temperament to find it easy to dilute his dreams with cold reality. His ideal vision was of course doomed in any case, but Conrad had himself wanted to be King in Ilyriand enough to sympathize.

But they were not a very impressive collection of subjects— five altogether, eight if you counted the dragon, the dog and the goose. And none of them would take orders from anyone, king or not. He had an image of himself sitting on a marble throne attempting to dictate to the companions of his travels, all of whom were quite capable of looking after themselves and more than capable of saying what they thought of anyone who tried to prevent them doing exactly what they wanted.

They heard footsteps returning up the rocky slope. Kerrin stood and wagged his tail, the others stared at the ground.

'Yours, I think,' said Ronan, smiling sweetly as he handed Mirim the key and sat down. 'I think you were going to tell us the meaning of the inscription?'

Mirim held up the key. It seemed to fit in her palm as if made for it. Slowly she spoke the words:

' "Whoso would Ilyriand see
Twist my tail and follow me." '

Deliberately she held it in her two hands and twisted. It came alive, throbbing, pulsing, moving beneath her fingers with its own inner urgency. She turned it this way and that, feeling its power grow and dim. Angled towards the cliff on her left the throbbing became compelling.

Following where it pointed she found, concealed behind a buttress of rock, an entrance.

She went in. 'Come on,' she said, her voice falling flat into the silence. She walked on without waiting to see if she were obeyed.

Ronan was after her immediately, Morgan just behind, calling, 'Wait, little one. Come back, it's dark in there.' He was engulfed in the blackness.

Ferdy paused, remembering another long journey underground; then he too, and Kerrin, and Emma in Derwin's arms, were swallowed up.

Prothero paused, doubtfully eyeing the size of the entrance. 'I never wanted to come in the first place,' he remarked.

Conrad grinned, drawing his knife. 'Don't worry, if you get stuck I'll help you along.'

Muttering darkly the dragon stepped into the tunnel. Conrad brought up the rear.

The darkness was absolute. Their eyes sought in vain for the faintest glimmer of a shadow. The passage was high and wide. Walking with arms outstretched they felt nothing, only a numbing chill. They might have been floating in water, or drowning in air.

The only sound, all but blotted out in the endless empty silence, was their shuffling footsteps. A tiny sound, yet persistent, like some small insect scrabbling, scrabbling at the fabric of night.

Mirim alone was confident, unafraid. Through the black unmeasured void she found her way with a sense that was neither sight nor sound, nor taste, nor touch, nor smell. Her steps definite, assured, she felt the shadows draw back to let her pass. The pulsing life in her hand was the only guide she needed to know that she was fated to follow this path. Of that at least— at last—she was totally certain.

Ronan followed always at her heels, and then the others, trusting in her trust. There was no sense in the heavy darkness, no warmth in the cold emptiness save the chill clasp of their companions' hands.

Stalking them, biding their time, hovering just past the fringe of hearing, lurked the nameless terrors of the monstrous dark, waiting with slimy tentacles, smothering webs, claws and fangs and bony fingers, waiting to choke and bite and tear.

Mirim allowed them no rest, and they asked for none. No one wanted to pause here, where their only sane fear was that of being lost under the immeasurable weight of the mountains, dying of thirst in this void beyond the world. Madness waited, not far off. Out of world, out of time, they walked on.

'The tunnel ends here.' Mirim's voice came out of the blackness. They stopped.

'Can't you give us some light, Prothero?' asked Derwin.

'No!' cried Ferdy. 'He's breathing right down my neck.' He tried to laugh.

Mirim put the key in her pocket and stretched out her hands. Her fingertips probed at the tissue of the rock, found a crack, followed it. She put her hands out flat and pushed.

A great slab of rock pivoted and swung slowly open. Grey light streamed in.

It was dawn in Ilyriand.

CHAPTER 25

A GREY DAWN. On either side the mountain wall stretched sheer and unbroken. Before them the ground fell into darkness.

A bird called, tentative, questioning. Another answered. The sky began to fade. The blackness took shape: dense forest, hung with silver mist. The sun rose on a land that rang and rang with birdsong.

No one spoke: no one could think of anything to say. They felt remote, unreal, too exhausted to begin to react.

Nearby a spring bubbled from the rock and spread into a quiet pool. They lay down on its grassy banks and one by one drifted into sleep. Mirim lay on her back for a while, watching the dark-edged leaves quiver against the blue sky; then she too closed her eyes.

It was mid-afternoon when they were rudely awoken: it was raining.

'I thought this place was supposed to be perfect,' grumbled Morgan, scurrying to the shelter of the trees.

'You can't expect anything to grow if it doesn't rain sometimes,' said Ferdy reasonably.

'I don't see why it has to rain on me while I'm asleep.'

'We'll have to issue a proclamation,' grinned Ronan. 'Clouds not to rain on Morgan while sleeping.'

'Most refreshing,' declared Prothero, wading out of the pool and shaking droplets from his scales.

Emma, paddling sedately round the pool, put down her neck, nibbled happily at some weed, then stretched up to the sky and clamoured triumphantly.

'I really thought we'd lost that bird,' said Conrad.

'You can't keep a good goose down,' said Derwin.

'Ah, but she was bound to head for the valley,' Prothero

222

pointed out. 'There was nowhere else to go. We who fly,' he added smugly, 'have a certain superiority. One has but to stretch one's wings and the world is laid out beneath one. One can read it like a map.'

'First I heard you could read,' said Conrad sourly.

Prothero contemplated him sadly and shook his head with the air of one much maligned. 'I suppose one shouldn't expect gratitude,' he said. 'Virtue is its own reward.'

'Next time I want to be rescued, I'll ask.'

'Can't you stop them bickering?' Mirim appealed to Derwin.

'What—and spoil their fun?'

'Mirim and I,' announced Ronan, 'are going to explore. You may come if you wish.'

'Lead on,' said Prothero. 'Nothing seek, nothing find. Anyone like to tell me what we're looking for?' he murmured.

No one responded to his invitation so, humming quietly to himself, tail twining between the trees, wing-tips brushing the branches, he fell in at the rear of the procession.

Mirim walked still in the dissociated clarity of dream. She felt, rather than saw, the forest. The bark, smooth or rugged or rough with lichen, of immense trees that soared beyond sight, their tops lost in the whispering canopy; the dark, leathery leaves of shrubs hung with fantastic flowers of every hue, brilliant as jewels; birds exotic as flowers, flitting, calling; butterflies in clouds; waves of sweet scents, intoxicating, drowsing.

Ferdy ran about like one possessed, distracted by first one marvel then another, exclaiming over an insect then driven demented by a tree, chasing after a bird then standing stock-still to gape at a snake. 'Look, Morgan!' he cried, as a butterfly as big as his head drifted through a patch of sun. 'Look at that!'

But Morgan, having woken up in a bad mood, refused to be diverted and stomped along in an ill-tempered silence. This place looked foreign to him; he missed his wife, he missed his home and he missed the sea—in reverse order.

Ronan still marched close to Mirim, his heels leaving deep prints in the soft ground, his mouth set in a determined line; but whenever he caught her eye he smiled gently.

Derwin, not looking where he was going, tripped and fell. Rubbing his ankle he sat up. 'Would you mind keeping your roots to yourself?' he enquired of the nearest tree.

'It's not a root,' said Ferdy, scratching at the moss. 'It's stone . . . carved, I think.'

'Look!' cried Ronan.

Then they all saw it. It was easy to miss, so luxuriant was the vegetation, mosses and ferns, climbing plants winding up and creepers snaking down, tufts of grass and pockets of flowers. They were standing in the ruins of a vast building. Immense pillars reared up, contending with the trees in height. Great archways opened onto nowhere. Walls stretched out, fretted with windows one above the other, many broken, all empty. The roof was long since gone: between the treetops they could glimpse the sky. The stones had once been intricately carved: from pillars gazed the sightless eyes of eroded faces; around archways twined the remembrance of the dreamlike creatures that decorated the halls of Fallond.

'I'd forgotten,' said Ronan slowly. 'Do you know, I'd really forgotten . . . *They* lived here, my forefathers. If only—wouldn't it be marvellous if we could rebuild it? Restore it as it was . . . '

Derwin raised one eyebrow. 'I think it might take us rather a long time,' he murmured.

'We'll clear the trees,' went on Ronan, staring about. 'And build a palace fit for a king!'

'Which king did you have in mind?' enquired Derwin; but Ronan was beyond hearing.

'Birds everywhere!' said Ferdy to Mirim. On every ledge was a nest: a neat mound, topped by two bright eyes and a curved bill. The birds seemed quite unafraid of the humans, watching them with an amiable curiosity. One landed on Mirim's shoulder, bobbed up and down, and trilled a long liquid bubbling call before flitting off to its nest.

'Have you noticed?' asked Ferdy. 'None of the creatures we've seen have run away. They just don't seem bothered about us.'

'We've given them no cause to be afraid,' said Mirim.

'Yet,' remarked Prothero, but no one was listening.

'Cheer up, Morgan,' grinned Derwin. 'At least there's nobody chasing us.'

'Have you seen the size of the spiders?'

Eventually Conrad persuaded them to move on. It was getting late, and they had to find water before they could camp for the night.

As they went downhill they met more and more animals, deer of sorts and others more difficult to name. None showed any fear, even of the dragon. Prothero smiled quietly to himself.

They were walking now on a well-defined path. Soon between the trees they caught a glint of silver.

The path, and the trees, ended at a sandy beach.

'The sea!'

'Or a lake . . . '

Ferdy ran down the beach. 'The water's fresh!' he cried.

'We could build a boat,' said Morgan, his expression lightening magically. 'Salt or fresh, there'll be fish to be caught.'

'At least,' observed Ronan, as a roundish bird the size of a goose wandered up, paused to peck shortsightedly at his boot, and then drifted vaguely on, 'at least we shouldn't have any problems in catching our dinner.'

'I shouldn't like to kill them,' said Derwin, taken aback. 'They're so tame. It would be like eating one's maiden aunt.'

Ronan looked at him, puzzled, then at the bird. 'Which aunt? I can't see any resemblance.'

'That's not what I meant. I meant, their trusting nature . . . '

'You do talk a lot of nonsense, Derwin.' And Ronan walked off towards the lake.

Derwin caught Ferdy's eye. 'That's me put in my place,' he grinned.

Ferdy smiled amiably. He felt amiable. Brimful of the scent of flowers, of tranquillity, achievement, well-earned repose.

Prothero stretched out on the beach. Conrad, damp and fresh from a swim in the lake, warm from the sun, lounged against the scaly back, gazing up at the sky.

'Prothero . . . '

'Mmm.'

225

'How far do you think you could fly with someone on your back?'

The dragon opened one yellow eye and squinted suspiciously over his shoulder. 'Are you thinking what I think you're thinking?'

Conrad grinned. 'Probably. I begin to believe there are no limits to your abilities.'

Prothero opened the other eye. 'Compliments from you I regard with a certain amount of mistrust,' he said. 'And that was altogether too blatant. What do you want?'

'You could do it, couldn't you? After all, we've only done half what we set out to do. You could carry me back to Fallond. You said yourself that from high up you can read the land like a map. On the way we could plan out a safe route for the rest of our people to follow.'

'Whose people?' muttered Prothero.

Conrad ignored him. 'I know what I want now. And I'm going to get it. I've wasted enough time.'

Prothero groaned. 'I knew it. I said to Derwin, if we ever got to Ilyriand I shouldn't be allowed to stay.'

'Very good,' approved Conrad. 'Such perspicacity you have, and such nobility of character. What would we have done without you?'

'That's what I think,' said the dragon.

The lake stretched out serene to a blue horizon. The shadows lay long on the land. The air was full of soft shufflings and low cries as beasts of all kinds padded to the water's edge to drink. Birds floated on the water, skimmed low over it, in countless myriads, white and red and iridescent green. The gold of the setting sun melted into the blue and silver water.

Derwin sat watching, idly running his fingers through the sand. I wonder what we'll make of this place, he thought.

He hadn't considered the matter before, had been too busy getting there. His mind shifted back to Fallond. Surely the wizard had given them some advice? He remembered the evening before they set out, the great hall, the wizard sitting on a stool. From time past and half a world away Derwin heard the wizard's quiet voice. 'Think of a world without men. A world where the sun shines, and the rain falls. Where grass grows, nibbled by deer in the early morning. Where the unwary deer is pounced on by the wolf. Where the wolf, when it dies in turn, is swallowed up by the earth. And where its body lies the grass grows thicker . . . There is a balance in the natural world that no other creature can upset. But you, you have that power. Power, endless power: but not the wisdom to know where it will lead. You can reach out your hand and change the world. Change one thing, and that may change another unforeseen, and that another, and another, until the world lies about you in ruins and you stand alone in the desert wind of your shattered dreams.'

Down at the lake's edge, Ronan and Mirim stood side by side. All was tranquil: the calm contentment of twilight. The sun seemed to hang still, poised in the evening sky. Long-legged waders probed the shallows with curving bills, their white plumage flushed with pink, each bird matched by its own reflection. Further out were tiny islets, each balanced by its image in the sparkling water.

Ronan reached out his hand to Mirim, and a flock of geese took flight, shattering the surface of the lake. The balance was broken.

In a blaze of red the sun began to sink into the water.